Text copyright © 2010 Published by Edward
Marcus

Follow the planetary patriot @
lulu.com/spotlight/planetpatriot

First Edition: November 2010 The characters
and events portrayed in this book are
fictitious. Any similarity to real persons,
living or dead, is coincidental by the
author.

The Planetary Patriot: a novel by Edward
Marcus.

ISBN:978-0-9567398-0-3

Time Travel : Science Fiction

Acknowledgments

For all the oppressed, occupied and beaten down people of the world! For the poor and the desperate. For those that have no voice and do not count. For all the victims of war and injustice across the whole world, in every far off corner and place nearby. This book is dedicated to you all.

"Humanities greatest downfall is being scared!"

"The Planetary Patriot"

Edward Marcus

Prologue

MISSION STATEMENT!

"A nation of one with six billion to come!"

THE FUTURE... Chance, fate, destiny, foresight, predestination. Even providence. The dictionary is full of words that tell of the forthcoming. That tell of tomorrow. But now tomorrow is not guaranteed, tomorrow is not an absolute. As in the last years of the twenty-first century. Time travel! Humanity's most powerful weapon of mass destruction, is now in secret use. With the rich using it to gain profit in slavery and misery. And the wicked using it for the murder of nations and their fellow brethren. Known as the act of temporal

terrorism. These men and women of evil, use
this technology to change the past too
their own selfish endings. But waging a
secret bloody war against this future
villainy throughout tomorrow, the present
day and past. Distant or otherwise! Playing
no favourites, casting no colour lines. And
having no religious or even Nationalistic
agenda. Jackson Carter aka "The Planetary
Patriot", battles throughout time itself.
Hoping to one day bring about a truly
effective and positive change in the world.
Fighting a war against war itself. Fighting
to once and for all achieve Humanity's
impossible dream of peace on Earth, and
good will to all men, and women as well...

Chapter One

VILLAINS RUN AND HIDE!

"Here enters the fastest man alive?"

The now as in today...

ORIGINAL HISTORY... With the local time being that of five minutes past two exactly. A brilliant blue moonlit night, the best moon lit night of the year so far. Rippled outwards over the German city of Berlin. Casting cold dark black shadows over a very menacing and apparently very abandoned, industrial complex. Whilst with the only signs of life nearby that could be heard. Were that of a cloister of stray black cats. Plus a single lone white one?

As meowing in a collective pattern of baby crying like communication. In complete choir like unison. All enjoying the competition of the hunt for scurrying rats in the gloomy distant corners! As in the far-flung background, many different places and spaces now became alive with the rumbling of loud music. That echoed in multiple directions. Sending faint rhythmic patterns over the dirty rainbow oiled street puddles. While three just parked, black on black Mercedes-Benz vehicles, sat with engines still running hot...

Seemingly just an unmarked and disused, broken down warehouse on the outside. Club Hate! Was a true haven of prejudiced and villainous bigotry, that stood completely invisible to anyone who would walk by. Just like the social diseases of racism and xenophobia themselves. While inside itself the atmosphere of the underground night club was electrified with the stench of intolerance and indifference. As the mother of all hate raves to end all hate raves, raged onwards.

With the décor inside mocked up to look like a Nazi death camp. Minus the smell of murder and beyond evil human destruction. A video wall of mounted television screens displayed in turn and in multiple rotations, sickening images of "the Nazi Holocaust", along with numerous hate crimes. One of which included that of the infamous L.A.P.D Rodney King beating. Only to then switch to numerous uncut, and very disturbing flash images of the 9/11 attacks on New York City. And the 7/7 London bombings...

Thus as these scenes of human destruction and misery played outwards. The feel of the place was hung semi-lukewarm throughout. Whilst the air itself inside was drenched with the sweet smell of warm German beer, sweat, marijuana and pure undiluted hatred!!! As raging uncontrollably onwards with a countless crowd of party goers. Made up of Nazi skin headed thugs and stupid young wannabe Aryan youth. That was three quarters male and a quarter female! These "amateur" racists were in continue motion and play. All now acting like wild animals. All dancing badly and madly to Germanic hate rock, leaping and jumping upwards, crashing into each other. As a live band played on stage...

"SIEG HEIL... SIEG HEIL!" Screamed the countless crowd, giving the vile Nazi salute in unison. As on screen images of the 9/11 Hijackers and the written words...

"Atta-Boys! The Magnificent Nineteen! Courage to do what we wanted too! City of Jews! Burn! Baby! Burn!" Flashed in unison over countless pictures of the smashed and burning Twin Towers!

Ten seconds onwards...

With flashing strobe lights cutting in and out! And the TV screens now displaying a picture in picture live News report of a burnout and smashed School in the Middle East. Five smartly dressed thugs, walked through the crowd. Who all in response, with the exception of one, stepped back respectfully in seeing their menacing presents.

Extremely skinny and pale faced, dressed up to look like Hitler himself, with a matching Charlie Chaplin moustache. The absent minded Nazi youth now danced badly, stepping and clapping on the offbeat.

"Glory, glory to the white man... The white man struggles on!!!" He yelled to himself. Accidentally blocking the exiting Henchmen's path!

Stopping dead in his tracks. With a faint Bullet burn scar on his shaved bald-head. Carrying a large Aluminium type suitcase that was of a strange design. And serving as a secret head enforcer to a mysterious and some would say almost mythical Neo-

fascist. Known only as--"The German."
Brutus! Who himself had the description of
a white South African male of Germanic
ethnic extraction. Now looked amused, as
the youth now turned around to face him.

Surprised and at the same time impress by
the sight of Brutus and his so-called Aryan
warriors. The youth now stood to attention,
giving the Nazi salute, extending out his
right arm! While a female Goth looking Neo
Nazi. Who incidentally was sporting bright
blood red trouser braces, along with laced-
up jack boots. And wearing a Black "Mickey
Mouse" T-Shirt. Now very quickly jumped
upon his position and person?

"You idiot!" She exclaimed only to then
yell a order in German. "Out of his way!
Now!!!"

"It's quite all right!" Responded Brutus
with a crafty cold smile, returning the
salute, while patting the youth on the head
like a pet dog. "Proud to be white, proud
to be pure!" He shouted to his accompanying
Henchmen, in his violently toned Afrikaner
accent. As they now exited the club. Only
for the music inside to now get played
louder and louder...

"NIGGER, NIGGER, NIGGER... OUT, OUT, OUT!"
Screamed the bands front man, as pure white
strobe lighting rained down upon them all
from high above. "GAS THE JEWS, GAS THE
JEWS, GAS THE JEWS! KILL THE FAGS, KILL THE
FAGS..."

"WHITE POWER, WHITE POWER, WHITE POWER!!!"
Screamed the crowd back in quick fired
hateful response.

"DIE MUSLIMS! DIE MUSLIMS! KILL THE
RAGHEADS!" Yelled the front man back. As
the set of the "censored" photos of Abu
Ghraib, minus the two thousand plus other
photographs we are not allowed to see. Were
now displayed on the video screens.

"FUCK ALL NIGGERS! FUCK YOU TOO!" He now
screamed out at the top of his spiteful
voice. As the infamous Danish cartoon and
other hate crime images were now displayed
on the wall screens too. As more things
were now yelled and screamed out in
venomous declaration. That included things
that were best left not repeated.

"FUCK ALL NIGGERS, FUCK YOU TOO! KILL THE
RAGHEADS!" Said the crowd back in return.

Thus delivering a last sentence of hate
speech that was not just unique to this

group of particularly misguided
individuals. That in itself was perfectly
acceptable too many "civilized" western
block people.

Therefore repeating this offensive hate
speech for over two minutes with screaming
madness. All now went silent! As suddenly
and without total explanation something
very strange then occurred???

STOP THE CLOCK! "TEMPORAL RESET"...

Consequently hanging frozen in place...
Drenched in the false purity of the white
strobe lights and their own racist
ideology. All of the party goers stood
completely motionless. Looking just like
living stone statues. Whilst droplets of
sweat and splashed beer hung in place
throughout the air. As now without warning
time snapped itself back by one whole
minute, just like an elastic band. With all
of the people moving backwards in full
reverse, as if they had all been video
taped.

HISTORY REWRITTEN... Hence with time itself
now jumped back to normal, and the party
goers all unknowingly reliving the same
said minute again. The rave continued to
rage ahead, as a mysterious unknown black
man now entered!

Sporting the highly attractive looks of a male model, with the matching hard body of an Olympic athlete. The handsome man of so-called colour walked undisturbed just for the moment! Coolly moving through the crowd...

YOUNG, BLACK AND VERY DANGEROUS... Serving as a hero, an avenger, and a champion to all. Set at a 6'3 tall fearless muscular bullet-proof build. This walking nightmare of a man goes by many names... To the wicked and good alike he's known as--"The Planetary Patriot." With some having nick named him as--"The fastest man on earth!" But to his friends and once living family he's Jackson Carter. A man who has personally declared war on all forms of terror, of all forms of injustice himself. Fighting the good fight in his very own bloody violent, killing time way! Serving as Judge! Jury! And Executioner! Against all men and women who would murder the innocent and terrorize entire nations...

"NUKE Israel! NUKE the Jews, NUKE the Arabs! NUKE them all!" Read a series of flashing words over cold war images of detonating atom bombs, on the video walls... As carrying on in continuance screaming a mixture of "White power!" And the so-called "N" word three times over in rapid succession. As well as other numerous detestable epithets. The hate rave raged

spitefully onwards. As a few of the party
goers now started to notice Jackson!

Going to danger seemingly like a moth to
the flame. And killing conversation as
always when he walked into a room.
Especially this time! Jackson stood strong,
very tall and very silent! Awaiting the
battle of the day, or rather the dying
night to begin.

Turning to each other in surprise, shock
and utter disgust. The crowd looked on, as
the Bands front man now stopped shouting!
As a wave of absolute silence now travelled
across the giant dance floor. With
Jackson's masculine cool image now
displayed on all of the TV screens.

"Jesus Christ! What the?!"

"Holy shit! What the hell is this?"

"Who's the SchwarzeNIGGER?" Whispered some
of the crowd under their breath, in a
mixture of German and broken English.

Suddenly as they all looked on, almost
frozen to the spot. Staring ahead as if
they were all deer's, stuck in the sights
of proverbial headlights. A large hulking
skin headed thug stepped forward...

"COME ON, NIGGER!" He shouted! Storming with fists flying...

Instantly responding to this racist insolence in just a split lightening charged second. Jackson unleashed a single powerful opened palm BITCH SLAP! Striking the thug backwards, like a evil pimp slapping an enslaved prostitute. Thus breaking half of his face and knocking out half of his teeth in the assaulting process.

Only for another thug to now attempt to punch him in the back of the head. Jackson instantly and coolly grabbed hold of the incoming fist! Thus lifting and swinging the thug around, sending him crashing into the crowd.

"Kill that, NIGGER!!!" Yelled some of the crowd, as half of them charged viciously ahead. Skilled in the ultimate fighting art of "Te Vu'Kra - Fu!" Which was also known as the Martial Art of Murder! Which was like a highly advanced form of Kung Fu meets Gymnastics. Jackson now bounced across the dance floor like Ali on fight night!

Unleashing a volley of single punches and spinning kicks. Faster and quicker than raw lightening and thunder itself. And thus

reacting faster than the legendary Bruce
Lee himself. Jackson now went about
defeating multiple opponents with beyond
total quickening ease. As a most disgusting
moment was now about to be put in play?

Immediately delivering and unleashing one
single kick into a Nazi thugs stomach!
Jackson instantly caused the racist
individual to turn and fall downwards.
While at the same time causing the thug to
let lose with a spray of vomit straight
into more incoming thugs opened mouthed
faces. Causing them all to fall back and
over each other in shocking momentum!

Five seconds later...

Breaking bodies and bones without a care.
And being a modern man of the new
millennium through and through. As well as
being a true equal opportunist in all
things. He now showed absolutely no
hesitation when it came to the female
opponents. Kickin' their asses and laying
the proverbial smackdown against them all.
Including the female Goth looking Neo Nazi!
With a equal back and body breaking
ferocity.

Increasing his speed and lightening
reflexes, Jackson now defeated even more

incoming thugs. As the other half of the party goers ran out of the club in total panic stricken fear! With all of the incoming thugs knocked completely out for the count! Jackson leapt upon the stage where all of the Band members stood anxiously welded to the spot...

"Never argue with the man holding the microphone! As he always gets the last word!" In general this was always a truth. But to Jackson this was not so. As beyond offended at the Band's lyrical content, he now snatched hold of the front man's Microphone!

Thus reacting with wanton violence, as the images of the Rodney King beating replayed above and all around on the video screens. Jackson now delivered the beat down from HELL!

That would have even made the L.A.P.D scream "Police brutality!" Breaking the said front man's teeth and jaw completely apart with just one violent thrust! Only then to turn and beat down the other Band members with their very own instruments.

Fifteen bone breaking moments onwards...

Finishing off the last member, by SLAMMING the drummers head into their drum set. Jackson now turned to see the extremely skinny and nerdy young, Hitler looking youth. Standing frozen in fear! As Jackson mockingly gestured, by raising his right eye brow. A puddle of urine ran rapidly down the young man's leg, causing him to now turn. (Scared straight?) Running away in total terror!

Looking ahead! Jackson now saw a single large metallic silver blast door, that lead to the clubs lower level. As a loud swishing sound echoed outwards the blast door now opened to reveal more villains!

Lead by wanted U.S domestic terrorist Lucas Walker. Who was kicked out of the Ku Klux Klan for being to racist! For being too much of a true believer. And armed to the teeth carrying an assortment of weapons. Ranging from axes, crow bars and baseball bats. A legion of badly dressed Nazi Henchmen now entered.

"I don't believe it! I DON'T, FUCKING BELIEVE IT!" Shrieked Walker in a deep southern accent! "THAT'S HIM!!! That's the Jew loving Nigger... Who stopped our crew from gassing all of those Christ killing kids, at the School today! Setting those ragheads up good and proper!"

As this was said all of the Henchmen, all
6' plus tall and of a muscular thuggish
build. Now looked ahead, with bloodthirsty
straight out of prison ravenous stares. All
acting just like a pack of Jackals,
snarling as if they were already to bite
the life out of Jackson's dark skinned body
themselves.

"Put that tree climbing Nigger terrorist
APE, back in his place boys... And when
you're done, bring me his balls..." Yelled
Walker, as the blast door now closed shut
behind him.

As the Henchmen all now violently charged
straight ahead with weapons blazing...
Jackson, being a former black man of a--"I
wish I was a slave mentality". And by that
I mean a truly unapologetic proud
individual of so-called colour, who refuses
to take any shit from anyone at any time.
And if to say... "Suck my dick Master! Suck
my Motherfucking dick!" Now smirked to
himself fearless in the face of the
incoming danger!

Instantly as the weapons were swung in his
direction. Jackson responded with no mercy
for the wicked! Unleashing a lethal volley
of KICKS and PUNCHES, killing half the
Henchmen with just one single strike to the
head or torso!

Now as seven incoming thugs viciously approached from behind with axes in hand. Jackson! Knowing instinctively that they were behind his fighting position. Now spun around with his arms fully extended outwards...

"TEMPORAL HELO SLASH!" He said loudly at a fast almost incomprehensible pace. Rotating his body in one fast singular motion, delivering a lethal power move of the martial art of murder. That itself instantly knocked down and cut through the incoming Henchmen. Just as if they had been struck down by a pair of Helicopter rotor blades.

With blood and murder on the dance floor a very much apparent seeing fact. The remaining thugs now attacked! Only to have Jackson turn the tables on them. Grabbing hold of their own weapons, using them to the maximum violent extreme...

Thus impaling their heads with crow bars and cutting their bodies down to size with their axes. Jackson now violently went about killing every single incoming thug. Destroying the enemy without mercy or care. Breaking and smashing the faces and skulls of the last few remaining thugs, with their very own aluminium baseball bats.

With all of the Henchmen laying outwards in a bloody broken dead heap! A cold metal rolling against stone sound echoed outwards. As Jackson now threw down a blood soaked baseball bat! Turning! Looking straight towards Walker with homicidal attitude... While at the same time gesturing him, as in you're next on my SHIT LIST, and you better recognize, Motherfucker! With two solidly pointed right fingers!

"You darky, coon, niggly nigga bastard!" Whispered Walker under his breath, shaking his head to himself in total stomach churning trepidation of imminent death. "I think I'm gonna carve me some dark meat today, boy! Ye Ha!!!" He howled in a higher intimidated pitched voice, pulling out a large Bowie Knife!

In almost a single fast motion, Walker now stormed straight towards Jackson. While Jackson himself stood apparently switched off?! Standing frozen in place as if he was a stone statue, waiting until the last second to react!

And react he did, by slamming his fist straight into Walker's stomach. (With a reduced strike!) Knocking the wind completely out of him. While at the same time flipping the Knife upwards out of his

hand... Taking hold off it, only to then
cut off his nose to spite his hateful face.
With just one violent swoop of the blade!

Instantly stepping back in absolute agony.
Walker screamed blue bloody murder. Wailing
for mercy that would not be given. As a
puddle of thick wet red blood gushed
outwards from his gaping wound...

Thus with Walker's blood dripping screams
for leniency going unheard, Jackson's anger
now increased.

"WHO YOU CALLING..." He growled, grabbing
hold of Walker... Lifting him upwards while
spinning around in one continuous motion.
Jackson now through Walker's whole person
forward...

Instantly lifted upwards and propelled
ahead. Walker now crashed uncontrollably
into the blast door breaking it open!

Tumbling inwards, rolling down a single
flight of solid marble stairs. Twisted
around with a hard bump at every turn. Only
to finally reach the bottom... Walker
looked upwards only to see the metal door
heading towards him.

"O' Shit!" He mumbled under his blood soaked bubbled breath, as the door now slammed into him. Knocking him out for the count.

Walking slowly down the stairs, almost as if he didn't have a care in the world. Jackson now entered the lower level. "Catch you later, Walker!" He voiced, coolly walking past him!

Now jumping into a unbelievably fast and incredible pace, like a sprinting athlete. Jackson stormed straight down a long darkly lit corridor, heading towards the owners office.

Ten seconds later...

Continuing to run through the dark as if he had night vision? Jackson now stopped dead in his tracks! Sensing some kind of lethal danger just ahead?

Therefore coming to a instant stop he now viewed eight pairs of glowing gem like eyes. As suddenly a loud, yet polite Germanic voice echoed outwards over a inter-com system...

"Bravo! Bravo! And bravo again!!!" Sounded
a voice clapping their hands together.
"What an impressive dark skinned individual
you are, fastest man on earth! A true
exception to the laws and rules of nature!"
Spoke the voice. As multiple ravenous wet
growling sounds, straight out of "The
Hounds of the Baskerviles", now echoed
downward through the corridor.

"Your Alpha Negro male status is truly
remarkable, my almost worthy opponent. If
this was the exercise yard you would be
king of the jungle by now. But now all that
will change!?"

Fixed in the dark! Coloured yellow! Eight
pairs of glowing eyes now shined through
the black pool of air clinging empty
darkness, that lay just ahead! Only to now
reveal themselves as a pack of ravenous
"White Dogs." A rare and evil breed of
horrifically abused Canine, that originally
hail from the wicked era of slavery.
Trained only to hunt and kill all those of
dark skinned African descent!

"My White Dogs here are trained to kill all
Negroes on sight!" Proclaimed the voice.

"It's too bad that you will be screaming
for mercy, when they rip the black flesh of

your body. ATTACK!!!" Thus instantly
reacting to Gideon's aggressive command of
violence, the eight snarling Dogs now leapt
upwards...

Not even breaking a single bead of sweat,
Jackson now calmly stood his ground.
Ripping off his tight fitting T-Shirt,
exposing his solid hard muscular smooth
eight pack torso.

As extending out both of his arms, just as
the Dogs were about to reach him. Jackson
now used his Temporal Abilities! A special
technique and ability that only he
possessed. That itself allowed him to do
strange and seemingly impossible things! As
inside a single passing second and inside
his body on a molecular level. Jackson's
D.N.A now rewrote itself...

Thus on almost instantly reaching his
position... The Dogs all now jumped back
down, walking around Jackson calmly!?

Standing absolutely still, in a MONEY-SHOT
moment! Jackson's whole appearance could be
seen to have changed. With his skin now
instantly altered from dark brown to light
white peach. As well as his eyes now
shining sparkling baby blue, and his hair
now being straw dirty blonde. Plus not

forgetting that his ethnic facial features
had now also changed. Matching perfectly to
that of a so-called white Anglo-Saxon male.

Firm faced, letting the Dogs know who was
the Boss. Jackson now pointed directly at
them, only to then turn his right index
finger around showing them the way to
safety!

Therefore causing all eight Dogs to
instantly run towards the exit of the lower
level.

Smirking coolly, knowing that more battle
lay just ahead. He now used his senses,
closing his eyes, running towards the
second door on the left... Changing his
skin colour back, Jackson now leapt upwards
kicking the door open with just one slight
tap!

Slamming to the ground with a thud, the
doors crashing impact echoed loudly
outwards...

As Jackson now walked inside the owners
office. He could now see that the interior
looked much different to the clubs main
level. With it's design looking like an old
European art museum. Having a classic solid

marble tiled floor and matching large
pillars hung coldly fixed throughout.

Apparently quiet of sound, with the
exception of the ticking strikes of five
perfectly precise Time Zone clocks on the
back wall. The office stood coldly silent
for just a moment!

"I would have thought that after four
hundred years of Western EDUCATION! You
people would have at least learnt how to
open a door correctly!" Said a loud echoing
voice with over the top racial suggestion.
The same voice that previously spoke over
the inter-com...

Looking directly ahead Jackson viewed the
clubs owner, Mr. Gideon. Who's description
was that of a middle aged white man.
Dressed smartly in a black tunic, sitting
at a desk surrounded by computer monitors.

"So you're the so-called Planetary
Patriot... The quickest Negro alive, and
all that." Spoke Gideon politely, clicking
his right fingers!

Thus reacting to his command, each armed
with the well known chosen weapon of war,
the weapon of peace and rightful

resistance. The AK-47 assault rifle. Thirty Henchmen in all now stepped out from behind each stone post.

Already knowing that the Henchmen were inside the office, as they now surrounded his firmly stood position. Jackson now looked from left to right. As all of the Henchmen now cocked their weapons. Already to open fire...

"VILLAINS RUN AND HIDE! Here enters the fastest man alive?" Mocked Gideon, as his Henchmen all now smirked, sucking up to the boss in instant response. "Or is it on earth!? Or whatever... KILL HIM!" He ordered, coldly raising his right hand!

Within just a second, the Henchmen now unleashed a unholy hellfire of raging white hot bullets. That all stormed mercilessly towards Jackson...

Living up to the nick name of "The fastest man on earth" in almost slow motion, as instant death seemed absolutely imminent. Jackson jumped upwards defying gravity itself! Spinning around like a tornado, upside down and upright in multiple fast almost light speed directions. Masterfully avoiding every single bullet!

"TEMPORAL NOVA CYCLONE!!!" He yelled,
coolly signalling the use of a Te Vu'Kra -
Fu Power Move! Thus thrusting the incoming
bullet projectiles back towards every
single gun firing Henchmen!!!

Just a single second later as Jackson now
jumped back down to the ground, all of the
Henchmen slumped downwards. With each of
their bodies completely ripped apart and
riddled with bullets...

Filled with total shock and horror, in
witnessing the ease in which Jackson had
just mercilessly dispatched his Henchmen
enforcers. Gideon reached for a concealed
Taser stungun, that lay strapped to the
under side of his table. Taking a panic
stricken, yet accurate aim, Gideon now
fired! As he pulled the trigger a projected
bundle of metallic claw talon barbwires
streamed outwards. Gliding forward,
sparkling with blue electricity straight
towards Jackson's position!

Reacting instantly to this in almost slow
motion, now twisting his whole body to one
side. Jackson! Masterfully dodged the
incoming fast speeding talons. Thus turning
around forthwith in one single blinking eye
moment. Grabbing hold of Gideon's arm. Now
breaking it instantly, with one single
twisting bone snapping clean crunch. While
at the same time confiscating the stungun.

"Wait! NEIN! I was only following orders."
Begged Gideon, like the true blue spineless
racist he was! "I was only following
orders."

"That sounds familiar! Where have I heard
that, before?" Voiced Jackson with
contempt, lifting him off the ground with
just one arm.

"Argh... Mercy... Wait! NEIN! NEIN!!!"
Pleaded Gideon, screaming NO! Praying and
begging for pity, like a gutless coward.

"Shut up, ADOLF!" He shouted back in
return, bitch slapping him in the face.
"I'm not in the business of giving mercy...
Especially to Fascist scum, who would try
to murder innocent children! To murder
little babies."

Thus looking at the Computer monitors.
Jackson now viewed a hit list of European
schools with high immigrant and other
minority population's. Thus in seeing this
Jackson's face fixed to that of solid cold
stone! As he now took a quick glancing
moment studying Gideon's right hand and
forearm...?

"Look! Maybe we can work something out... I have a Swiss bank account. Let's... Let's talk about this... Let's work this out!"

"I DON'T DO PEACE TALKS! I DON'T DO WHITE FLAGS!" Said Jackson back in perfectly spoken German, with a violent snarl.

"You give your Boss a message from me... You tell THE GERMAN that it's open season on all Nazis... And that none of you death camp lovin', Goose stepping, Hitler worshipping, non-professional racist Motherfuckers are safe!" He voiced with very fast paced syllables that themselves were verbally soaked in murderously charged aggression...

"ON SECOND THOUGHTS... I'll pass on the message, myself!" Said Jackson returning to his cold and disturbing, bitch I'm gonna kill you next, American accent.

OPEN WIDE AND SUCK IT... Living up to his well earned violent reputation of dealing out fatal punishment, to all men and women of evil. Jackson with a "SUCK ON THIS" collective looking mannerism, now SLAMMED the Taser straight into Gideon's mouth, firing it instantly!

As this happen the projected talons stormed straight down Gideon's throat. Causing him to convulse in absolute murderous pain. Then within just a few savagely revenge filled seconds, he now slammed to the ground dead! As a mixture of blood and vomit poured out from his mouth.

"Guilty as charged!" Voiced Jackson with ice cold contempt! As taking no pleasure in Gideon's death, he now walked up to the Computer monitors...

Using his mental Temporal Abilities, placing his right fingers onto the main computers systems monitor. He now interfaced with it's hard drive. Thus causing a list of multiple high valued attack targets in the US, to be rapidly displayed...

"Come on, come on." Said Jackson annoyingly as if he was looking for something in particular. "GOT YOU!" He now yelled collectively. As a secret directory knownas a NOC-list, now displayed a roll call of hit men, known as "The Crew" (Aka Slaughter Crew) now appeared on the screen. Along with a digitally encrypted code key algorithm, that displayed a number of strange, ancient Nordic like rune symbols.

Thirty seconds before...

Meanwhile back inside the Club's dance floor, loud thudding echoes rang outwards, along with the sub supersonic booms of just detonated flash bang grenades! As a G.S.G-9 strike Team. Germany's very own elite counter-terrorism and hostage rescue team. Was locked and loaded with all actions on for a fully armed tactical assault. As making a violent glass smashing abseiling entry in complete unison, via the club's sky lights. Whilst Armed German Police officers dressed up in the full riot gear of green coloured jumpsuits, with white and black coloured helmets to match, stormed inwards below!

Thus as the Police Officers now secured the dance floor level. Special Agent Robert Lysander, cautiously entered...

An Agent of America's world famous and some may say infamous FBI, the Federal Bureau of Investigation. Lysander, a white male of Southern Memphis Tennessee extraction. Now walked about the dance floor viewing all of the damaged done. As the Paramedical support entered, checking out all of those who lay unconscious or half dead.

Carrying a side arm and wearing a bullet-proof vest. Special Agent Lysander, now walked ahead, tapping his right fingers against his leg nervously. Viewing the just

ensued carnage, which included countless
puddles of blood and chips of broken teeth.
Plus the freshly cut tissue of Walker's
severed nose.

"It's him! He's here!" Lysander forcibly
dictated. "With me... NOW!" He yelled, to
the strike team. Drawing out his Government
issued Handgun! While at the same time
sliding a bullet into the gun's hollow
metal chamber...

Fifty-five seconds later...

Back inside the Owner's office, with his
mission of violence and gut wrenching
justice almost completed. Jackson now
finished memorizing the download, as the
sound of loud running and soon to be
incoming footsteps rang outwards.

"PATRIOT!!!" Echoed Lysander's pursuing
voice in the narrow distance. Thus with
only one way in or out! It would have
normally seemed that Jackson was about to
be caught?

But this would never be a fact or a truth.
No way! As in hearing and knowing instantly
who the voice belonged too. Jackson turned,
looking towards the direction of the doors
entrance. Smirking with a almost "Catch me

if you can" cheeky arrogant yet perfectly
smiled grin! Only to then... Instantly run
straight towards one very solid stone
wall!!!?

A single second onwards...

Empty of anyone alive inside. As Agent
Lysander now entered, with the strike team
taking point! The lay of the room rang
silent and devoid of the living throughout.
With the interior décor looking more like a
cross between a war zone and a butchers
slaughter house...

"Good Christ...!"

"Shit!"

"JESUS!" Responded a few of the strike team
members in whispered muffled German, as
they now went about securing the room.

Taken all aback, at the horrific sight of
the walls inside. That were riddled with
bullet holes and drenched throughout with
wet blood and grey dank brain matter.
Lysander! Knowing that he was too late, and
that death had just called for the wicked!
Now lowered his weapon, placing it back
into his black leather holster. Walking up
to Gideon's dead body.

Not at all surprised at the murderous
manifestation of justice that had been
delivered. As he had witness even worst
displays that had been unleashed by "The
Planetary Patriot", many times before.
Lysander now leaned over Gideon's dead body.

"Mr. Gideon, I presume!" He said placing
his right hand over his mouth nervously.
While at the same time looking down at
Gideon's diamond encrusted, ultra expensive
Swiss watch. Which itself now ticked
backwards!

Taking off her Helmet and goggles in one
quick motion. The strike teams leader,
Detective Helena Munich, now walked up to
Lysander.

"The room is clear! I don't see how he
could have got by us?" She said in a strict
feminine German accent.

"O' he was here!" He mocked with the cold
failed wit of dry sarcasm.

"Where do you think he went?" She politely
asked in return.

"The Question's not where... But when???"
Responded Lysander, cryptically saying too

much. As he now stared upwards at the
clocks on the wall, that also now ticked
backwards!?

STOP THE CLOCK...

Chapter Two

INTRODUCING THE WHITEST WOMAN IN THE WORLD!

"Mirror, mirror on the wall! Who's the
purest of them all?"

The next night and ninety minutes later...

ORIGINAL HISTORY AGAIN... Austria! That was
the place and spot of physical description.
A place of glorious Vontrapp landscaping
majesty. A place of snow capped tree laden
mountain sides that all now sat drenched in
cleansing white blue moonlight. While in
just one particular mountain sided corner
of that nation. Substantial patterns of
black shadows stood cold and frozen, like a

spider waiting on a web for it's prey.
Casting themselves outwards from a massive
Château. That itself sat menacingly silent.
With a disturbing dead stillness in the
winters near Christmas night.

Thus evil in the far backdrop like a lair
in an old world war two movie. With
detonating burning amber sparks up high in
the night sky. Fireworks now began to
cascade with a multitude of rippling
coloured lights over the Château's grounds.
While the faint white patterns of fast
exhaling. And almost out of breath sounds
of a physically fit running individual now
sounded out!

Holding a bullet empty Pistol, plus
silencer. Barefoot in a tight fitting-sexy
red, Ms. Santa Clause outfit. A young
woman, with the drop dead gorgeous look of
a white Mediterranean. Now ran ahead,
trudging through thick layers of cold damp
snow. As clouds of cold coloured breath
continued to be expended from her over
worked lungs.

Throwing down her empty Pistol, running
like a hunted and nearly cornered animal.
Powering herself relentlessly forward. With
her hands covered in the red blood of five
just disposed Nazi thugs. That itself
looked more like wet coloured black ink,
due to the descending moonlight. The

unknown woman pushed herself forward, like a marathon runner reaching the last mile. As countless Henchmen, aided by German Shepherd guard dogs, now searched the Château's grounds by torch and searchlight.

Lead by head enforcer of violence, Brutus. All dressed up in military like snow camouflage fatigues. The Henchmen all searched onwards, like hunters looking for their prize kill of the day, or rather the night!

"Wolf to base! Wolf to Base!" Spoke Brutus into his com-link radio. "The Doctor is dead! Five men down... Juden escaping on foot. In pursuit! OVER!" He yelled!

Continually drenched in the echoing light of the detonating fireworks high above. The woman now reached a clearing of snow capped trees, half way up the mountain side. Sensing danger with fox like cunning skill, in seeing some of the snow on the tree branches had been displaced. The woman's spy like? Senses now kicked fully inwards...

Jumping into a quickly preformed duck, tuck and roll. The woman just narrowly avoided a burst of semi-automatic Pistol fire, that came from six hidden anonymous Henchmen! Who themselves stood concealed just ahead...

Snapping back upwards, straight to her feet. The woman, skilled in the violent and blatantly sadistic martial art of Krav Maga. Now battled against the six armed thugs...

Knocking out two of them with just a couple of fast placed punches. While grabbing hold of the third thugs gun. Killing him and the remaining three others with quick fast shooting instant aim, to the head and the face...

Looking ahead through a pair of Night vision digital binoculars. A skinny stick thin young thug, going by the name of Lars. Brutus' last in command. Now sighted a fast moving green lit silhouette. That was heading towards the edge of the mountain side.

"Herr Brutus! I see her, I see her!" Said Lars pointing and shouting loud in German.

"Target sighted... Taking action!" Shouted Brutus, taking instant aim with his Night-scope Sniper rifle!

A SHOT IN THE DARK EQUALS...? Masked by the just detonating fireworks. As the woman now reached the top of the mountain side, a single loud thunderous gunshot rang out!

Striking her dead in the chest! Sending a sticky-wet stream of blood and heart tissue spraying upwards through the cold night air. Thus in the throws of death and blood choking demise, taking one dying step forwards. Trying to still push her just dead body ahead out of sheer instinct. As her soul now emptied from her body. The now dead young woman's lifeless corps, slumped downwards...

Falling over the mountain side. Still beautiful even in death, with her arms both fully extended outwards. The young woman's body now sailed gracefully downwards, tumbling through the cold mountain air like a fallen angel. Heading towards a raging ice river below...

Lowering his Rifle Brutus now walked up to the mountain side edge, as more Henchmen ran up to his moving position. "Target! Eliminated!" He spoke coldly.

"All to easy!" Responded a cool and cold Germanic feminine accent, back over Brutus' com-link!

STOP THE CLOCK! REWIND THE TIME! TEMPORAL RESET!

With the just past events now playing
backwards. Time itself now rocketed ahead
at a full eye blinking, fast pace reverse.
As unknowingly to all, time now resets all
the way back to the days cold setting
winters evening sun!

HISTORY REWRITTEN... A hot air balloon of
18th Century design, sailed gently with
grace over a gigantic man made lake. As the
cold winters day sun now began to set over
a colossal white marbled Château. Which
itself once served as a lair to Hitler's
villainous Third Reich. Now owned by the
European corporation of business, Avatar
Industries. And serving as one of the many
homes to it's C.E.O Aryana Avatar. Who
herself had an uncanny knack for predicting
the highs and lows of the stock market? The
Chateau stood as a monstrous fortress to
capitalistic wickedness and pure corporate
greed.

A KEYSER SOZE OF A SORT... That's who "The
German" was. As just like that fictional
movie character. This particular unknown
super villain, was indeed a mystery to the
world of intelligence and anti-terror law
enforcement. With most, if not all
concerned not even really believing them to
be so. Thinking that it was just something
cowardly neo-nazis and white supremacists
alike collectively wished for but would
never have. With "The German" being in

villainous/heroic legend like Osama Bin Laden (Depending on who you ask!) to the misguided evil world of white supremacy! Ticking seconds replayed onwards...

With the sun now almost set. A ribbon of lights throughout the Château now switched on like clock work. Illuminating the whole mountainous grounds, in clinical man made light. As a giant Christmas tree stood tall, brightly lit outside the main wide stretching entrance.

"The greatest prize in war is art!" Just ask Hitler! Just ask The President or the Prime Minister! Former or current! That is what was on display all throughout. As inside the Château's many countless rooms and dwelling places. A large master study sat filled up with volumes of dusty books. Newly painted pieces of art that were worthless for today. But would be worth a small fortune by the near end of the century. And a large antique globe, that displayed the world of old. That itself stood as if newly just brought?

Holding a half filled or half empty (Which ever way you look at it?) Brandy glass. Walking past the globe trailing his pale skinny, middle aged right fingers along it's surface.

While a wall mounted flat screen, next generation 3DTV played on mute. Julius Kruger, Financial Director of Avatar Industries. And evil two-faced, back-stabbing business magnet. Stood proud yet short. Engaging in a conversation with a unknown person, over some kind of wireless like communications-link...?

A INVENTION OF TOMORROW, TODAY... A voice activated device. A Cellular phone without buttons? That was smaller than small in design. A nano phone of nano phones. That went by the highly creative name of a Red-Cell in the near future. That in itself looked just like a hands free kit, and yet looked very different?

"Gideon's dead! That idiot Walker's in I.C.U... O' hell no!" Spoke Julius Kruger with slight disappointment. "Well no matter, I've got the 411 on the situation! And we'll keep the rest on the what if and lo for the moment! Then we can move ahead... As that uneducated impure, inbred hillbilly hooligan. Knows nothing of our forth coming plans. We'll just give the job to his cousin instead." He stated taking a momentary pause. "O' and don't worry! Gideon was just the middle man. Serving his purpose... His death will not hold us back." He said sitting down at his solid oak desk. Tapping open a number of file icons on his computers ultra, ultra thin plasma monitor. Thus opening an encrypted file. Which itself displayed a flickering digital code key of ancient rune symbols. The same symbols that were displayed on Gideon's Computer.

"Bang on! It was him... The Patriot of the Planet... Or whatever it is he calls himself." Said Kruger, conservatively estimating what to do next. "No! He seems to be unaware of our plans for New York. Although? We will have to do something about that dark skinned individual very soon... Until then! We'll continue on with--THE PLAN!" Hanging up the line Kruger removed his Red-Cell. As Brutus now entered carrying a Aluminium briefcase. The same case he was carrying at Club Hate the night before.

"Holla!!! Brutus!" He greeted politely, clapping his palms together. "So what up blood!? What up Money?!!!"

"Err? I have the items you required!" Brutus declared not rolling his eyes as he wanted too, in hearing Kruger's use of "ghetto" street slang.

"Marvellous! The case!" Exclaimed Kruger taking hold of it.

Opening it up Kruger now sat amazed at what was inside. Amazed at the said items inside that where themselves over thirteen thousand years old... That were all encased in strange looking glass like sealed cylinders.

"Resurrection knives! All real. All mine. One down two to go." He uttered taking hold of one of the cylinders, making Brutus very nervous!

"Chill homie! These things cannot hurt you... Whoops a daisy!" He mocked pretending to drop it.

"Mein Herr!" He yelled clearing his throat speaking on. "The knives are one hundred and ten percent authentic as you said. They are more sharper than obsidian blade edges that themselves can reach almost molecular thinness."

"Science!!!" Mocked Kruger with a friendly smile. "I know Brutus. Aryana will be pleased."

"Where is she?"

"O' she's just finishing off her daily work-out!" Exclaimed Kruger, like a would-

be proud father! As he himself now tapped
open an E-Mail that was written in Arabic?

Elsewhere...

Meanwhile, as the night finished off
setting inwards outside. Loud almost
thunder like sounding high impact punches
and kicks! That were followed by violently
aggressive feminine power grunts. Just like
an female tennis player. Now echoed
outwards through the Château's Gymnasium.

"BOUDICCA THUNDER STRIKE!" Yelled a cold
yet sexy Germanic voice in perfectly toned
English. Signalling the use of a Te Vu'Kra
- Fu Power Move...

**INTRODUCING THE WHITEST WOMAN IN THE
WORLD**... "If Barbie was a Nazi she would
look exactly like this!" That was just one
of the many of the ways you could use to
describe her. This Valkyrie of evil! This
wannabe Amazon warrior Queen! This
Sovereign of the fake and beyond phoney
Master race. As skilled in the "Boudicca
Fist" technique of the martial art of
murder. And drenched in ice cold sweat.
Dressed in a tight fitting white cotton
vest with white metallic track suit bottoms
to match... Aryana Avatar, supposed good
Samaritan to the world and profiteer to
philanthropy. Looked downwards with a

sparkling ivory white smile, projecting a
shivering reverence of definitive evil.

"Same time tomorrow, boys!" She said in her
sexy smooth, femininely wicked voice. As
thirty muscular Henchmen now laid out
dotted around the room, half unconscious or
half dead...

Strikingly beautiful, in a absolutely
filthy gorgeous way. With symmetrical
beauty! That is the mathematical kind of
the Hollywood A-list and supermodels. With
the look of a young Nordic goddess. And
standing out at a sexy tall 6'f. Aryana now
peeled off her vest, throwing it down
without a care.

Exiting the echoing Gymnasium topless!
Smiling to herself with a cold glare
Entering one of the Chateau's forty seven
luxury spar like bathrooms. Aryana now
ripped open the studs on her track suit
bottoms. Stepping into a strange looking
power shower, that was made from solid onyx
and pure platinum.

"Shower On!" Spoke Aryana, as the fully
automated Château's in-house computer
systems activated, blasting out multiple
jets of hot soft pure spring water. That
gave a almost instant skin exfoliation! As
a digital wall unit next to the shower now

displayed the words "Music! Aryana's mix one!"

Gleaming like flawless marble through the wet fogged shower glass. Aryana's whiter than white skin began to almost shine. As it became immaculately pure, enveloped by white soapy foam bubbles. That were repeatedly washed away by the showers high intensity power heads.

As the music now cut out, Aryana stepped out of the shower. Wet and naked through and through. And not shamefully bashful, Aryana charged into her walk-in wardrobe with a cold despondent glare. Just like a cocaine snorting heroin shooting, and way to thin runway supermodel.

Echoing in size, her walk-in wardrobe stood as a corner stone to greed and self wanting. Containing countless glass cabinets filled up with priceless diamond and platinum jewellery. As well as millions upon millions of dollars worth of designer clothes and an infinity of footwear. That could have made even Imelda Marcos or Mariah Carey jealous with green eyed envy.

Looking at her naked and flawless body, lustfully admiring herself. While at the same time licking her lips. Aryana now stared deeply into her own reflective,

cobalt baby blue sparkling eyes! As her
personal assistants now entered with
collective poise.

Just turned nineteen years old, and of so-
called white ethnic Germanic extraction.
Come ladies in waiting. The set of blonde
blue eyed twin sisters, named Strawberry &
Platinum. Each now gracefully walked up to
their Queen.

Serving as her Girl Friday's! Dressed
looking like beauticians, wearing white.
And matching all of Aryana's clothing and
footwear. That themselves symbolized her
affinity and obsessive compulsion to that
particular suggestive colour of racial
purity. Strawberry and Platinum each now
stared at their boss. Come living Goddesses
bare naked body. As if they were looking at
a white marble statue of so-called Aryan
perfection!

Extending her arms upwards, Aryana now
stood in place enjoying every single touch
and soft rubbing sensation! As both
Platinum and Strawberry now dried her wet
smooth body softly, with large white fluffy
towels. As if she was royalty.

Dried off wrapping a towel around her waist
just like a man. Proudly unafraid to show
off her bare firmed full breasted chest.

Aryana moved up closer to her mirror. Enjoying her reflection...

"Mirror, mirror on the wall! Who's the purest of them all???" She spoke in a sultry, yet cold questioning manor. Looking closer, clapping her hands together in a prayer like manor. Aryana now stared even deeper into the full length digital mirror. "You are. You are!!!" She whispered to herself!

Three hours later...

With the night sky now cloudless, for just a while to come. A long and lengthy convoy of sports utility vehicles, Black limousines. And an assortment of one of a kind luxury cars, travelled towards the Château. As fallen moon beams now casts patterns of bright clean white light, all over the snow capped mountain side. All things seemed to be playing out the same again? As high above the sea of traffic at the top of the mountain. A shadowy silhouette of a Commando now snowboarded towards the Château...

Twisting and turning fast through the hard crisp current of snow and solid mountain ice. Dressed up in navy black assault gear, wearing the latest in hi-tec spy wear. In the form of mini Night vision goggles. That

themselves looked like across between a
pair of chunky swimming goggles and
designer sunglasses. The Commando now
stormed ahead towards a dead drop!

Speeding up! The mysterious Commando zoomed
to their seemingly imminent doom, storming
straight downwards below. As with certain
death almost a reality. The said Commando
now pulled open their concealed parachute
ripcord!!! Thus instantly deploying just in
the nick of time. The specialized parachute
now cast the Commando forwards on a silent
entry, over the lake below.

Just gliding over the ice cold lake with
bouncing hard pressed ripples, the Commando
sailed straight towards the gardens of the
Château.

Eighty-eight seconds onwards...

Armed with concealed automatic weapons that
themselves were of the latest design. And
bored with the tedious and very ordinary
routine of guard duty. Three anonymous
guards now patrolled the edge of the
gardens...

"Checking in... All clear!" Responded the
first Guard into his com-link in bored to
tears German...

"Clear here!"

"Yeah... All clear here as well!" Responded
the others back. As the first guard now
turned around to retrace his snow laden
steps. A silent hard thrust glove covered
fist now slammed into his face, knocking
him out for the count. Delivering the quick
blow with ease the Commando now ran
straight towards the neighbouring Guards.

Leaping upwards like a dynamite skilled
gold medal winning Olympic gymnast! The
Commando instantly delivered two single
spinning jump kicks. That each in turn
knocked out the two remaining guards, with
total quick hard hitting ease!

As both guards slumped downwards into
instant unconsciousness. The Commando now
coolly pulled off their black navy ski
mask, and mini Night vision goggles... Thus
revealing their identity to be that of
Secret Agent, Inari Gellar. That same woman
who was shot and killed while trying to
escape from the Chateau in the previously
original timeline!

An operative of the Zionist state of
Israel's very own secretive and highly
aloof. Come barbarously efficient
intelligence agency. That could give the

Waffen SS a run for it's money. "The
Mossad." Inari with the official title of
Officer Gellar! Moved with stealth and cat
like cunning, hiding away her gear.

A spy, come killer and walking war
criminal. Readying herself for her mission
of infiltration. Peeling off her black navy
jumpsuit in just one motion. Inari with one
cool twist and flick of her right wrist,
now pulled open her tied up silky smooth
Dahlia black hair. As living up to the
meaning of her first name, she now looked
immaculately beautiful. With her raven jet
black wavy hair now riding up slightly into
the night's cool winter breeze.

WORK IT GIRL! WORK IT... Dressed in a sexy
one piece, yet almost not revealing outfit.
Always "cooler then the red dress", with an
hour glass body and a runway walk! And most
definitely a perfect ten with a hollow
point, Teflon tipped bullet! Inari! Walked
ahead with ice glass cutting girl band cool.

"Let's do it!" Inari said in her mixed
American/Israeli accent, puckering her full
luscious ruby red lips together. Checking
her reflective appearance in a small make-
up compact. Only to then snap it shut in
just one motion, heading towards the party
that was now beginning to start inside.

Sixty seconds onwards...

As the gigantic Christmas tree continued to
stand proudly lit outside. More just
arriving guests now walked up to the
Château's main entrance. Only to be greeted
graciously by young female servants. Who
were all dressed up in tight fitting sexy
Miss. Santa Clause outfits, plus matching
bobble hats. As the guests, all handsomely
beautiful. From super rich elite
backgrounds, money new and old. Now
prepared to enjoy Aryana's newly famous
Winter Balls pre-Christmas party.

Broken into two distinctive sections. One
that contained displays of Avatar Industry
technologies and products. And the other
that contained a banquet fit for a million
Kings as well as a classical orchestra. The
Château's ballroom itself stood at a
monumentally reverberating size.

As three sparkling crystal champagne
fountain's placed in the centre of the
ballroom flowed downwards! Crowds now
talked amongst themselves, waiting for the
party to get into full swing. Waiting for
the arrival of Aryana.

Leaving the Ballroom, turning a corner.
Looking downwards... Not wanting to look
anyone directly in the eye! A servant now

walked towards the Chateau's Kitchens, accidentally bumping into Inari.

"O' I'm so sorry... Please... Please forgive me!" Responded the servant fearfully apologetic in a light east European accent.

"That's all right." Said Inari kindly, with reassurance. "I've gotten a little lost, could you tell me how to get to the ladies room?" Pretending to gesture with her hands, Inari now readied her sleep inducing needle ring! Which itself serves as a handy piece of spy gadgetry, designed to induce a non-lethal long deep sleep of up to six hours.

"Of course!" Responded the servant girl, raising her arm up to give directions. "You just head down..." Stopping instantly in mid sentence, she now collapsed downwards into a quick unconsciousness. As Inari delivered a fast and firm tapping hand press against her just extended arm.

Catching the servant girl in her arms just before she could hit the solid marble floor. Inari now went about putting the final plan of her infiltration into action. Taking her into an adjoining empty room!

Laid outwards upon a long stretched chair,
the servant girl still remained incomplete
unconsciousness. As Inari went about
undressing her.

"Now! Don't take this the wrong way. But I
need to borrow your clothes." Said Inari
whispering into the servant girls ear.
While at the same time removing a small
metal hair clip from her own hair! "Ho, ho,
ho! Here I go again. I hate this job! I
should have gone to dental school!"

Nine minutes later...

Meanwhile back inside the master study. A
state of the art CD player now silently
played a track at the highest ear drum
cracking audio setting.

Thus with "MP3 is not for me!" Wearing a
pair of headphones, preferring the CD
Players quality of sound over that of the
in-house computer system. Kruger now leaned
against his desk. Gesturing with his right
hand like a conductor, listening to his
music. While at the same time picking up a
Cuban cigar off the table, with his other
hand. Lighting the hand rolled Cigar up
with a one thousand dollar bill. As he
always did. Kruger now began to blow smoke
rings upwards. Only to then walk over to

the antique globe opening it up. Pouring himself a Brandy, taking a very large sip...

"I GOT 99 PROBLEM BUT THE BITCH AIN'T ONE! IF YA HAVING GIRL PROBLEMS I FEEL BAD FOR YOU SON." Said Kruger gesturing with his hands, bustin' moves like a teenager at a rap concert. "HALF A MIL FOR BAIL COS I'M AFRICAN!" He voiced gesturing towards his face.

"I GOT 99 PROBLEM BUT THE BITCH AIN'T ONE! HIT ME!!!!!!!!!!!!!" He commanded aloud to a empty room? Walking up to the CD player now taking out the disc. "Now that's what I call music!" He said to himself, placing a CD back into it's plastic album case. "I always enjoy da classics."

Turning around as he now stared downwards, taking another sip of brandy. Kruger now noticed a slightly shimmering feminine reflection...

"Hello my dear, child. I...?" He said politely, turning around. In thinking that the reflection belonged to that of Aryana. Surprised! And almost taken a back, Kruger now stared into the barrel of a Modified Desert Eagle 357 Handgun. That itself projected a green lighted laser sight, that reflected of his forehead.

"Merry Christmas, Motherfucker!" Cursed
Inari with hate. With a wanting of
vengeance for the actions she knew the
German had been responsible for? And had
profited in!

DON'T EVER MAKE IT PERSONAL...? That was
the silent advice of the moment and a rule
that should nearly always be obeyed. But
things never ever seem to be that easy when
your heart and human emotions are running
sky high. As now thus dressed up in the
Miss Clause outfit. Standing fixed in place
holding her gun tightly. Inari was almost
making the bad mistake of dropping her
guard...

"The charges are as following..." She
announced standing ready to pull the
trigger, about to perform an execution!
"Mass murder of Jews and Arabs alike...
Supply of arms to terrorists..."

"Takes one too know one!"

"The... The supply of unlawful and illegal
arms to my nation... The..."

"I don't know what you're talking about,
young lady!" Voiced Kruger acting as if he
was a so-called made man, and she was
wearing a wire.

"The start of a new wave of anti-
Semitism... And..."

"Anti-Semitism? That's a misleading notion!
As most of you aren't really from them. Are
we! You know, those Arabians. No! That's
just something that was made up to make you
stand out! As you're just diluted...
Polluted racial throwbacks of Poles, Slavs.
And those very racially inferior, Russians,
and of..."

"THE PLANNED, attack against a school full
of innocent children yesterday! The..."
Inari said ignoring Kruger's prejudice...

"What exactly are you accusing me of again?"

"Cut the SHIT! I've been onto you for a
while. And I know who you really are,
Julius Kruger. Or would you prefer to be
called by your ALIAS?"

"My alias?" Responded a pretending to be
puzzled Kruger...

"Don't play games you Nazi dumb fuck! Good
people died on all sides and in between
because of the likes of you. We fought a
WAR that shouldn't have been fought! My
friends died because of you... And my

people are never going to know peace, because of you! You!!!" She said tightening her grip on her gun. "And I've got the blood of countless civilians. Of innocent people on my hands. That I can never wash off! NEVER!!!" Uttered Inari with tears almost formed in her eyes. "FIFTY TWO PEOPLE! You've tainted my soul... You've..."

"Like you ever had one of those!"

"You've! You've dammed the children to hate! You've dammed us all..."

"You've dammed yourself, Juden... You let yourselves be consenting house slaves to the End-Timers, to the west and their Machine masters... You and your whole ethnically backward people are doomed! You're done! As in. Well, done!" Mocked Kruger. Making Inari force herself to not take violent reactionary offence.

"I'd tell you to suck it!" She uttered pointing the gun towards Kruger's mouth. "But you probably would!"

"Did I hit a nerve...? To close to the truth for you, Juden!? As... As--The one who will destroy you, you have made and they will come. They will make what is left

of the river Jordan run with the blood of
countless Jews... They're won't be an
Israel by the time it's over..." He voiced
laughing after...

"Cut the prophecy!" Announced Inari,
ignoring what exactly he was referring too?

"O' it's a fact! As the only thing that is
really going to be left of you people when
this is all over... Will be that Anne Frank
Diary, and those very disagreeable
Spielberg movies." He uttered with extreme
malice. "Although I did like the one he
made about, Peter Pan! But I digress. As
when all is said and done, you'll be
extinct! You'll be gone just like the
proverbial dinosaurs very soon. Or though,
then again it might not happen!? That's if
a certain someone intervenes, like he does.
As word has it he's quite the Judeophilic!
O' that's a person who loves you Jews.
Although?"

"Someone?" Inari declared confused. "Don't
you dare act crazy on me! You're THE
FUCKIN' GERMAN himself." She then spoke,
taking one single step forward, forcefully
looking Kruger dead in the eye!

"You crude speaking, vile, foolish child...
You dirty little social... I may be a

German. But I'm not THE GERMAN"! He mocked
laughingly. Stepping back at a single
smirking pace, Kruger now accidentally set
off Inari's spy skills!

One motion of reaction onwards...

Instantly knowing that their was another
person in the room. Inari! In just one said
movement, now spun around taking instant
lethal aim... Firing one single shot!

Standing at the opposite end of the room,
dressed to kill, quite literally. Aryana
now stood firmly in place! As the speeding
bullet violently cut through the air at the
speed of sound. And yet seemingly in slow
motion?

"BOUDICCA BULLET-BLOCK!!!" Shouted Aryana
coolly raising her hands upwards! Using a
Te Vu'Kra - Fu Power Move. Thus crossing
her arms and opened palm hands past each
other, as if she was performing some
strange type of yoga movement. She now
stopped the bullet in mid-flight!!!

With only just a single second passing,
Inari now looked on in a what the hell? Or
rather what the Fuck was that? Amazement!
As the bullet hung motionless, frozen
perfectly in place!

Just before Inari could now react by firing again. Aryana stormed onto her position. Delivering a single powerful uppercut! That seemed not to even connect with Inari's jaw...?

Dropping her gun, lifted off her feet completely. Inari had only one given destination. And that was of a hard impacting crash-landing straight into Kruger's solid oak table, breaking it in half. Knocking herself out for the count!

"Well done my dear!" Said Kruger proudly, with a quick given clap of his hands. "Who is this troublesome Judaic individual, anyway?"

"She's an ISRAELI Agent!" Said Aryana with contempt, looking down at Inari's gun.

"Tell me about it!" Politely commented Kruger, staring downwards at Inari as well. Thinking for just a moment! Just a single moment! "You know! I would say then, that this... Not so pretty and very impolite Jewess! Needs to be taught some manners."

"I agree!" Exclaimed Aryana. "I'll have the dirty little girl sent to, Dr. Soap. He knows how to clean up such, DISEASED FILTH!"

"Quite so. And very good my child."
Remarked Kruger in agreement, touching the
side of Aryana's face with soft, almost
Fatherly love!?

Now cold clocked, sucker punched and
beaten! Unable to even use her Krav Maga
combative skills! Inari laid trapped in
defeated unconsciousness. As Aryana stood
masterfully over her. Looking downwards,
like a predator enjoying the kill of it's
just slain prey!

Chapter Three

AND THE KEY WORD IS INFRASTRUCTURE!

"Are we expecting rain, Kruger?"

Fifty eight minutes later...

ENTER THE FASTEST MAN ON EARTH!...Therefore with nearly just an hour gone by, and the party now beginning to jump into full swing. With a display of Austrian culture, that included a Viennese waltz dancing floor show. That itself was of high performing excellence to world championship extreme. Jackson Carter! Sporting the appearance of a late twenties something white male. Now arrived fashionably late to the Winter balls party.

Unchallenged entering the said Chateau.
Dressed, styled like a Secret Agent
straight out of some old nineteen sixties
spy novel. Wearing a classic black tuxedo.
Jackson now walked towards the main
ballroom. That itself echoed with the sound
of friendly conversation!

Looking upwards as he entered, Jackson was
not even slightly impressed at the
ballrooms massive size. But knowing all
eyes of visible and invisible surveillance
were upon everyone inside and out. He now
gave an award winning performance of an
impressed man. As a very two-faced Kruger
now greeted U.N ambassadors, from around
the world.

"Doctor! How are things coming with the aid
package that we supplied you with?" Said
Kruger, to a UN African Ambassador, who
went by the name Dr. Victor.

"There going great Director Kruger, just
great! I don't know what the UN would have
done without you and Ms. Avatars help!"
Said the Ambassador, in his politely toned
Ethiopian English accent.

"O' it was our pleasure... As if we cannot
help one another, who can?" Laughed Kruger,
with a false friendly reassuring smile!
Standing at a distance, using his lip

reading skills and temporal sixth sense
abilities. As if he was all alone in the
room with Kruger and the Ambassador.
Jackson now noted the ongoing conversation
between them both.

"You must let me find a way of repaying
you... Yourself and Aryana must be my
honoured guest at the UN next time you're
in New York for a visit!" Responded the
Ambassador.

"New York? Well it won't be any time soon.
But be reassured that when we are next in
that magnificent city again. We'll take you
up on your more than gracious offer,
Doctor." Said Kruger, causing a still
watching Jackson to doubt this very much.
As Kruger's body language and vitals showed
that he was lying!

With the conversation ended Kruger now went
about greeting more guests. Thus seeing
this false and sickening exhibition of fake
tax-right off philanthropy, Jackson kept
his disgust to himself. Turning away, only
to see an interesting display of Avatar
Industry products...

AND THE KEY WORD IS INFRASTRUCTURE! The
apparent "IT" word of this already blood
soaked, early twenty first century. That
being the phrase. As in roads, schools,

Hospitals, water and power stations, urban centres, and shopping malls that sell over priced slave laboured goods. Of "foreign policy" in practice. Of democratic freedom. Of capitalism in blood drinking hot coffee motion!

Therefore thus the said it word of the now, as with extreme convenience just after a few so-called "civilized" people, come chicken shit bullies and cowards. Spinelessly bomb from high above and murder those who are not strong enough to fight back on a equal playing field. Then illegally occupy and do all things vile, that we will never know what truly has been done! While other "civilized" people stay silent with their apparent self loathing guilt on hold!? And whilst countless spaces and places on Earth. From New York's world trade centre and New Orleans. To the sovereign nations of Iraq and the Lebanon. And all in between. Have to now be rebuild and re-sculpted with reconstruction? Thus the said word of infrastructure has truly become a new or rather an updated art form of selective racist capitalism. And corporate fascist greed. In this brave new world. In this brave false new world order itself!

A one minute view of interesting things...?

Highly prolific and very instrumental with
apparent partial rebuilding throughout the
said places and spaces in the world. Avatar
Industries was itself seemingly a
"corporate psychic" when it came to being
prepared for crisis management. With the
export of much needed equipment for
disaster relief and war zones. As thus
making themselves a tonne of money out of
the recently made to occur on purpose
recession aka "the credit crunch." Come
undeclared depression. That has netted
AmeriKKKa and the rest of the western block
nation rapists a secret total that was into
the sky high billions and trillions.
Financing certain US and U.K government
special projects? (Celestial and otherwise.)

Thus with Avatar Industries bank rolling
over half of the power players in the rooms
business ventures and so on. Gluttonous
blood sucking come blood drinking Captains
of Industry from around the world. Avidly
sized up their impressive competition with
money lusting envy. Jackson now studied the
displays closely... That themselves ranged
from plastic model kit miniatures of world
famous super structures. Including a G.M
(Genetically modified!) Crop Laboratory and
Solar farm power plant (Yet to be built?).
To a range of communication and spy
satellites. And digital canvases of
gigantic prototype Cargo blimps and sub
orbital space planes. Plus not to mention a
large holographic 3D projection of a

strange looking half rocket, half jet
engine vehicle.

Instantly in seeing the projected image.
Jackson immediately recognized it as a
Stealth missile system. That itself was
originally designed to be used in
"Operation Iraqi freedom..." aka the Iraq
War! (Or the rape of Iraq as the history
books of tomorrow record it as.) But was
mysteriously cancelled on the eve of
congress approving full funding?

As Jackson continued to look at the
displays, a river of whispers now instantly
spread through the other guests?

"Ladies and Gentlemen!" Echoed the voice of
a hidden announcer as if he was about to
introduce a championship Boxer. "Honoured
guests! The C.E.O of Avatar Industries...
And Humanitarian of the year... Who herself
refused that particular title, giving it to
the runner-up instead... Introducing,
Austria's first and new favourite daughter,
Aryana Avatar!"

Thus--"The greatest trick the Devil pulled
was fooling the world into believing that
he did not exist!?" And Aryana was that
Devil. Not the kind of misguided vile
worded White Devil of reverse racism. But a
true definition of the word of devil

itself. As thus dressed to kill once more,
looking like a Classic Hollywood movie star
on Oscar night. Aryana! Who herself was a
practising racial hygienist! Was now
immaculately wearing "virgin white",
including long sleeve gloves. So she did
not have to touch the hands of any non-
white or Jewish guests, while greeting
them. Now smiled graciously. As a ripple of
approving applause echoed outwards.

"Thank-you, thank-you very kindly ladies
and gentlemen." Responded Aryana, as Kruger
now stood one step behind her.

"If you would be kind enough to step
outside, just for a moment! Myself and our
very lovely host. Aryana would like to show
you a very special demonstration. That is
sure to wet all of your appetites!" Said
Kruger politely hinting.

As the guests, Jackson included, now
curiously walked outside to gather on the
steps of the Chateau. Jackson himself now
noticed countless art works from statues to
paintings all dedicated to the myth and
legend of the seven sisters. From Greek
Mythology and beyond.

Two minutes and five seconds onwards...

Looking through the gathering crowd of
guests. With the night sky still remaining
cloudless, drenched in white blue
moonlight. Jackson now made eye contact
with Kruger himself! As the only true way
to gage the devil is to look him in the
eyes and get ready to say no!

Thus in thinking that Jackson was really a
white male, with the appearance of a more
than likely racially pure so-called Aryan.
Kruger gave him a sincere nod of friendly
greeting and approval. Not wanting to give
any hint of knowing or disapproval. He
instantly returned the nod back, giving a
friendly smile!

Turning to look slightly upwards Jackson
now noticed the large antique hot air
balloon moored just above the Château. As
the servants now went about handing out
countless umbrellas to all of the guests.
Kruger and Aryana included!

Taking hold of the just given Umbrella,
while at the time giving a friendly kind
smile back to the young servant girl. Who
herself shyly smiled back in returned.
Jackson now stared down at the umbrellas
bright yellow colour, wondering? Along with
the rest of the guests, what it was for? As
the sky seemed to remain completely
cloudless?

"Are we expecting rain, Kruger?" Said one of the guests loudly, puzzled! As everybody now went about opening their umbrellas.

"Just wait and see!" Responded Kruger, cryptically, as the guests including Jackson looked onward, all slightly perplexed?

With her hair styled short and wavy gracefully. Aryana now stood at a distance, in front of all of the guests. "Hello to you all... My name, as you all know is Aryana Avatar. And I am here to show you my very special gift to the world. Just in time for Christmas." She said politely holding a blood red coloured umbrella.

Gesturing gracefully with her right free arm, Aryana pointed towards the night sky over the giant man made lake. That stood opposite to them all. As the stars twinkled through the dark blanket that was the night. A single flashing falling star now sailed through the sky. Heading straight towards the Château.

"What you see before you in tonight's sky is a stealth missile!" She voiced loudly to the guests, jumping into a staged theatrically performed speech. "Designed to be used in the very sad mistake that was the Iraq war, this weapon of destruction

proved to be to powerful, to costly to the
preciousness of human life... Having full
stealth capability, powered by Hyper Scram
jet engines, that are able to travel seven
to ten times faster than the speed of sound
itself. Thus shattering the sound barrier
this weapon of murder. This weapon of chaos
has now become a weapon of... LIFE!"
Shouted Aryana at the top of her voice.

As within an instant the missile itself
detonated with a rippling thunderous RAW.
Sending outwards a cascading velvet puddle
of multi coloured light, that instantly
folded in on itself... As this happen all
of the crowd with the exception of Jackson,
stood watching with jaw dropping fear and
absolute amazement.

Just as soon as the puddle of light
finished folding inward. A massive burst of
pure, clean white light silently flashed
outwards...

With just a few seconds passing, seeming
like a lifetime. The crowd continued to
look on as a rumbling of thunder now
sounded out.

"And thus project RAINMAKER was born!" Said
Aryana loudly with royal predicting grace,
as a deluged of hard rain now fell from the
heavens above.

Looking shocked and totally amazed as the
falling rain bounced off all of their
Umbrellas tightly bound canopies. The crowd
all looked towards Aryana, almost as if she
was a living God!

"Thus we will be able to quench the world's
thirst! Thus we will now be able to cleanse
the world of all it's ills..." She supposed
with mysteriously hidden sub cryptic
suggestion?

Clicking her right fingers together, while
at the same time collapsing down her
umbrella! The rainfall now instantly
stopped, almost as if by her command.
Standing proudly with closeted racial
pride. And not a drop of rainfall on her
head. Aryana now looked ahead into the
amazed crowd of guests... While an
unimpressed Jackson Carter stared directly
at her, with a fearless superhero like
conviction of justice. As then with the
rain fall suspended! And the sky completely
cool. Sparkling with a clean night blue,
the crowd now all looked on clapping with a
sea of magical applause! All acting if
they'd just seem some kind of Vegas magic
show. Not realizing the full implication of
the outstandingly impressive, yet beyond
disturbing technology.

Feeling that she was being watched. Almost
with instinct, thinking, or rather knowing

that a pair of eyes were trained on her?
Aryana looked through the crowd, only to
see a chorus of applauding encore from the
guests??? Thus as she now graciously
accepted the continued applause. Jackson
Carter, with his standing position empty!
Now seemed to have disappeared completely
into thin air?

Three seconds later...

Meanwhile as the party continued above,
deep below in the château's sub levels.
Which themselves were designed with a clean
white clinical look of a Hospital. Drenched
throughout in dim night economy light. The
sound of shoe polished foot steps and loud
voices now echoed outwards.

"The Israeli agent is waiting for you
inside, Doctor!" Said Brutus. As Dr. Soap.
A young and extremely creepy looking skinny
fellow now walked along side. While three
Henchmen followed respectfully behind.

"A Zionist Agent you say... Indeed! That
sounds like a pleasant challenge! I haven't
had one of those in ages!" Responded the
near white blonde hair Doctor, carrying his
suitcase.

"Yes! She is very dangerous..." Voiced Brutus with concern.

"A she? A JEWESS! Exclaimed Dr. Soap, like a child receiving a surprise birthday present. "How Delicious! It's quite a rarity to get hold of a Mossad Agent. As they normally don't allow themselves to get taken alive!"

"Quite so! But never the less take caution, Doctor. As she broke through security with ease and almost assassinated Herr Kruger!"

"What a troublesome child! I do hope that she is still in one functioning piece!" He said looking down at his limited edition Mickey Mouse watch.

"O' do not, worry Doctor. As she is racially impure, Ms. Avatar has left the dirty Juden unmolested!"

"That's good to know Herr Brutus. As one could say that I have something in my case for the Jewess, that has a real STING in it's tail!" Exclaimed the Doctor laughing loudly. While Brutus and the other henchmen all looked wondering what was so funny?

"This way, Doctor!" Said Brutus, gesturing the way just ahead...

Thus reaching the end of the corridor. As they all now stood outside of one of the sub-levels many labs.

"You two stand guard. YOU! With me!" Ordered Brutus to his subordinates. "Enjoy your Jew! And Doctor... Don't forget that the room is completely proof of sound!" He voiced in misspoken English. "So remember... That when you carve her up like the BEAST she is. Make sure you make her SCREAM!!!"

"O' she will! Her kind always do!" Voiced the Doctor with a cold cutting, I've done this nearly a million times before stare. With Brutus and Lars now leaving to rejoin the party high upstairs, Dr. Soap walked into the Lab. As the two remaining Henchmen stood guard!

Eight seconds before...

Emptied of all equipment inside, with the exception of a small table and chair in the foreground. The Lab itself stood drenched throughout with bright clinical white fluorescent light. That reflected off the labs black tinned glass entry doors.

Still dressed up in the Miss Clause Santa
suit. Bound and secured by a single white
coloured strip of "Guantanamo" plastic
cuffs. Inari sat in the up right position,
with her head tilted downwards. Sleeping
silently in cold clocked unconsciousness,
as Dr. Soap now entered!

Being a true blue living monster, vile in
villainy. And the kind of person that when
they were a child they would pull the wings
off insects. And burn ants alive with a
magnifying glass on a sunny day. Dr. Soap
stood evil and twisted. As surprisingly
young, being just twenty-two years old in
body! With his mind being that of a fifty
plus years old man. And his descriptive
self being that of eyes cold dead blue
grey, hair Aryan blonde and skin pale
white. The Doctor now placed his suitcase
down onto the table, opening it up!

On closer inspection the well travelled and
worn leather like suitcase now revealed
it's contents. That consisted of a variety
of torture devices and instruments, that
all looked immaculately clean. Ranging from
two bars of surgical soap. Scalpels, an
assortment of surgical instruments and
drills. To Needle knives and Barber razors,
and a number of different coloured medicine
vials. That each in pigment and number
represented the seven colours of the
rainbow.

Plus not forgetting a plastic wrapped Ham? Sandwich and a single shiny red apple! Thus with matching old fashion syringes, placed upright next to a strange metallic container that buzzed with a mysterious humming, inside the case as well. The aforementioned Dr. Soap now removed a Polaroid instant Camera. That itself dated back from the early nineteen seventies. And yet looked brand new?

Walking up to Inari, the Doctor now stared at her sleeping beautiful image through his cameras viewfinder... "Rise and shine, my dear!" He exclaimed, taking one flashing picture! Awakening from the bright white light of the camera's flashing single pulse, Inari now blinked her eyes. As the doctor now peeled back the cover to the wet, just developed Polaroid picture.

Having a disturbed fetish for the smell of just developed Polaroid film, Dr. Soap now began to sniff and lick the side of the picture. As if he was tasting the temperature of just prepared soup.

"Think I'll save this one for later!" Spoke the creepy Doctor. Placing the picture in his top left breast pocket. Walking over to a sink at the back of the lab.

Removing his jacket, rolling up his
brilliant white shirt sleeves. Taking hold
of a bar of Surgical soap! That itself was
made from the fat from his previous
murdered victims. Dr. Soap now lived up to
his name. As he now begun to wash his hands
and arms all the way up to his elbows.
Washing his hands thoroughly, over and over
again nearly to the bone.

"My name is Dr. Soap..." Said the overtly
clean and beyond obsessive compulsive young
Doctor. "I have a few questions to ask
you, my child. It should not take to
long... But be reassured that it is okay
for you to SCREAM!"

"BITE ME!" Shouted Inari, with a face
filled with hate! As the Doctor put on a
double pair of white latex gloves, picking
up a old fashioned barber razor! Sharpening
it on a old leather? Strap.

"All in good time my dear... All in good
time!" Spoke the Doctor, now biting down
taking a chunk out of his red shiny apple.
Like the big bad wolf of grim fairy tales
himself.

"Thought you were quite the clever Jew,
concealing that hair clip, didn't you?" He
voiced throwing down the said item... "To
bad you did not count on German efficiency

with the use of the modern wonder of plastic cuffs."

As he now approached her with murderous intention, holding the razor up. Inari showed no sign of fear or panic. Preparing to break free and escape from her restraints, as she had unknowingly done before in the original timeline.

"I don't think that's the right tool for the job. As I think that soft JEWISH skin is too good too ruin by carving you up!" Said the Doctor, putting away the razor. "NO! It has much better uses! As I could always do with a new pair of Lamp Shades!!!" He laughed with a sickening anti-Judaic flare.

"DROP DEAD! YOU NAZI, MAMZER!" Shouted Inari with extreme anger. Calling the Doctor a bastard to the tenth generation degree.

"No! No! I Think I'll take you to a much higher level of pain!" Voiced the Doctor coldly walking up to his suitcase. Taking hold of a pair of tweezers! He now tapped the strange looking metallic container with two strikes of his left middle finger...

Swishing open with a cold icy swirl. The metallic container now revealed its contents...

A row of glass vials, each containing a single Killer African Honey Bee. Wingless Bees that had all had their wings removed by Dr. Soap himself. Now sat next to each other in a perfect symmetrical row. Thus removing a single Honey Bee! Holding the tweezers in his left hand. The Doctor now clasped tightly on the tweezers metal forceps, holding a Honey bee forcibly crawling in place. As he now took hold of a surgical scalpel with his free right hand. Walking over to Inari, planning a murderous dose of torturous interrogation...

"I personally guarantee you, my dear. That you won't die with the TENTH STING! Or the TWENTIETH! Or maybe not even the FIFTIETH... As somehow, I think you're going to be a record breaker!" Said the Doctor moving up closer to her...

PLASTIC NOT SO FANTASTIC... Knowing a trick of instant escape to her present captured situation. Inari with spy, come mad Houdini skills. Broke free of her plastic cuffed holding. As if she was double jointed, or at the very least had wrists of twistable rubber...

"Let's say we begin with your PRETTY LITTLE
EYES... Shall we!"

"No! Let's not!!!" Said Inari with charge
feminine aggression, holding up her now
free hands... Thus delivering one single
violent kick! Inari knocked the Doctor
completely backwards...

Now in just one fast motion she leapt
upwards towards the Doctor. Slamming his
whole left arm and hand that still held the
tweezers, that held the bee. Straight into
his left ear! While at the same time
snatching the scalpel out of his right hand
as well.

A supercharged kosher Bratz doll for adults
only. That swears like a sailor with guns,
knives and Girl Power attitude to match.
Inari now handled her business, as always!

"FUCK YOU AND DIE!!!" She screamed with
NEVER AGAIN conviction. As the tweezers
themselves now half jammed into the ear
canal and head of the Doctor. Who himself
now riled about in absolute pain, as the
bee had stung his inner ear drum. Thus
causing a river of blood to run out of his
wounded ear...

"GUARD!!!" He instantly screamed as Inari with scalpel in hand, now slit his throat from ear to ear. Sending a gush of fast projected blood jetting upwards. Splashing on the labs white clean ceiling tiles.

As the Doctor's just dead body, now slumped downwards. The tinted black glass entry doors to the lab now smashed open with the arrival of both Guard duty dwelling Henchmen, from just outside.

Slammed inwards as if they have both been hit by a fast moving vehicle. The Henchmen now crashed into the back wall of the lab. Dead! Both simultaneously impaled! With their bodies welded together by a "yellow" umbrella...

With everything now seemingly moving in slow motion. Inari now took a single one quick looking glare at the just slain Henchmen. Turning to view the just smashed entry doors?

"Officer Gellar..." Said Jackson, coolly stepping inwards into the lab. Just like a white hat wearing cowboy entering a western Saloon.

But before he could even finish his sentence, Inari mistakenly took him for the enemy. Throwing her just acquired scalpel straight towards his head!

Reacting with his martial art skills with sheer split second instinct. Raising his right hand upwards, Jackson now caught the spinning scalpel with just two right fingers...

"We need to talk!" He said throwing down the scalpel, taking a single step towards her.

Not believing him, in thinking that she is being set up in some kind of staged Nazi plotted "let's see her escape with false information" plan. Inari reacted with the bane of a spy, and paranoid to trust absolutely no one killer! Leaping forwards with a fast volley of spinning high kicks and high impacting punches...

Instantly blocking her Krav Maga skills with instant ease, reacting as if he was practising dance moves. Jackson instantly made apparent who was the master! And who was the student! As Inari herself now went for a last ditched, down and dirty move. Pressing her hand against Jackson's neck with all her might! Trying and failing to use her still wearing needle ring against him.

"Fuck no?" Was the look on her face as the needle ring failed instantly to knock him out? Jackson himself now violently grabbed hold of Inari. Slamming her body hard yet softly into the side of the wall...

"Listen to me, listen to me!" He said, holding her athletic feminine person tightly next to him.

"Go Fuck yourself, Nazi!!!" Cursed Inari pressed against the wall, one step away from snarling almost like a trapped animal trying to chew off it's own arm!

"No thanks! I don't love myself that much!" Voiced Jackson, continuing to firmly hold Inari against the wall. "Now listen, Officer Gellar. Listen good! Cos I'm only going to say this once! I'm a friend and soon to be ally to you!"

"You're no ally to me! You're just another soon to be dead, Nazi!" Inari said ready and wanting to kill Jackson were he firmly stood.

"I'm no Nazi, Officer Gellar!" He voiced.

"Prove it! PROVE IT!!!" She exclaimed, preparing herself to fight Jackson as soon as he released his iron vice like grip...

Spinning her whole person around to face him in just one single quick turning moment. Before she could even get a free thinking chance to react. Jackson now looked Inari dead in the eye... Thus activating his skin colour changing Temporal Ability. Turning his skin, hair and eyes back to it's natural colour and state...

Thus with her mouth one step away from a jaw dropping state of total disbelieve, Inari now looked with a--"What on Earth?" Manor.

"How the hell did you do that?" She said, now placing her hand gently against the side of Jackson's smooth and soft dark brown skin. As time itself almost seemed to stop still for both of them, for just a split second instant.

"Save the questions for later, Officer Gellar." Said Jackson with near suggestive haste. "For now...we have to get out of here!"

Chapter Four

OFF WITH THEIR HEADS!

"I'll take the three on the left!"

Two minutes and seven seconds later...

PARIS, FRANCE... Set amongst the Metropolis
of lights and high romance that was the
night life of the famous city. A large and
anonymous banking headquarters stood still.
All very much apparently closed for
business? As in the backdrop of the said
night. The Eiffel tower remained tall and
beautifully magnificent. Owned by a
international criminal organization, known
as the Order of Egret. That in itself had
ancient roots and origins. The bank stood

as a unified secret base of operations to the world's second most vile pocket of white Supremacy. With Neo Nazis, Euro Fascists, and KKK in unified service... Who together, having a hypocritical and unjustified hatred for nearly everything and everyone else on the planet. Who themselves were different to them. Including as unbelievable as it sounds, a vicious hatred of Wicca and all witches!? For some unknown or rather some never to be asked question?

INSIDE A BUNKER... Thus located inside the bowels of the unnamed and undisclosed bank. A hi-tec and cold grey stoned designed boardroom, stood respectfully quiet... As a committee of middle aged business men, along with one business woman. Sat upright in hard backed leather chairs, around a solid black table. That itself was equipped with rows of flat panelled computer monitors.

Acting as if they were members of a fortune five hundred company. This wicked congregation dedicated to some of the worst aspects of humanity. Looked the very model of respectability. Having giving themselves a daytime TV talk show makeover. Replacing their brown shirts, shaven heads, white sheets and pointed hoods of their failed history. In favour of the super high priced disguises of business suits, with three hundred grand Swiss watches to match. Going by the highly original name of "the committee!" The groups main members were highly proud to be representing racism. And all other prejudices that you could imagine to the ninth degree. And then some... As now all respectfully silent! Wearing their badges of bigotry and hate with racial pride. The chairman of the board. A Mr. Ran, now studied a number of digital photographs via his computer screen.

"Our Human trafficking operations in Dover, England! Last week! The destruction of our HIV experimentation clinics in Johannesburg the week before that... The Judaic children's School incident yesterday. O' and not forgetting Club Hate in Berlin early this morning. Death, freedom! Death, freedom! Death, freedom, death, destruction, death and mayhem. More death!" He voiced over and over again in a polite South African accent. While tapping through countless ultra violent blood letting crime scene photos. That themselves showed a high number of slain thugs and henchmen.

"This Planetary Patriot! Still pursuing his foolish crusade... A supposed deacon of defence! Declaring his very own Jihad! His very own personal war... His one man war on terror... On us and the rest of the whole wide world! Even governments too." He questioned loudly...

"He seems to know so much about us. And yet we know so little about him. Not even his real name." Remarked one of the Euro-fascists sitting next to him.

"We've tried pulling our resources with others out there. Even putting out feelers with our business rivals. And racial enemies in neighbouring territories, and still nothing... I mean The Russians, the Chinese, Nigerians... Hell even the Zionists no absolutely nothing as well!" Voiced another member.

"He's a complete mystery..." Said the Euro fascist.

"What about THE MACHINE! Do they?" Quizzed a Neo Nazi member, making a commenting query.

"Nothing! No word from them or rather their middle men. They refuse to even consider his existence. Considering him just a myth! A made up bogeyman." Voiced the KKK member, in a polite deep southern accent.

"This will not do!" Said Mr. Ran. Thinking to himself for just a fleeting moment. "Get our associate on the line!"

Same time... Different place...

AUSTRIA CONTINUED... With the festivities of the winter solstice going ahead without apparent incident. Aryana now engaged in the false niceties of small talk, and Christmas Yuletide banter. With the last of the guests gathered outside. Just as the fireworks began to detonate high up above in the night sky.

Looking up and ahead in amazement at the spectacle of colour, light and sound. All of the party goers stood watching in ore of the grand, and some would say absurdly fanciful. Multi million Olympic opening like fireworks display. As Brutus, with Lars in tow. Now calmly approached Aryana.

"My apologies for the interruption, Ms. Avatar!" Said Brutus whispering next to her.

"What seems to be the problem?" She whispered, with a straight faced smile!

"We have a slight infestation problem down below." Voiced Brutus, with extreme hinting politeness. Thus instantly causing Aryana's facial expression of innocent immaculate beauty. To turn into that of annoyed hidden hateful spite!

"I think we need a solution to our new found infestation problem! Don't you think so?" She questioned rhetorically with a sexy smile of sinless evil... "A final solution! Brutus!"

"Consider it done!" Exclaimed Brutus with an evil all is at hand glare as he now walked away.

Elsewhere and below...

At the very top of the Chateau's upper sub levels. Jackson and Inari now firmly walked ahead, travelling down the narrow and clinically cold corridors. Heading straight towards a secret exit point!

"O' shit! You broke my ring!" Declared Inari looking at it closely. "My ring!!! You know my people don't hand out things like this to everyone! Junk!" She now exclaimed in Hebrew about to take it off, only for it to not come off? "O' great! It's stuck!" Inari voiced not getting any return comments from Jackson himself.

"So--Err? I didn't catch your name back there!" She asked, politely wanting Jackson to introduce himself. "That's right! You didn't!" Exclaimed Jackson, not saying his name...?

"So who are you, Agent?" She quizzed on,
tittering near the verge of interrogating
Jackson with twenty questions or more!
"CIA? NSA? Home-Sec." She Said in reference
to the US Department of Homeland security.
"FBI? BBC? MTV? PBS? HBO?" She mocked with
a hinting smile. "O' I see! MI6? On her
Majesty's secret service... Great cover!
BLACK tuxedo. Highly original! I never
would have guest?" Mocked Inari once more,
with her very own specially styled
cynically cut to the wire, dry humour.

Firm faced and completely ignoring her
sarcastic banter, as they now reached the
end of the last corridor. Jackson with
protective instinct, now rudely pushed
ahead...

"This way!" He voiced firmly pointing the
way towards a secret exit. That was shaped
in the form of a large antique mirror. That
then silently opened...

Two seconds onwards...

Exiting with cooled and composed caution!?
Both Jackson and Inari now walked inward.
Straight into a large, echoing art gallery
styled section of the Château. That itself
stood quiet, with the exception of the just
detonating fireworks outside.

With a very large painting of the seven
sisters chalk cliffs located in Great
Britain. And being Cathedral like in
design, with a ceiling that was hung
higher than high. Along with a balcony
level half way up. This part of the Château
looked more like a history museum,
dedicated to European art. Filled up with
countless rare wall mounted paintings and
white marbled sculptures. All once more
dedicated to the myth of the seven sisters.
As well as being decorated throughout with
antique weapons from the middle ages. That
themselves were all loosely fixed to the
long stretching walls.

Looking around, Inari now sighted four
exits. That each were in the form of a
large solid door, spaced on each opposite
side of the room. "Okay hero! Which way?"
She said.

Not answering her, knowing that they were
not the only two in the gigantic room.
Jackson instantly realized that a trap was
being set for them both.

"Stay close! Follow my lead!" He said
quickly, knowing instant danger and a
violent death for them both was imminent.

"What?" Said a momentarily puzzled Inari.
As her spy senses kicked instantly inward
once more...

Hidden! Laying in wait inside, ten Henchmen
now jumped onto Jackson's and Inari's
position. All dressed in black suits and
armed with metallic batons. The thugs now
attempted and immediately failed to defeat
their intrusive guests. As Jackson and
Inari instantly held their ground, back to
back like would-be super heroes. Knocking
out six of the incoming thugs within a few
fast pace violently charged seconds...

"SWITCH!" Yelled Jackson with collective
cool, ordering Inari to change position.

Instantly and almost unconsciously obeying
him, as three of the remaining thugs
stormed toward her. Inari pushed against
Jackson's back. As they both spun around,
changing positions... As Inari now faced
just one remaining thug. Knocking him out
with two quickly unleashed Krav Maga
strikes. While Jackson now delivered one
single eye blinking fast kick. That itself
instantly impacted into all three incoming
thugs from the opposite side. Thus knocking
all of them down and out for the count!

"Well that was easy!" Said Inari taking a
quick breath. As now without warning, all

four oak doors now slammed open! To reveal
a countless number of Henchmen.

Looking from left to right Inari now turned
to Jackson. "I'll take the three on the
left!" She said with a sexy wicked straight
faced grin. As Jackson now raised his right
eye brow...

Remaining back to back with Inari, a calmly
composed Jackson stood ready for Battle!
Knowing he had the situation ON-LOCK as
always. As he now fearlessly engaged the
enemy... Knocking down and out multiple
opposition, with either a single quickly
delivered punch! Kick! Face breaking head
butt or high knee to the torso.

Trying and instantly failing to wrestle
Jackson to the ground. As he himself just
shrugged of their twelve handed grip, with
just one slight lift of his arms and
shoulders. The six thugs now accidentally
ripped away the whole of his black tuxedo
jacket.

Causing Jackson to react by instantly
unleashing two quickly performed spin
kicks... Thus knocking out all six thugs.
As Jackson himself now threw down his black
coloured bow-tie, unbuttoning the top
collar of his brilliant white shirt.
Engaging even more opponents!

Standing her ground respectfully and having an incendiary temper. Inari now fought with violently laced feminine aggression. Screaming out with a number of highly charged power grunts, as she unleashed a number of fast and hard hitting Krav Maga moves.

With the last of the thugs near her position defeated, and standing not far from beneath the balcony. Inari now spun around. As the sound of a bouncing metallic object now echoed outwards...

Staring downward frozen in place, as a single waiting second seemed too last forever. Inari now looked to see a just thrown flash bang grenade, that was a split second a away from detonation!

Seemingly doomed to a instant concussive super heated filled death. And as fear and panic were just about to fill Inari's almond honey brown eyes... Jackson now somersaulted through the air towards her. Lifting! Throwing Inari straight upwards, as if she was a rag doll...

Feeling herself lifted up from the ground, as if she was a acrobat leaping from a trapeze. Inari's face now filled with elevated surprise! As the grenade now detonated. A loud booming nearly sub-

supersonic wave of sound, now echoed
outwards throughout the Cathedral like
structure. Only being partly masked by the
increasingly louder detonation of fireworks
from high outside...

Now thrown almost as high as the ceiling,
Inari now began to fall downwards... Only
to be caught just in time by a still
somersaulting Jackson. Who himself seemed
to masterfully nearly fly through the
air!...

"GOT YOU!" Jackson said, thus catching her
with one arm just like a Trapeze artist. As
he now threw Inari straight into the path
of four just entering Henchmen!

Thrown through the air, Inari's
horizontally level body now slammed into
the thugs Knocking them down. Just like a
perfect strike of ten bowling pins. As she
now landed with a perfectly delivered
twisting turn like a Gymnast. Inari now
jumped up to her feet! Only to see Jackson
now land safely downwards from an
impossible height!

Now standing at opposite ends of the
lengthy room. Both Jackson and Inari stood
ready for more hand to hand combat. As the
next wave of thugs entered, all
simultaneously running to armed themselves

with the wall mounted weapons. That ranged from swords and a few shields, to axes and lances...

Possessing the manuscript to professional ass whoopin' in every way. Taking on all comers, Jackson now fought onwards. As so did Inari... Hitting them all so hard, that they would never get up again. Jackson destroyed all of the approaching enemy, with head breaking body hits. As Inari just managed to dodge and duck incoming weapon strikes and cuts. Fighting back with a hard impacting technique of Krav Maga!

"DIE!!!" Yelled a thug in German, charging towards Jackson with a long lance.

Just twisting to avoid the approaching villain, Jackson slammed his right elbow into the thugs face. Breaking it apart completely, with one single bloody crunch.... Now taking hold of the lance he now rammed it straight into another incoming villain. Thus impaling the approaching thug with a violent thrust, Jackson now through the lance straight upwards. Just like an Olympic athlete. Sending the now dying thug vertical! Causing him to be slammed upwards straight into the high ceiling!

As she now battled against two more
Henchmen, knocking them out. Another with
sword in hand, now went to stab Inari in
the back!

Turning! In somehow instantly knowing that
she was in danger, Jackson now jumped
through the air. "TEMPORAL CONCUSSION
KICK!" He shouted, snapping into a lethal
power move!...

Instantly impacting into the thug just
before he could kill Inari. Jackson's
skills lived up to the true meaning of the
martial art of murder. As the thug was now
propelled through the room. Lifted off both
feet as if he had a rocket strapped to his
back, just as if he was in an old cartoon.
Hitting the wall at a high impacting speed.
The thugs body now hung broken and smashed
apart, embedded into the once solid now
cracked apart wall. As now dodging a few
sword thrusts with lightening ease. While
the final wave of weapon wielding Henchmen
approached. Jackson went for the proverbial
jugular, quite literally.

Taking hold of a incoming villains sword,
stabbing him in the stomach with it.
Jackson somersaulted over the thugs fallen
impaled body... Now taking hold of the
sword itself and thus using it against the
last of the Henchmen.

Killing three of them within just a few
seconds. He slammed the sword straight into
another incoming thug. Turning and spinning
around, only to kick the sword that itself
was still impaled into the thug! Sending
his dead body backwards through the air.

In shock at the violent ease in which he
could kill. One of the thugs tried to use
his shield to protect himself. Only to have
Jackson lightly punch the shield! Thus
causing it to break apart... Revealing a
bloody mouthed and very much just dead
cowardly thug!

Thus with just three Henchmen left, Jackson
ducked and dodge two of them who tried to
cut him down with their swords. Only to
have him kill them with each others
weapons... As the last sword wielding thug
stormed towards him. Jackson grabbed hold
of the villains weapon carrying arm,
snapping it apart. While at the same time
flipping the sword upwards!

As the sword itself now spun through the
air, Jackson went airborne!

"I'm the MVP, you know me!" That was the
order of business. As just like a Most
Valued basketball Player making a point
winning slam-dunk! Grabbing hold of the
sword while at the same time holding it's

pointed end downwards. He now jumped back
down to earth, with a hard hitting bump.
Thus slamming the whole of the sword
straight into and through the thugs skull.
Cutting all the way into his spine... Dead!
Murdered and killed without mercy where he
stood. The thug now fell to the ground in a
large puddle of his own blood!

Standing firm faced with vicious
conviction, Jackson now turned to look at
Inari. Who herself was slightly taken aback
at his just delivered act of violence!

"O` my, God!!!" She whispered to herself in
Hebrew, under her breath... As another
voice now echoed outwards?

"And I just had those floors cleaned..."
Said Aryana, who was now standing at the
top of the balcony level of the room. "I'd
send you the bill, but they say you can't
get an E-Mail in hell!" She announced
giving a falling flat joke. As more
brightly detonated fireworks screamed
outwards outside...

Now covered in the multi coloured flashes
of light. Jackson and Inari looked upwards
as Aryana spoke again... "We meet at last,
future boy!" She voiced slightly annoyed,
with racial suggestion. "Some how I thought
you'd be, DARKER!" Aryana mocked politely.

With her racial suggestion bouncing off his
persona like bullets hitting Superman's
chest. Jackson now responded. "And somehow
I'd thought you'd be THINNER. But I won't
hold it against you!" He remarked coolly in
return. Thus causing Inari to instantly
smirk with a cheeky grin, at his smooth
quick given comeback! Hiding her continued
annoyance with a false perfect smile.
Aryana now looked up for just a second, to
see one of her Henchmen impaled into the
ceiling...

"You know you both shouldn't have gate
crashed my party. As now... I'm just going
too have too ask you too leave. Let me
introduce you to Platinum and Strawberry.
My girl Fridays!" Echoed Aryana's voice, as
both twin sisters now stepped out onto the
balcony. "Girls! Show THEM, the door!!!"
She firmly ordered, clicking her fingers.

"NORDIC DRAGON JUMP!" Shouted both twins,
leaping off the balcony, simultaneously
performing a Power Move!

Instantly realizing that they were skilled
in Te Vu'Kra - Fu. Jackson now readied
himself for battle. As Brutus, armed with a
silenced automatic weapon. Now entered
through one of the lower doors. Taking
instant aim for a cornered Inari!!!

"AMBUSH!!!" Shouted Jackson in hearing
Brutus take aim. Just as he was about to
engaged Platinum and Strawberry.

As a single ticking second now felt like a
frozen moment. Jackson almost seemed to fly
and slide across the room with both his
feet still on the ground... As he now
preformed a speeding dodge slide glide,
reaching Inari's position in an instant.

Proving himself to be every bit the living
real life "Superhero" his secret reputation
said he was. Jackson now grabbed hold of
Inari tightly, spinning her whole person
around into his muscular arms. Just as
Brutus unleashed a continuous burst of
nearly silent automatic gunfire!
Bulletproof throughout in body with his
back turned. Jackson now shielded Inari
from a violent instant death. As every
single white hot incoming bullet now fell
to the ground!

Whilst the rain of gunfire now ended as
nearly as fast as it had begun. And Brutus'
attempted to reload. Jackson, with the back
of his brilliant white shirt now a cotton
Swiss cheese, having a high number of
bullet holes. Now released his protective
grip of Inari.

Turning to instantly crush Brutus' weapon into a metal mush with one hand. As at the same time striking him with a half closed hand. Almost as if he was waving away a fly from his vision!

"OFF WITH THEIR HEADS!" Ordered Aryana with violent grace, to her girl Fridays, just like a Elizabethan Queen.

Knocked back hard into the ground. Brutus now laid unconscious, as Inari foolishly now engaged Strawberry...

"NORDIC SCISSOR KICK!" Yelled Strawberry, pouncing through the air like a Cat...

Thus proving to be no match against the Martial Art of murder. Inari's Krav Maga skills failed to protect or defend her. As Strawberry's power move now impacted. Instantly injuring her and knocking her out and down for the count!

Just as she was about to finish her off with a lethal power move. Strawberry found herself ejected in full reverse through the air. As Jackson himself now violently lifted her off the ground, by pulling her backwards by her very own blonde silky hair...

Thrown almost half way across the room.
Strawberry now slammed into Platinum! Who
herself was just about to try and unleash a
power move against Jackson himself.

TWO CHOICES INSTANTLY AHEAD...? With Inari
now injured and his only remaining options
being that of fight or flight. Jackson now
decided the latter of the two. As he now
powered forward in one single fast motion,
just like a sprinter running at a track
meet!

Grabbing hold of Inari by her limp right
arm. Exiting straight out of the room, at a
eye blinking fast running pace. Jackson now
pulled her unconscious body just behind
him, as if he was rescuing a fallen comrade
from a War Zone? While jumping back to
their feet. Following them with great speed
and increased quickness, Platinum and
Strawberry now violently stormed ahead in
full pursuit.

Three seconds later...

Running into an adjoining pool room. That
contained as you would expect a number of
large gaming blue felt covered pool tables.
And sliding Inari unconscious body forward
across the floor. Jackson now spun around
in one fast quick turning motion. As he
with unbelievable strength, kicked one of

the pool tables upwards! And straight ahead
towards the rooms doorway! Only to turn
around once more within just the same
second. Lifting up Inari in one fast
running scooping motion. Cradling her in
his arms to a rapid escape!

Just as they both ran towards the room.
Platinum and Strawberry now jumped upwards
in seeing the fast moving kicked table,
that was heading towards them...

"NORDIC HAMMER STRIKE!" They yelled,
instantly breaking the table completely
apart!

Entering at a cautious running pace, as the
last of the fireworks completed their
detonation sequence outside. Both twins now
scouted ahead, as if they were Lionesses on
the hunt. Turning around at exactly the
same time. Strawberry and Platinum now felt
a gusty breeze sweep across the room. As
the doors to an outside balcony now hung
blown wide open. And an unnoticed high
mounted wall clock now ticked backwards???

Chapter Five

WELCOME TO THE WONDERFUL WORLD OF TOMORROW!

"The future is sadly always sighted in
innocent blood!"

Seven years and two days, to the 22nd
Century... And the end of the World?

DAWN... December 30th 2092 was now the date
in question, with the exact day itself
being a Tuesday. As rising over a seemingly
endless and some would say forever
stretching ocean. The morning sun now
glowed anew, reborn as always in perfected
glowing amber orange. As standing just
outside of time and reality. Located on the

edge of the world, a place some where
between nowhere, anywhere and everywhere.
The Islands of Promise, or Promise Island
as it had eventually come to be known.
Stood mysterious and untold to the
unknowing outside world of tomorrow.

Wrapped in a shield of invisibility that
cloaked it's presents. Drenched throughout
with white beaches, tropical landscapes and
a sleeping volcano dead centre. The Island
stood as a secret base of operations to
Jackson Carter. Equipped with all kinds of
modern wonders and advanced clean
technologies of the future and past as
well...

Standing alone watching the just rising
sun. Jackson's Dog, a white wolfhound who
went by the name of Sherlock. Now commanded
the moment of the newly arrived morning as
he always did. Only to now raise his ear's
up like as if he was expecting his master,
and his best friend to come home!

Turning around with a happy go lucky
gallop. Sherlock! Now ran towards the
Island central bubbled domed complex. As
countless leagues beneath the sea. Laying
on the ocean floor, half covered in sand
and silt. An alien object and living entity
to beautiful to describe, sat all alone.
Nearly the size of a small city. Known only
by it's coded nickname as--"The Submarine!"

This piece of mysterious and cryptic
Extraterrestrial technology is now home to
the fastest man on earth. Serving as his
would-be fortress of solitude, as well as
his base of temporal operations.

Thus this unimaginable object had the
ability and projected will, to send Jackson
Carter to any time in past Human history it
wishes to... Fixing right what once went
wrong. Or what has been changed for the
worst!

Time in silent motion...

Inside it's inner chambers the Submarine's
crystal cold structure. Resonated with the
perpetual peace of pure serenity. As a row
of portals, that served as gateways to the
past, sat still and silent just for the
moment... Now almost just like a scary
scene in a movie, that would normally make
the average person jump out of their seat.
A single solitary portal now activated!

VIEWED IN LIGHTSPEED TEMPORAL DELIVERY...
Hailing the arrival of the fastest man on
earth, plus one. A description to
beautiful. To immaculately amazing to be
foretold, and verbally described. Or even
imagined by anyone. Was now in molecular
motion. As a doorway through the 4th

dimension, a doorway through time itself
was now momentarily opened...

Through the portal, that was instantly
closed shut behind him. Jackson! Still
cradling an unconscious Inari in his huge
arms, and taking a few more steps forward.
Was now greeted by one of his assistants!
Who went by the nickname of "Techy!" Happy
to see his best friend safely back as
always. Whilst wanting to act like some kid
in an old war movie. Greeting the door to
his Dad or big brother that was coming
home. Techy instead kept it cool!

"Hey! J.C's is in the House! In the House!
In the House!" He exclaimed like the super
fan he was. "Peachy keen, J.C! Back on the
dot as always..." Techy now said looking at
Inari! "Who's your hot date?"

"Cut the humour, Techy!" Said Jackson with
firm faced concern. "This is Officer
Gellar! She just received a scissor kick
blow. Nordic style!"

"Nordic style!" Said Techy walking up to
them. As Jackson now stared downward at
Inari. Who herself looked even more
beautiful asleep, trapped in
unconsciousness once again...

"Was it the German, herself?"

"NO! One of her flunkies!"

"She's lucky to be still alive."

"Yeah! She is... I'll take her up to Liz in Medical!" Voiced Jackson.

"Don't worry, J.C. She'll be, A-Okay!" Uttered Techy, with his tone now completely serious.

STOP THE CLOCK! BACK TO NOW...

Two hours after midnight...

AUSTRIA CONCLUDED... With the party long over and the guests all gone, the halls of the Chateau stood empty, washed clean of the spilled blood and murder on the floors. As all alone in her monumentally gigantic walk-in wardrobe, Aryana stood looking as if she was the only person in the world...

"Am I putting on weight? Am I fat?" Was the look on Aryana's face.

With herself secretly purging her last eaten meal just minutes before! Only to now look at her perfect ten Nazi Barbie, come runway model reflection in a full length mirror. Acting as if it was her very own and personal magic mirror of grim fairy tales?

Staring up and down again and again. Studying herself very closely. Looking for any faults in her purer than purer mind set. Thinking that she was overweight (Even though she was a zero!) with Jackson's passing comments having messed with her head. Just a little! Well maybe? Just maybe quite a lot!

"Mirror, mirror on the wall, who's the purist of them all!" Said Aryana, having a wanton vanity personality disorder of Hollywood proportions. This time not giving herself the answer?

Dysmorphic syndrome was her physiological condition. But racism, or skin colour and religious bigotry was her social disease. Thus one step away from tears. Aryana now turned around taking one last look at herself in the mirror. As her girl Fridays, Platinum and Strawberry now entered. Ushering inwards a near to tears servant girl. The same servant girl who had been knocked out earlier that night by Inari.

"Well who do we have here?" Asked Aryana rhetorically and aloud.

"O' forgive me! O' forgive me! Please... I didn't know, she got...I..." Muttered the young servant girl!

"Not a word!" Voiced Aryana with a disturbing hush, placing her right index finger over her own mouth.

"I didn't..."

"Shut up! She said silence!" Yelled both Strawberry and Platinum.

"That's all right, girls. She's just a little scared! Frighten even." Mocked Aryana now walking up to them. "Come on, this way, it's quite all right." She said, as both girls now looked disappointed that they would not get a chance to harass her themselves.

An emotional wreck! Shaking, just one step away from passing out. The servant girl mumbled with her mouth closed shut! As Aryana now placed her arms around and over her person in a very, very and O' quite so not appropriate way...?

"What do you see...?" Asked Aryana... "Do you see perfection? Do you see the purist of them all?"

"I...? I don't understand?" Uttered the servant girl, now with just forming tears in her innocent eyes.

"O' they will... You, them and everybody will... BOUDICCA STRIKING PUNCH!!!" She exclaimed. Thus instantly unleashing one violent and very deadly Power Move of the Martial Art of Murder. Killing the Servant girl. Sending her body crashing straight into the mirror.

Dead before she even slammed into the mirror breaking it into a shattering half. The servant girl's body now slumped down, bloody and broken from within.

Thus seeming to reaffirmed her false superior stance once more, with regained confidence! Aryana stared forth as if she was looking ahead for a hundred miles. As with her own reflection now broken and distorted in the remaining pieces of the shattered digital mirror.

"Mirror, mirror on the wall. I am the purist of them all... Aren't I?" She announced, like a mentally disturbed child?

Answering her own question with a answer,
only to doubt it all once more!

Showing that her vile and evil ways of
racial bigotry had cracks in it. That were
bigger than the valleys and canyons on
Mars... And they were pretty big!

Four hours and three minutes later...

BERLIN CONTINUED... Now symbolizing a
returned and fully unified city, as well as
an entire nation. Germany's Brandenburg
gate stood imposingly tall and yet
beautifully structured in the distance. As
a row of plain and seemingly unimaginative
office complexes stood indifferently
boring. Built coldly clean throughout, all
standing out as a stereotypical model of
German efficiency. That themselves abided
quietly still, in the just arrived
morning's dying winters night.

Sculpted out of steel and glass, occupying
an uninteresting part of the city. The
FBI's central Berlin field office. Remained
asleep yet secure, with only half of it's
armoured glassed windows lit up. As inside
standing at the end of a brightly half lit
corridor. Taking a five minute break. And
wearing the start of a just developing
would-be five O' clock shadow. Lysander now

finished off drinking the last of his black
with two sugars coffee.

Just like "the Mountie" of Canada, he was
dedicated to always getting his man! A
would-be Javert straight out of the Victor
Hugo novel Les Misérables. Meets Lt. Gerard
out of The Fugitive, in his pursuit of "The
Planetary Patriot!" Lysander was known for
leaving NO case unsolved and no stone
unturned. As he now walked with his head
slightly lowered, trying to hold back a jaw
gaping yawn. Slowly heading back to his
make shift office that was at the end of
the corridor...

Usually kept for file storage, the
makeshift office remained quiet and
seemingly uninteresting inside. As
Detective Helena Munich, dressed in a
stylish black trouser suit. And sporting
wet blonde cropped hair. Now stood with
wondering eyes, walking around the room.
Acting just like a Mother nosing around her
teenage daughter's bedroom for the hidden
secrets of a diary.

Sighting a briefcase out of the corner of
her right eye, that itself had been left
opened. Detective Munich now approached it.

Placed on top of a collapsible table next
to a plain closed shut white cardboard box.

The opened briefcase could now be seen to hold a number of red Notebooks as well as a switched off PDA.

Picking up the top red note book, flicking through it. Munich now was surprise to see that it was in fact a scrapbook. That itself contained countless newspaper clippings from around the world, written in many languages. As only fluent in English and French as well as her own native German. Munich now read through a number of the clippings...

"LIGHTENING STRIKES TWICE!!! TERROR PLOT FOILED AGAIN! THIRTY THREE SUSPECTS (WHITE MUSLIM CONVERTS?) FOUND MURDERED AT LONDON'S HEATHROW AIRPORT. SCOTLAND YARD ANTI-TERROR SQUAD SEEK UNIDENTIFIED BRITISH ASIAN MALE FOR QUESTIONING?"

"MANIAC COP!!! UNKNOWN AND UNARMED? POLICE OFFICER FOILS VEGAS BANK ROBBERY. VIOLENT HI-TEC CRIMINAL GANG KILLED AT SCENE!

HOSTAGES & SWAT TEAM SAVED BY SAID UNKNOWN POLICE OFFICER? HIGH SPEED CHASE AFTERMATH LEAVES TWO HUNDRED MILLION IN GOLD BULLION MISSING?"

"THE HILLS HAVE EYES! HUMAN HEAD HUNTER HORROR REVEALED! SERIAL KILLERS FOUND DEAD

IN AUSSIE OUTBACK, BUTCHERED BY UNKNOWN
ABORIGINE MAD MAN! AMERICAN BACK-PACKER
FOUND ALIVE REFUSES TO CONFIRM EVENTS TO
LOCAL POLICE AND THE FBI!"

"BLACK SUNDAY! BLACK SKY!!! OIL DEPOT
EXPLOSION... POSSIBLE TERROR ATTACK? OR
GOVERNMENT EXPERIMENT GONE WRONG???"

Closing the notebook shut, looking across
the room as if something had just caught
her eye. Munich now walked up to a large
whiteboard. That itself had a working
profile of "The Planetary Patriot" on it.

Written in black and blue marker pen the
working profile of Jackson Carter himself,
read as...

Real name unknown?

Alias' "The Planetary Patriot!"

A.k.a "The fastest man on earth!"

Who is the--"The German!???"

Planetary Patriotism?

Sane!/Yet seemingly insane motives?

Actions of violence...

A tactical method in his madness.

Plays no favourites!

Lethal unknown martial art...

No guns?

Loss of loved one to...terrorism?

Height: 6'3ft

Weight: Muscular build...

Eyes?

Hair?

Race/Ethnicity: ?

"Race/Ethnicity???" Commented a puzzled Detective Munich.

Apparently surprised at the fact that there was a blank space on that particular last line...?

Now acting almost as if she had a photographic memory and was taking a mental snapshot picture. Munich stared deeply at the board. Taking one single stepping pace backwards, reading the last written line on the board...

"A nation of one with six billion to come!?" She said, reading the motto and mission statement of "The Planetary Patriot."

Putting down the notebook back where she had found it. Munich snooped towards the white box placed next to the suitcase... Hoping to find out more information on what exactly Lysander was investigating? And what did he exactly mean by "the question is not where but when?"

One step and one hand motion away from opening the box. Just like a child taking a sneaky peak at their Christmas presents. Munich was now about to discover more on the fastest man on earth...

No longer holding back his fatigue. Yawning
with a loud gaping opened mouth, Lysander
now walked inside the office.

"Good reading, Detective?" He said knowing
that she was just about to snoop through
his case files.

"Nein! Well! Err? Actually I hear you're
going back to the states this morning." She
said trying to change the subject quickly.
"And I just wanted to catch you and say
good-bye. And..."

"And???" Responded Lysander, knowing that
she was fishing for information, as many
other Law officials he had momentarily
worked within the past had done before. All
wanting to know the WHAT? WHERE? And most
of all the WHY? To "The Planetary
Patriot's" violent blood letting actions.

"I just wanted to know why all of the
bodies from Club Hate have been put on ice.
And are being shipped off to the US!" She
questioned. "But somehow I think you're
gonna tell me that it's classified, or
something?" She asked...

"Yeah! That's about right, I'm afraid I
can't say much on it!" Said Lysander.

"Well can I get you a car? Or give you a ride to the airport? Agent Lysander!"

"NO it's okay I am booked in on a transport." He said looking at his watch. "Gotta leave in thirty-three minutes!"

Standing at a slightly taller height to Lysander. Munich now walked up to him. "Can I at least ask you one thing, off the record? Before you leave." Asked the detective.

"OFF! THE RECORD?" He said firmly letting her known that it was going to be. "Shoot!"

"Err?" Said a puzzled Munich not speaking English fully?

"O' please do." He voiced in realizing she did not fully understand.

"Why bother worrying about a few dead Terrorists or dish bags, as you Americans would say..."

Knowing the correct term as dirt bag. Lysander did not correct her, but politely listened on.

"Those Nazis have caused my people and country nothing but past shame and historical regret! And for what I might have read about the rest of those gutter dogs... Maybe they had it coming!"

"That's easy too think. But you have too remember that both our nations, are a land of laws, with NO one above or supposedly below them."

"Yeah right!" Mocked Munich back in return. Only too get a firmer tone reactionary response from Lysander himself. "He... He doesn't have the right to play judge, jury and executioner! No one does!"

"No one? What even your President?" Asked Munich not expecting a honest answered response to that particular question.

"Yes! Especially if their, the President!" Lysander declared with the articulation and conviction of a "Good American", who really lived up too his countries supposed we the people, we the good guys ideals and values! As he continued... "Even for those terrorists who attacked the School, the other day?" Questioned Munich! "As they were well armed. Carrying assault weapons, grenades and even canisters of nerve gas. Ready to do evil. And yet this fastest man on earth... Defeated them all! Saving the

children and teachers at the School...
Arabic people would have got the blame for
it. And there would have been another
Lebanon. If not for him stopping them and
exposing them."

"And drenching the schools halls with
blood!" Announced Lysander with certitude.
"It doesn't matter that this time it was in
self-defence of others. He thinks that he's
above the law. And that he gets to decide
who lives and dies!" He expressed nearly
letting more slip than he should. "Like him
or loathe him, he's still a murderer...
He's nothing but a Butcher for a more
better word!" Commented Lysander, pausing
just for a moment. "LOOK! It doesn't matter
that they were terrorists, criminals, sex
offenders or killers themselves. Life is
still life. And taking a said life in anger
or vengeance is a mortal sin! God decides!
Not him, or me or anyone else come to think
of it." Lysander voiced pausing for a
moment. "NO! I've constantly witness the
violence he unleashes. And all I can say is
that no one deserves to die like that! No
one! To be butchered! Murdered where they
stood in cold blood! No!" He said like a
western sheriff in some old TV show or
Movie. As Munich now glanced at him with
listening eyes.

"Somehow he's... He's got to be stopped!"

STOP THE CLOCK... BACK TO THE FUTURE!

Twenty four hours into the next day...

PROMISE ISLAND... Still trapped in
unconsciousness. Floating in and out of
rapid eye movement sleep. Laying like she
had been anaesthetized for what seemed like
just a few hours, when in fact it had been
nearly twenty four! Inari's closed yet
rapid moving eyes now began to flutter...
Dreaming a dream that she had dreamt every
night for the past ten years plus. Inari
now remembered back too her last surviving
childhood memory...

"HAPPY BIRTHDAY - INARI" That's what a
large hand painted party banner read in
Hebrew. That was hung high up above the
entrance to a Hotel Ballroom. As inside the
said ballroom a party of the family kind
was in motion, with the play of music...
The same mix of songs old and new, that
themselves could be heard at any family
function anywhere in the world. At that
said time of the start of the new
millennium era.

Cutting out in an echoing instant, the
music now stopped as a loud and happy
chorus of "Happy Birthday!" Was now sung
out. As young looking, teenage cute in a
absolute innocent way. The birthday girl

herself, Inari now smiled with a mouth full of metal, being that of the braces kind, that is.

Thus with a very near perfect grin with her fixed braces. Laughing, being the centre of attention. Inari reverberated in total enjoyment of the ice cream and presents given on this very special day.

As she now looked downwards at her large birthday cake that itself was covered in pink icing sugar, with lit candles. Inari's Mother and Father now lovingly approached...

"Make a wish! Lamb Chop!" They both said in Hebrew with a kind smile, saying their collective pet name for her.

In what seemed almost like a frozen moment. Just before she could close her eyes and make a secret wish... The twelve gleaming candles now seemed to blow themselves out without explanation. As in under a single nearly earthquake like second, an explanation was given. Delivered in the form of a cascading river of light, and waking pulse of sound that ripped and roared outwards across the room in any and all directions. Sending Inari's raven jet black hair riding upwards in the concussion of the just detonated BOMB!!!

A single second onwards...

With eyes wide open, Inari now awoke in a
cold sweat. Just as she did every time she
had the same near waking Nightmare from her
past! As drenched half in near darkness and
still dressed up in her stolen Miss Santa
suit. She now found herself stretched
outwards on a strange looking Hospital Bed.
In a room that seemed quite echoing in
silent size...

"Did anyone get the number of that truck,
that hit me!" She voiced, as she then
coughed! Clearing her dry throat!

Getting up off the bed, feeling half like
she had the hang over from hell. And like
she had been in a car wreck! Inari now
stood up to her feet completely. Taking a
couple, then a couple of few more steps
forwards...

Looking downwards and not paying much
attention to her surroundings at first. But
noticing that her needle ring had been
removed. Inari now thought she could hear
the faint sound of conversation in the far
distance? Only to then think that she was
just imagining it!? As going the long way
around with her arms folded walking ahead.
She now advanced as if she was travelling
down a cold and lonely street.

One minute onwards...

Getting closer, walking past "wardrobe" and a few other sections without giving them any notice. The sound of the voices in the near distant backdrop now echoed outwards once more...

"You know! You took the words right out of my mouth, Techy!" Said Liz in her soft yet happy Japanese-English accent. As Sherlock, who was standing next to them both now barked in instant agreement.

Representing a few of the closest living people to Jackson in the world. In this future and in the past too. Techy and Liz sported very different looks and styles. With Techy himself not being what you would expect.

As for a would-be sidekick even though Jackson did not do those. He was not like a nerdy intern out of some medical TV show, or some computer science geek! As minus the wearing of thick rimmed black rimmed glasses. Which he made look fashionable. Techy was a very handsome young man, with male model looks! Who's only draw back was his super intelligent type of personality!

While Liz, having a strange, a very strange
fusion of Gothic and Animé in fashion and
believe. With the absence of any jewellery
or body piercing. Well! Any that could be
seen anyway. Was dressed up in one of her
many mix and match black & white styles,
old School and new. Looking half like a
character out of a wacky Saturday morning
cartoon show. Wearing jet blue bottle/black
lipstick and twisted pig-tails to match.

"See even Sherlock here, agrees with you!"
Said Liz with a cute chuckle... As all
three of them stood inside a gigantic sub
level of Promise Island.

Imaginatively nicknamed "The Batcave" by
Techy himself. The massive sub-level
structure was filled up with weird, and
wonderful looking futuristic scientific
equipment. As well as clusters of strange
in spherical retro design Computer screens.
That themselves hung in the air,
holographic wet in projective shape and
structured fabrication. And would not have
looked out of place in any episode of Star
Trek or some hyped up sci-fi summer
blockbuster.

"Can you believe what it's going to be like
for her? I mean knowing the what? The why?
Or the when?" Remarked Liz.

"Yeah! A lots happen over the years..."
Said Techy, thinking for just a fleeting
moment in thinking of Jackson's battles and
missions to the past... "The future is
sadly always sighted in innocent blood!" He
said in a serious manor, quoting something
that was said when he very first met
Jackson. And remembering all of the Twenty
first centuries man made horrors and crimes
against humanity.

From 9/11 to the rape of Iraq and all of
the other forced wars. Come human horrors,
that happened across all points on the
compass that followed. That are still
denied by "civilized" people even in this
future. As well as the world's natural
disasters that claimed countless innocent
lives too.

"You were in for quite a shock when you
first arrived." Said Techy to Liz. As Inari
listen on slowly getting puzzled in what
she was hearing?

"In shock!" Voiced Liz with slight sadness.
"Yeah! But Karen helped me through it,
along with Jackson and yourself, Techy!"
She uttered, taking a caring stare at him.
Ready to blush! Wanting to give a raised
smile, wanting to say something back. Techy
tried to keep a straight face about to say
something. Something from the heart! Only

for Sherlock to now bark, wanting Liz's
attention also.

"O' yeah, and you too boy!" Said Liz. "You
too!" She remarked stroking Sherlock's
head, now turning to Techy. "But I would
say that I was more excited to say the
least! I mean... Welcome to the wonderful
world of tomorrow." She uttered, quoting
the first thing that Jackson said to her
when she first arrived herself. "It may not
be Flying cars, Phaser guns and rocket
ships to the Moon. Well okay it's maybe all
that. What with Jackson having THE set of
rocket ship wheels going. And trips to the
Moon cost a fortune... But the future is a
nice place to live."

"Except for all of the..." Said Techy
stating the facts on the future.

"Yeah! Well nowhere is perfect!" Said Liz
interrupting with gesturing hands, in her
own quirky way. "O' anyway... I just hope
she can take it!"

As Inari now moved closer she could see
that both Techy and Liz where watching some
kind of news broadcast. That projected
itself high and gigantic above their
position.

"Peachy Keen! You're watching Channel
93,359, Europe's thus the world's number
one Entertainment Channel! Brought to you
on the Carter-Beck Hyper-Network! A
division of Carter-Beck Industries. A
conglomerate of Carter-Beck Global! Making
the World a smaller and safer place
everyday!!!" Said the announcer in a over
the top English accent. "Coming up the News
with Suzy Sol. But first, a word from our
sponsor on this Morning of Dec 30! 2092!"

"Dec 30... 2092???" Mumbled Inari
whispering to herself.

Watching from a close distance Inari now
looked on. As a Commercial for the world's
number one soft drink "Carter-Beck fresh
water Elite Colä", now played on screen.

"2092!!! The future? It can't be!" She said
nearly aloud.

As the commercial played on, Inari's just
given whispers now instantly caught the
attention of Sherlock. Turning with a growl
the wolfhound Dog barked towards Inari's
direction. Thus causing Liz and Techy to
turn towards Inari's near distant position.

"O' Peachy Keen!" Liz remarked giving the future saying for Hi or Hello. "O' I mean, Hello!"

Looking at her surroundings, over come with what she had just heard. Inari now turned around only to run out of the socalled Batcave, back the way she came. As Sherlock now gave direct chase.

"Wait! Wait! Sherlock no, here boy!" Shouted Liz! "Techy, where's Jackson?"

"I locked down the training bay and... I think he was about to go practice in the KILLING ROOM!" Said Techy.

Two seconds onwards...

As Inari with an instantly delivered rush of adrenaline, now powered ahead. The sound of a "RED ALERT" styled siren now screamed outwards.

Taking a quick turn around a corner with Sherlock almost catching up to her. Inari now ran unknowingly straight into the Killing Room!

Knowing that with the exception of Jackson, no one was not allowed in there. Sherlock

stopped dead in his tracks at the Killing
Rooms doorway. Only to bark loudly with his
head extended upwards, as the rooms entry
door slammed shut.

CRASH! BOOM! BANG! Strange in design and
construction. Straight out of a video game!
"The Killing Room" served as a blueprint to
wanton murder and destruction. Filled up
with death-traps and lethal gadgets, that
even James Bond or The Batman himself
wouldn't be able to escape from. As now
within a second after it's doors now closed
shut. The aforementioned Killing Room
remained quiet for just a silent moment, as
Inari took one single near fatal foot step
forward!

Thus stepping forward, Inari just managed
to avoid danger as a number of booby traps
activated!

"Shit! Shit! Shit! Mother... Fucker
FUCK!!!" She cursed. Ducking! Diving!
Rolling and completing two instantly
perform back-flips and one very high
somersault. As a number of traps that
involved blades, knives and swinging pits
of razor spikes now opened themselves up.

Just avoiding death! Inari now jumped
downwards to a lower level, landing like a

cat. Only to be greeted by the deployment
of two high powered machine gun cannons!

"Fuck it!" She cursed... As now trapped in
what seemed like a frozen moment, just as
the cannon's now spun activated! And the
first volley of high velocity bullets
screamed out!!!

Jackson! Quicker than a blink of the eye.
Jumped upon Inari's standing position...

"TEMPORAL NOVA CYCLONE!!!" He yelled,
grabbing hold of her person! Shielding her
as he did before from a bullet laden death.
Experiencing the Temporal Nova Cyclone's
full force at first hand, for herself.
Inari was now spun around and around in
fast and multiple paced, high G-forced
directions! Just like a child on a rocket
propelled merry-go-round!

As the seemingly frozen moment jumped into
a few violently laced seconds. The gun's
now emptied of their ten thousand round
each payload. Instantly allowing Jackson to
jump back down to the floor, still holding
Inari next to his person!

Feeling sick to her stomach, as if she'd
now just been on the roller coaster ride

from hell. And eaten a metric tonne of ice cream, as well as a river of cotton candy. Inari now still held onto Jackson's hard bodied torso.

"Welcome to the wonderful World of tomorrow!" He said holding her up onto her feet, taking a slight step back. "Officer Gellar! We do need to talk!" He voiced with concern, softly moving her wavy jet black hair aside. Checking to see if she was all right.

As feeling a spooky? Or somewhat strange déjà vu emotion, that he had earlier tried to dismissed when he first met Inari. Jackson now almost knew to himself that he had met her somewhere before?

"I don't feel so good!" She said, as she now quite literally tossed her proverbial cookies! Throwing up all over Jackson's person. Just like a drunk Taco take out munching girlfriend after a night on the town...

As now in what too some could only be described as a funny or disgusting moment. Take your pick? Jackson now stood with half of his top person covered in just projected vomit! Lost completely for all or any words. For one of the few times in his well travelled life!

STOP THE CLOCK... BACK TO NOW...

Chapter Six

AND NOW FOR SOMETHING ELSE!

"How quaint! Papa Smurf!"

Many hours into the morning...

PARIS, FRANCE CONTINUED... Having a crisis
of false self so-called racial identity.
Forgetting that they have the coolest
sounding language in the world. Along with
their Josephine Baker break through! This
land of Hijab banning rich elitist Liberty?
Is quite very often reported to have only a
welcome to black people on it's fashion
runways and soccer pitches. Reducing even
the worlds first black female

billionaire/most "powerful" African
American woman in Hollywood to just a
"Window Shopper!!!" Plus not to mention
Arabian Muslims and Non Arabian Muslims
alike given no real welcome at all!?

Thus sadly learning nothing from it's past.
Ready to "deal" with the Iran problem too.
As quite happy to be proud of it's colonial
history of raping nations. As with France
part of the living cancer known as western
civilization. This Country of supposed
independence and enforced counterfeit
secularism, served "the Members" most
excellently! And would continue to do so
for countless years to come? Until that day
when France would decide to do the right
thing. With freedom of equal opportunity
across all colours and believes!

Three traffic vibrating seconds onwards...

Now as employees entered the Bank. A
regular work day was on the cards for all
concerned. As down below it's secret sub
levels a early morning meeting of "the
Committee", was already taking place.

AND NOW FOR SOMETHING ELSE! "THIS IS MEDIA-
NET NEWS! Europe's fastest growing on-line
news channel on the web and beyond...
Brought to you by our sponsor Carter-Beck.
Building a better tomorrow for all our

tomorrows." Said the pre-recorded announcers voice. A voice that belonged to a very famous classically trained actor!

"Now, for real news. For real facts... For real truth!" Exclaimed the announcer, as flashing CGI images of world events now pictured themselves upon a large wall mounted TV. While the said "Members" of "the Committee" all sat in silence glued to the screen.

"Good morning! And here are this mornings headlines." Said the News anchor politely. As recorded images of up coming stories played out.

"TERROR ALERT! U.S Homeland Security sets a condition of ORANGE this morning after Al-Qaeda E-Mail promises more attacks on US Targets over Christmas... MAKING RAIN! Scientific fact or seasonal hoax? As Avatar Industries reveals a incredible new technology last night in Austria... STRANGE WEATHER? Conspiracy bloggers blame chem-trails? U.K Met office reports of irregular weather heat patterns! And Oscar hopes for new hit British film revealed... But first..."

As the members watch on, News images recorded of a School, half burnt out, smashed and bullet ridden, now played...

"Israeli authorities are still refusing to comment on the terrorist attack unleashed upon a middle School two days ago... Only stating that the attack was in NO WAY committed by Islamic extremist militants!" Spoke the News anchor. As a number of high angled "eye in the sky!" TV Helicopter camera angles and images of the damaged School were now shown.

"However! This network has exclusively learnt that a number of unconfirmed witnesses reported on hearing gunfire, and the sounds of explosions from inside. Followed by the sighting of a single unidentified Israeli? Male, who somehow foiled the gunmen's attack! Thus allowing all of the children and staff to safely escape!" Read the Newscaster, taking a second to pause as the autocue/teleprompter now rolled ahead with new information.

"Denying these events the Israeli Government have sworn to reveal the truth, after a full investigation."

"As this strange case unfolds... Comparisons are being made to the breaking of a Human trafficking ring in Dover, England last week. And the still unexplained disappearance of over one hundred and forty seven undocumented refugees... Thirty-three of them children.

And the unexplained deaths of nineteen guards at a U.K immigration detention centre. Who themselves were under investigation for the alleged racist abuse of detainees, as well as the severe mistreatment of said detainees!"

"Dam you to hell fastest man on earth! A nation of one with six billion to come... That's his supposed motto, isn't it?" He questioned rhetorically. "Another three hundred million in the red, again!"

Muting the TV Mr. Ran now sat silent for a moment, as a one of his assistants now entered. "Kruger on the Sat-Link, Mein Herr!" He Said walking up to him.

"O' it's about time..." Mocked Ran as a live video feed of Kruger was now displayed on the large TV screen, as well as the computer monitors on the table.

"Nice of you to get back to us, Kruger!" Said Ran with contempt!

"My apologies, Gentlemen!" Kruger stated. "I had some problems with my personnel... That just had to be severely dealt with!" He remarked with cheese. Just dropping a hinting fact that Aryana's girl Friday's, on his and her orders! Had killed the guards on duty who all let Inari get by them!

"A day late and a dollar short, as the Americans would say!" Mocked the British fascist sitting next to Ran. With a smirking over friendly hidden smile towards him.

"Yes! Quite so..." Remarked Ran. "You and Aryana better have one hell of an explanation to what is going on... Revealing our Rainmaker project before it can be perfected! Failing to produce a working prototype of your Cargo lift Airship. And space plane you promised us... O' and allowing this Crew to unleash an all out attack on a School. In Israel of all places... Without getting permission from The Machine!"

"Is that all!" Said Kruger. "You called an emergency meeting just to tell me this. Just to waste my time." He mocked like a teenage child back talking his parents.

"To waste your time... YOUR TIME, Kruger!" Said Ran with cold annoyance. "No! You and Aryana are to come here within the next 24 hours. And explain yourselves fully, or..."

"Or what?" Said Kruger, with disregard.

"You know what!" Uttered Ran saying so much with only a few small words.

"Just like that!" Mocked Kruger.

"Just like that!" Gestured Ran. "O' and bring your cheque book!!!

Two silent signing off seconds onwards...

Thus with the video link-up terminated, Kruger now sat opposite Aryana. As being an expert in all of the Computer Sciences, he now began to type rapidly with super speed...

"Bring your cheque book! That man sounds more like a individual of the gutter faith, everyday!" He remarked, now reading through a number of computer coded files...

"He does... Doesn't he!" Exclaimed Aryana with a cute grin, reaffirming her vile racist superior stance. As Kruger now tapped open a classified file menu. Hacking into the Israeli Intelligence central computer network.

"Just like I thought. Like the CIA, the Pentagon and MI5. Their KUNG FU is a joke.

Primordial Firewalls to the extreme! The neo Phoenix system... God that's so old, old school, it's stupid!" Mocked Kruger using his computer skills to gain access with an informative ease. "ZERO TRACE! They don't even know that I'm... IN!!!" He commented, waiting for just a few seconds.

"Here we go!!!" He said as he gained entry. "Honey-pot traps and terrorist profiles. Off-shore accounts. The Israeli mobs monthly payments for the holy-land. Double Agent NOC-lists! Allies and enemies alike. Hit lists! Malcolm X..."

"Malcolm X?" Said Aryana in a mocking preacher man voice.

"Dr. King!" Voiced Kruger reading onwards.

"Dr. King?!!!!!"

"JFK! Don't!" Mocked Kruger with a fatherly smile. As Aryana now bit her top lip with a playfully mischievous smile back.

"Err? Slaughter crews. Infiltration units to encourage violence. Standing assassination orders from the Machine, to kill anyone promoting Palestinian peaceful non-violent protests or resistance... O'

Princess...da, da, die! U.S Neo Cons and
the Vatican. Something about plans for a
join increased Christian-Judaic cultural
infiltration into India and China.
Hopefully effecting a takeover within a
single generation..."

"I guest we're not the only ones who thinks
that white, makes right!" Remarked Aryana.
"Even though their really not!

"I guest so. Err? Government report on how
one in four Israelis are living far below
the poverty line. And pollution damage to
the dead sea and rest of the environment
are suffering from permanent neglect!"

"Well they shouldn't be wasting their
millions of US tax dollars, plus a day
extra. On crap they don't need..."

"Joint project with Egypt on Red sea
environmental repair? A number of Israeli
politicians looking in secret for new
backers. Trying to back out of their end-
timer sponsored prophecy. You know, the
seven years of tribulations that is still
to come. Wanting, readying themselves to
jump ship from the U.S. Probably looking at
Norway and Australia under the counter!
Knowing that Rome is about to fall..."

"Burn, baby, burn!" Smirked Aryana with a cold knowing grin. "Although this is just a roper-dope play by the US. Wonder will the Muzzies realize before they send their devils army into the trap."

"No! They are to stupid for that, My Dear!"

"O' this is very interesting! Very interesting. Something about a Robin Hood hacker, named Heat-Seeker!"

"Now that's a silly name!"

"I kind of like it. Err? Wanted in Europe and by the FBI for computer crimes, netting the theft of millions in holocaust funds. That were seized from Swiss bank accounts by Zionist pressure groups and certain Jewish charities. Placed into US/Israeli government holdings. That themselves were not all given to the so-called victims of that marvellous event!" He said with referring vile.

"Wait? I thought that not all of those chosen people were rich back then. Before that little house painters British and End-Timer backed adventures begun."

"Yes! That's quite true! Most if not nearly all Jews were not rolling in paper at all!"

"So who's money was it then?"

"O' I remember this backfiring event!"
Expressed Kruger with recall, forgetting to
answer her. "A planned working proposal to
the Machine for Hollywood studios to have
full open control of Bollywood. From the
twenty percent plus and undeclared rest
they already control..."

"Why on Earth would those Jokers want a
racially retarded thing like that for?"

"O' good grief!" Kruger expressed with
interruption. "Countless cold case files
old and new alike, half of a mysterious and
completely unsolved nature." He voiced
reading on. "O' he's been a very busy boy!"

"Who?" Asked Aryana.

"Our friend the fastest man on earth. Bombs
defused by someone with expert knowledge of
explosives!" Kruger read, flicking to the
next page. "Honour killings avenged by ski
masked wearing insurgent. Some Arab girls
targeted for said honour killings. Missing
without a trace before they could be
murdered by their own families... Failed
female suicide bombers missing after
arrest? Palestinian children, and Lebanese
war orphans pimped out by their own to high

paying Arab officials. Israelis, and
foreign sex tourists, a few politicians,
Peacekeepers and some other names best not
mentioned...? Abuse taking place at safe
houses and a few high priced Hotels etc!
Across countries... Said activities
sponsored by--The Arab Underworld... The
Israeli Mob! Including numerous Drug,
prostitution, and Human trafficking
rings... That were smashed across the
middle east... By Person's unknown!?"

"A ski masked wearing insurgent! A
TERRORIST!"

"You guest it, Sista!"

"You're right! He has indeed been very
busy! Where does he find the time?" Uttered
Aryana with a mocking smile!

"Arms dealers and Jacob Diamond financiers
in Africa... Who were all trading in
conflict! Or Blood diamonds... Killed in
unexplained circumstances?" Voiced Kruger
with a suspicious mumble?

"Te Vu'Kra - Fu in other words!" Stated
Aryana knowing that the martial art of
murder was used to kill them.

"Indeed!" Announced Kruger, as he typed up more files. "Multiple hits in Gaza! Of course!"

"O' of course!" Said Aryana back in return!

"Then more hits later on. Err? Hamas members that were informers and secret double agents for the Mossad. Training up youths to be suicide bombers. Members murdered in strange explosive circumstances? A few counts of Hizbollah agents, some double-agents killed too. One Murdered a Israeli child settler who begged for her life. Little girl then beaten to death! Hizbollah member found beaten, to death as well. Coroner said it was as if someone had taken a pneumatic drill to his head."

"Pneumatic drill?"

"Err? Something else... Something about chemical weapons and a botched drone missile attack! Before that. Smugglers tunnel explosion? Pregnant woman saved in Gun attack by unknown Aid worker? Ambulance diver, or rather driver, rescues nuns? Err? Ski masked Hizbollah terrorist. Or resistance fighter as they will be know in the tomorrow, saves Chinese UN observers? IDF Soldier saves Palestinian civilians and child!? The child's name seems familiar? O' and so on." Articulated Kruger reading through scanned images of newspaper articles. Including some that were suppressed and pulled from circulation. Just as Aryana was about to make a fake yawn!

"O' this is sick. Some Israeli Centurion Stormtroopers using the blood libel myth in their favour... Using it to install fear into Palestinian citizens, including the children. O' here's a weird one... Jewish Extremists plotting hate crimes? Against? Non white Jews. Ethiopian Israelis... Asian Jews etc? Considering them not equals? Not true Jews?" Said Kruger in puzzling surprise! "Don't they know the first Jews were of black and Arab colour? Strange?"

"How amusing they're doing our job for us!" Remarked Aryana about to give more of an insight to a feeling and viewpoint of hate! "A Jew is still a Jew no matter where their from or what colour they are!" She mocked giving hate speech quote from the not to distant future...

"Factual actual!" Uttered Kruger with future talk. "Err? They--the said Jewish Extremists. Some kind of Ashkenazim group. Had some kind of mass terror attack involving nerve gas in the refugee camps..."

"O' one of the Hornets nests. I believe the good tolerant moral people of Israel like to call it..."

"Yep! I believe some do..." He uttered reading more. "Plus something about a double event plot to simultaneously strike upon..." Said Kruger having a realization. "O' sounds like they were probably from tomorrow like us!"

"It's a mad small world!"

"Quite so! And something with a neutron bomb! I think they were those Neo Zionists. Probably trying to get back their failed and cancelled Machine social experiment..."

"O' them!"

"Yes! They don't like it that most, if not nearly all Jews in the tomorrow are back to being of colour... And are Sephardic in practice! Err? Once again, they... The Extremists were killed by person or persons unknown?"

"Future boy!" Exclaimed Aryana in return!

"For real!" Uttered Kruger in agreement!

"Murdered by... Now that's painful!" He
remarked not telling how they died! "Err?
Countless more cold cases. Shooting Murders
of Aid workers and subsequent cover-ups,
etc. Some avenged!? O' onto The X-Files."
Kruger said whistling the theme tune to the
same named TV show! Now reading through
files that had been classed and classified
as unsolved?

"Err? Israeli Tanks and Bulldozers crushed
or destroyed without explanation? F-16
Fighter jet missing? Loaned U.S stealth
sub-boat prototype stolen and destroyed.
Cargo plane carrying experimental cluster
bombs, hijacked? Plane slammed into
Mediterranean sea." He voiced going onto
another page. "One case of thirty-three
homeless refugees disappearing without a
trace? Interesting! Jenin massacre
aftermath! " He remarked reading onto the
next page. Switching to even more
classified Israeli government reports.

"The standard occurrence of children, boys
and girls as young as five taken in for
questioning? Facility 1391. More than one
occurrences when they went missing before
they could be quizzed? Cells empty, still
locked???"

"Really! So how exactly do you question a
five year old child anyway?" Expressed
Aryana with disturbing yet very truthful

commentary. "My guess, it's not with colouring books and the offer of ice cream or video games. Or whatever the kiddies dug back in these old school days."

"O' you don't want to know! Nanny Cam!!!!!" Said Kruger, skimming over more reports. Stating just one of thousands of true and undisclosed apartheid styled hate crimes against Humanity. That Israeli society would not want to admit too, or ever acknowledge!

"My goodness. What a savage! One case even has about the death of an UK Military Doctor who was continuing the work of Capture Nazi physicians. Experimenting on Palestinian children and babies.

Something about Organ harvesting. Torturing Terrorist prisoners and experimenting also on mentally Handicapped Israeli's for medical research... All for our business rivals and future rulers of the planet. Carter-Beck Inc, who in turn are doing it for the Machine."

"Just like in the black sites legal cases and Git-mo scandals lawsuits, and record breaking WHITE CHRISTIAN GUILT payouts... In two thousand and?" Stated Aryana knowing yet nearly forgetting the dates of importance's to the history of the future?

"Err in?" Said Kruger turning and failing to remember as well?

"Ja! Quite so! Nein! O' poor man." He stated moving on. "The said Doctor was killed by persons or person unknown. Murdered by..." Kruger voiced, taking a nearly correcting pause. Pulling a strange face as if he had seen something that even made him feel a little sick! "O' that's even worst than before. Very brutal and very, very, and one more very over the top!"

"Quite an extreme death to say the least... Even for a Jew!" Aryana commented, reading the said file as well!

"Time to move on! As we could be here for hours... And a few more hours!" Remarked Kruger exiting the cold case files.

While typing once again at a fast key thumping pace. Kruger now opened the NOC-List directory for active and inactivate Agents. "O' this is very interesting, very interesting indeed!" He remarked studying a top secret Israeli Mossad mission report. That itself now displayed a striking ID photo of Inari and a working profile of her. "Inari E. Gellar! Age? Expert in counter-terrorism! Master in all weapons, guns, knives, explosives etc... Qualified

fighter pilot, Helicopter Gunships etc...
"Second language is French."

"Bonjour!" She exclaimed with a French
accent in continuance.

"The language of cowards and Frog munching
sellouts. And the people who's greatest
cultural contribution to the world was? The
Smurfs!!!" Mocked Aryana with playful
prejudice, while then switching back to her
normal voice with a smile!

"Indeed... But they do make great
croissants. And...? Wait? I like the
Smurfs!" Said Kruger with a smile back to
Aryana. "I got the movie and the old school
cartoon show on DVD!"

"That says it all!" Exclaimed Aryana with a
perfect smile.

"Err? She has the given nickname of Ball
Buster. As she was constantly sighted for
violent and reckless behaviour!"

"Like what?"

"Fighting fellow soldiers. Motorcycle
racing on base. Showed impressive

leadership skills in stopping regimental bullying. And a suicide attempt by a new recruit."

"How quaint! Papa Smurf!"

"Funny!!!!!!!!!!!!!!!" Smirked Kruger back. "Her Father was Israeli, Mother a French Jewess! Both Mossad Agents as well!"

"O' what a family affair!"

"Both deceased!" Remarked Kruger! "Close friends to assassinated Prime Minister, what's his face. Both on a watch list of Israeli's and non-Israeli's alike, deemed as sympathetic to the Palestinian plight. Names past onto, O' dear! No wonder it all ended bad for them!" He voiced clicking a current version of the list, going back to Inari's file. "Daughter's Mission status?"

"What is it?" Quizzed Aryana.

"She's been disavowed by her Government! She's a rogue Agent!"

"A renegade! That's good!" Aryana declared.

"Yes! Apparently she went rogue after the aforementioned Patriot of the Planet foiled the attack at the School! After her superiors refuse to believe her theory. On how I, Julius Kruger. Was really the mythical Neo Nazi Terrorist known as THE GERMAN!" He stated with a mocking theatrical glare.

"And not a best friend to America and all of it's kept whores, like Great Britain, South Korea and the aforesaid vile state of? O' I mean Israel!" Remarked Kruger, correcting his near slip remark of knowledge of tomorrow, as he now completed a few more key strokes. "And who could forget, Japan. Why did that Hitler loser have an alliance with those inferior bandwidth hogging olive coloured, whale munching individuals again?" He mocked in rhetorical racist passing...

"I don't know!" Said Aryana back in smiling return. "What else is there?" She questioned!

"Joined IDF, Israeli Defence Forces a year before she was technically able too. Lied about her age! Fake ID, and everything!" Mumbled Kruger reading through the report.

"Scored higher than high in her tests... A exemplary soldier... Given fast track to special forces and aerial combat training. "

"Not found out until summer 2006... Err? Court marshalled, during the Israeli-Hizbollah war of the same year...or as it's known as in the future the ransack of the Lebanon. Something about a hospital. Civilians... Children! Charged with refusing direct orders. High treason! And attempted murder of superior officers! Branded a sell-out and a traitor to Israel for standing up and saying the truth in court! Declared herself as an anti-Zionist Israeli!"

"How amusing! Is their really such a thing!?"

"I suppose it's a bit like a Gay Catholic. Or an African-American... Or a British Muslim!" Joked Kruger back. "Err?Found guilty. What a surprise!" He uttered with sarcasm.

"Sentence to twenty-five years to life in the Stockade. Countless escape attempts and Prison Breaks. Sentence lifted after joining the Mossad in secret! As they were quite impressed with her skills... And mad moves!"

"Wow! She really had her grown woman on!"
Said Aryana. As mumbling through a few more
personal facts Kruger now stopped! Sitting
up in his chair, taking more of an
absorbing read.

"Marked for use on expendable missions
list. Her next mission was going to be? O'
well there's no way she would have got out
of there alive." Kruger said flicking to
the next page. "Well go have sex with a
duck! This is interesting. Very interesting
to say the least!" He remarked turning the
monitor towards Aryana.

"Yes... It is!" She said cryptically, not
saying aloud what she was now reading.
Whilst holding Inari's Desert Eagle handgun?

STOP THE CLOCK... BACK TO THE FUTURE AGAIN!

Chapter Seven

HERE ARE TODAY'S TEMPORAL THREAT MATRIX
REPORTS!

"Thanks very much for the Newsflash, Hero!"

Twenty minutes later...

PROMISE ISLAND... Standing still, closing
her eyes shut! Taking a seemingly heaven
sent, steamed filled futuristic power
shower. Inari now relaxed inside the vortex
of swirling rainfall.

"Stay close! Follow my lead... SWITCH! We
have to talk! We have to talk?" She said

mocking Jackson's growling cool pattern of speech. "Temporal leaping lizards!? Or Whatever it was he said! I didn't mean to throw up all over him!" She remarked with a mumble, now taking a moment to think! "THE FUTURE??? It can't be, can it!?" Questioned Inari. "And who would have guest that The German was a woman. That Be'yatch Aryana, Eva Braun Avatar! Although he seemed to know already?" Voiced Inari aloud and to herself! Only to continue! "O' you got yourself in one huge puddle of shit this time, Girlfriend!" She voiced annoyed to herself. "How the hell did those bullets not kill him? He didn't feel like he had a vest on? He felt like all muscle. Solid rock-hard muscle... Whoa!" She uttered in thinking of Jackson's perfectly toned physique.

"HEY! Lizzy? Or Liz! Isn't?" Yelled Inari, as the shower now deactivated. "Could you pass me a towel?" She asked, dressed only in droplets of water...

"You don't need one!" Voiced Liz standing just outside. "Computer! Drier on!" Now encompassing every single wet point, and crevices of Inari's athletic perfect body. A rush of hot air now zoomed upwards from the showers smoothed floor beneath... Causing Inari's just dried raven jet black hair to hover upwards, riding the current of warm air. And her eyes to bulge just slightly!

Immediately dry completely from head to toe. Inari now stepped out of the shower drying off nearly instantly! As Liz, with a very pale complexion and eyes oil slick black, yet warm and friendly in colour. Stood a few steps away...

"Wow! I've never had a shower like THAT before!" Exclaimed Inari.

"A girl could spend along time in one of those!"

"Yeah! I guest she could!" Said Liz finding her humour quite vulgar. Looking down at the floor, as Inari stood naked in front of her.

"Do you have some clothes for me, Liz! Or is the naked look in for 2092! 2092! That still feels so unreal! Don't take this the wrong way, Liz. But do me a favour and pinch me!"

"Okay!?" She said pinching Inari's left arm.

Feeling the slight nip of the pinch. Inari now knew for sure that she was not dreaming and this was all apparently real!

"No! This is all real!" Voiced Inari, as Liz now passed her some clothes.

As she now started to get dressed. Topless wearing only a pair of denim like trouser bottoms. Inari now held up a T-shirt in front of her. "What the fuck is this!" Exclaimed Inari in seeing the T-Shirt had a Swastika design pattern on it's front...

"It's a Buddhist Swastika! You know life, luck love and death and so on... It's high fashion in India!" Said Liz. "What's your problem?"

"Hello! I'm Jewish... A Jew!" Stated Inari with aloud attack! Sounding if she was almost ready to punch-out her lights, quite literally! "That's my fuckin' problem!" She then mumbled.

"O' I'm so sorry I didn't think. Well actually I didn't know! But I'm sorry again anyway! Although I really didn't get to read up on your file!" Voiced Liz with apology. "Although you shouldn't really take offence."

"I shouldn't?" Mocked Inari.

"No! You should not!" Liz voiced with polite yet forceful reassurance in return.

"As we got the symbol back off the white false Christian supremacists years ago... I mean we had it first before them. And now that we've got it back! It causes no offence, as it has no negative power. In fact it's a symbol of peace..."

"Peace? Peace?" Declared Inari twice with malice. "Shit! Tell me what kind of symbol and flag gets people thrown into ovens? Gets women and children raped. Gets people turned into fucking bars of soap and tables with matching lamp shades... Can you tell me that? Can you tell what people would slaughter the innocent?"

"Well where do I start? The blood soaked stars and stripes of imperialistic baby raping America. To the we know our princess was murdered but we don't care. Sloppy seconds loving. In it just for the cheque. Bloody union Jack of not so Great Britain. My own former nations symbol of the rising sun. The Zionist blue star of Da... Never mind!" Said Liz about to increase a awkward moment into a very difficult one.

"Look? I didn't think..." She now spoke changing the subject back onto the T-shirt.

"Save it, kid! I guest the holocaust doesn't mean anything in this future anyway..."

"The Holocaust!? O' you mean World War
Two." Said Liz. "In--in which well over
sixty million plus Human beings lost their
lives... What with the Nazi holocaust,
and..."

"The Nazi Holocaust?"

"Yeah! As the word holocaust can be applied
all throughout human history! What with the
four hundred years of the Black African
Holocaust. You know slavery, false
colonization to civil rights. Getting left
behind to die in Katrina, and black on
black Genocide throughout Africa sponsored
by the western block to keep them in the
gutter... And the East Asian Holocaust of
the Japanese Empire in world war two. That
killed more people than the said Nazis, but
it didn't really count back then as most of
the people murdered weren't white! To
the... O' never mine?" Voiced Liz realizing
she was about to put her foot in it!

"What? Go on? Don't stop on my account!"
Said Inari with intentional sarcasm.

"Well to the Islamic Holocaust..."

"The Is...? When was that?"

"When wasn't it!" Said Liz shaking her head in all. "You murder million's of white Europeans, it's a holocaust. You murder people who aren't. It's just foreign policy."

Thus with the air having almost a feeling of awkward declaration to it. Liz now broke the tension by offering up more clothes.

"Try this one." She said passing it onto her.

"Twilight!" Inari remarked, like a teenage girl in love. Now putting on the said T-shirt. "So can I get a toothbrush? My mouth tastes like old carpet that's been used by super-sized Sumo wrestlers as a practice mat!"

"Thanks for the mental picture!" Was the saying look on Liz's face, trying to undo the just imagined visual. "A toothbrush?" She now puzzled, taking a moment. "No! We don't use those anymore... Well most of us don't!"

"What do you use?" Asked Inari.

"We use these..." Said Liz walking over to the strange looking sink bowls, opposite the shower.

Holding up what looked like a strange designed Candy dispenser. Liz now popped out two small looking tablet like capsules...

"Just pop two of these into your mouth!"

"What are they?" Said Inari, studying them closely.

"There Tooth Pills... Well capsules actually! Brought to you by Carter-Beck Industries, a division of Carter-Beck Inc. A conglomerate of Carter-Beck Global! As the Channel 93,359 commercial says!" Said Liz, mimicking the voice of Channel's announcer.

"And they clean your teeth?" Quizzed Inari.

"Yeah! Splash, splash! Minty fresh clean!!!" Said Liz mimicking the Tooth pills jiggle tune. "Just like those old Alka Seltzer! You know? Those dissoluble tablets that sleazy ho's would take, after a drunken night on the town or something... You know!"

"Yeah I do! I certainly do!" Laughed Inari in thinking of the past wild nights out on the town she'd enjoyed! Only to then stop as she thought to herself, silently mouthing the word. "Ho's?"

"I'll get this cleaned for you!" Liz said, as she now picked up Inari's dirty Miss Santa suit. "O'! And don't forget to spit out the white creamy stuff when your mouth feels clean!"

"I will!" Exclaimed a cheeky smirk Inari, placing the two capsules into her mouth...

Elsewhere on the Island...

With the Temporal Threat Matrix now set to stand-by. Techy now waved his open palm over a lit up display panel in the would-be named Batcave. While washed and dressed in a new set of clothes. With the look of a cool looking Island tourist. And his shirt cuffs unbutton. (As was the fashion in the future!) Jackson! Now stood next to him going over a number of mission reports on possible "FUTURIST" activities.

"Here are today's TEMPORAL THREAT MATRIX reports!" Techy said as he did every morning, always reading through them. "Still no location on FUTURE TOWN in the now. It could be anywhere!? Activity is high in past but low across the board in this now..."

Doing the same thing they had both done for what seemed like a million mornings. Jackson and Techy now went through the names and list of groups set on changing the past to their total favour. Of FUTURISTS themselves. With some set to even destroy the world of the past as well as the world of tomorrow.

"Neo End Timers. Still wanting to bring about the apocalypse..." Techy then said turning his head again towards Jackson. "If only they knew that they didn't have to go back in time for that to happen!?"

"Tell me about it!!!!"

"O' by the way. Liz said she wanted to know how's that new power move you've been working on?"

"Great! But not good!" Stated Jackson giving the particulars. "I can't quite focus the combustion strike to it's flaming potential!"

"O' I'm sure you'll get it in the end..." Said Techy like a true friend giving a not need, yet very much appreciated encouragement!

"O' swell! Not so innocent not so Stupid!"
He uttered waving into the next file...

"Her again!" Jackson said with a familiar
not again tone! As they both now looked
slightly upwards at a holographic type
image...

"You know, J.C! It always amazes me that
unlike all of the other FUTURISTS out
there, all she wants to do is just be
famous! Just be a star! Not take over the
World, not hurt anyone! Not make war and
make herself a trillionaire! All she wants
to do is just sing, get number ones. And
just be famous!" Techy said as he now
zoomed in by one, to her crystal clean holo
image.

"Next time I run into her. I'll get you her
autograph!" Uttered Jackson with a humours
rhetorical asking growl!

"Although no wonder she does what she
does... As POP music is no longer popular
in this time!" Techy stated giving facts on
the future. "So does that make it still pop
music???" He voiced as he always did with
puzzling yet true to ask comments and
queries.

"Although at least original Hip Hop is
finally making a come back! After Middle
America and the suits running the network
killed it!"

"Word!" Remarked Jackson with a growl and
hidden wit. As flicking through her vital
statistics, Techy now studied her image
closer.

"Is it me or has she put on a little
weight? And are those real?" He said
looking improperly closer at her chest.

"A little! But it looks good on her! And
yeah! There a hundred and ten percent
natural, and real to the eye seeing touch!"
Said Jackson, not giving an explanation to
how he knew for sure?

"Yep! Okay!" Techy said not asking anymore
questions, flicking to the next file.

"Jackpot and Bingo! Or Bingo and Jackpot
which ever way you want to look at it!"
Exclaimed Techy, one step away from
babbling on as he sometimes always did. As
a working profile of both Aryana and
Kruger, now appeared.

"AVATAR!!!" Snarled Jackson with a Kick
ass, I'm gonna git you sucka mentality!

"Aka THE GERMAN, the whitest woman in the world... Aryana Avatar. And her partner in TIME crime! Hey! That rhymes!"

"Yes it does Techy. Please continue!"

"Dr. Julius Kruger." Said Techy reading the report... "The Order of Egret's highest ranking members in this time of tomorrow... Or rather time of today?!"

"Order of Egret?" Asked Inari, as both her and Liz now entered...

"What kind of dumb name is that?"

"There a group of White supremacists. That lean to the status of educational racists." Said Techy, as Jackson now switched off the temporal Threat Matrix. "O' and there name is reference to..."

"There name is unimportant for now!" Voiced Jackson with firm and yet not rude interruption. So that Techy did not accidentally say more than he should...

"What are they like those weird other Nazi groups out there... Like so-called Good Nazis, commie Nazis... Or even gay Nazis?"

Quizzed Inari. "You know I never figured
out how that last one actually worked! I
mean, do they throw themselves in the
ovens. Or what!?" She remarked with her own
style of crude and almost vile humour...

Ignoring her apparent joke, finding it
quite offensive. Jackson now spoke. "Let's
just say they think there better than your
common garden variety Nazi because they
apparently don't use racial slurs..."

"Wow! That's interesting..." She said with
a typically laced sarcastic flare. "Thanks
very much for the Newsflash, Hero!"

"You're welcome, Officer Gellar!" Said
Jackson back in return.

"So this is really tomorrow?" Inari asked.

"Yes it is!" Responded Jackson coldly back
in return. Not wanting for his own private
reason, to get too close to her.

"What! I'm just supposed to believe all of
this... People doing Kung fu straight out
of The Matrix? Stopping bullets in mid-air?
Jumping! Up up and away, like Superman?"
Inari said looking up and down at Jackson.
"Not to mention changing the colour of

their skin like a lizard or something!" She said. "How the fuck did you do that anyway?" Quizzed Inari.

"You don't need to know all of that." Said Jackson. "What you do need to know is that we are fighting a real WAR ON TERROR... That must be won whatever the cost! A war on..."

"Yeah! I kind of know that!" Said Inari with sarcastic knowing. "I mean 9/11! Hello! Nineteen Box cutting Mother fuckering Hadji muzzie ATTA-BOYS! Go do a Islamikaze and murdered three thousand innocent people on a blue and sunny September morning..." She said putting her foot quite literally in it. Not even realizing she had made racial slurs towards Arabs and Muslims alike. That itself carried the same given weight of stupid misplaced hate and spite as the words of all racial/ethnic slurs, ever did!

A Human lie detector, usually knowing when someone was lying or false. Jackson thus stood surprised at Inari's comments. As thus having a hundred and ten percent belief in the true philosophy of his very own Planetary Patriotism. And therefore instant anger at any and all offensive racial slurs that were said in his present. That's if anyone dared to. Jackson's face now turned to that of withdrawn stone, for other reasons as well.

"Box-cutting! As in Box-cutter, and... As in..." Said Jackson shaking his head in instant disgust at her racist comments...

"And the H-Word too! What a surprise! No surprise! Do judge a book by it's cover!" He voiced disappointed at Inari, expecting more from her. While Techy and Liz, shocked to hear someone speak so vulgar! Also looked at her with collective distaste! Excepting Jackson to take extreme personal offence.

All forgetting that is the normal talk of most and nearly all "civilized" people of the early twenty first century.

"WHAT A SURPRISE?" Inari repeated back loudly, taking a misunderstood stance.

"O' I see, cos I'm JEWISH! An Israeli! I must automatically hate all Arabs. All Muslims. Must I? You probably think that I like to bathe in the blood of little Palestinian children... O' God! Why don't you just call me... Why don't you just call me that word that rhymes with bike... Just call me a CHRIST KILLER! Or why don't you just get on with it. And call me JEW!" She

said with hate, knowing that she had gone
too far, knowing that she was lying to
herself. Not realizing how fortunate she
was. As Jackson feeling very let down by
her comments, and then some! Now spoke back
in return...

"Just call you..." Expressed Jackson in
disgust. "You know. If you can't say
nothing nice. Don't say nothing at all!" He
remarked with anger at the mere suggestion
that he would ever, ever say such a wicked
thing!

Surprising Techy and Liz. As his usual
response to someone who had spoken in that
offensive manor, using those words of hate.
Would have lead to them at the very least
spitting teeth! Both now looked onwards.
With Liz now thinking to herself that maybe
it was a mistake to keep Inari around on
the Island. Whilst Techy looked on like a
child watching their Parents argue. One
step away from smashing the family china.

While standing firm with his stance of
disdain. As he himself had seen the Nazi
death camps when they were fully
operational! Jackson now said nothing back
in response. As about to run off at the
mouth, as she nearly always seemed to do.
Inari now realized too herself what she had
said!

"Wait! God! Did I just say all of that...?
I didn't mean it like that. I...!" She
exclaimed, feeling a little ashamed.
Feeling a lot ashamed!

"I don't care what you meant!" Said Jackson
as his voice got louder. "YOU! DON'T EVER
GET TO TALK LIKE THAT. NOT EVER!"

"Look! I didn't..." Inari said, as Jackson
now instantly cut her off.

"Maybe I was wrong! Maybe we don't need to
talk! I don't need your help!"

"Why not?" She asked.

"You're useless! That's why!" Said Jackson
with out a care.

"O' FUCK YOU!!!" Cursed Inari back.

"FUCK ME... NO!!!" Jackson exclaimed.
"FUCK-YOU!"

"O' you wish, Motherfucker, you wish!" Said
Inari back in quick response. As she now
walked up closer once more to Jackson.

Sparring for a fight! It seemed and sounded
as if both of them were one step from all
out mortal combat. Or on the flip side
ready and about to jump into bed with each
other?

"YOU! Better grow up!" Voiced Jackson,
taking charge of the argument. "The world
and time you're from was a fake! A phoney!
An illusion." He growled. "There's a real
world, a real time beneath all of that.
Beneath the bullshit of race, of abuse of
religion, of power and all that country
shit! There's a world where FUTURISTS are
trying to rule!"

"What are futurists?" Quizzed Inari, taking
a step back trying to take it all in.

"People from this time... People from the
FUTURE to you!" Said Techy, accidentally
interrupting. Answering her just before
Jackson could.

"You can always tell who they are!" Said
Jackson forcefully. There just a bit
cleaner, a bit more leaner than the rest of
you!" Responded Jackson, causing Liz to
accidentally smirk!

As instantly staring at him with a look of
attitude. Just like a wife cross at her

husband, who himself had said the wrong thing when she asked. "Do you think I'm putting on weight? Or do you think that girl over there looks sexy!?" Inari now listen onwards.

"Know this, Officer Gellar! Let me give you a MOTHERFUCKIN' NEWSFLASH!" He said moving closer. "Yours and the other so-called civilized nations... Long war? World War Four... That false so-called and very fake War on Terror, come prejudiced. It's okay to be a racist, and bomb the shit out of unarmed Men, women and little children and babies all alike! And giggle about it, then deny just how many people were butchered, and count all your BLOOD MONEY afterwards. While pretending you were sorry! Has been erroneously declared over and done with for a long, long time..."

"Erroneously? Over and done with!?" Said Inari puzzled. Acting as if she did not know the meaning of the word. "Who won?"

"Who won?! Everyone lost! But it's all over now. Onto more things more important with no lessons learnt by everyone. All my... Everyone died for nothing!"

"Well at least it's all over! Isn't that a good thing?"

"You'd think so wouldn't you." Voiced
Jackson in his typical misanthropic way.
"The trouble is, it didn't go away, it
wasn't really won, done or even over with!
They didn't want it to be. Despite what
those murdering knowing assholes at
Plantation House... O' excuse me! That's
the White House to you civilized people...
Said at the time... Techy! Fill her in!" He
ordered with anger, turning his back on her.

"Yeah! Err? Well... Well it's like this."
Said Techy a little unnerved by J.C's and
Inari's exchange of words. As he now was
about to give the low-down on the world of
tomorrow.

"With the devils army, the third temple and
the fire falling from the sky! All things
played themselves towards..."

"Towards what?" Inari asked with extreme
interest.

"Techy! Don't bother. As she's too STUPID
to even get it anyway! Just get to the end.
Leave out the middle!" Said Jackson with
interruption, elevating his voice by one,
reminding him to stay on topic and target!

"What middle?!" Declared Inari without
getting an answer back.

"O' yeah... Err? Where was I... O'
right..." Spoke Techy trying to remember.
"Well let's just say that events of a very
hidden history transpired..." He declared
taking a quick staring hero-worshipping
look at Jackson himself! "And that-- the
rain came down again, giving a permanent
and absolute peace to be declared in the
Middle East. That then eventually lead to
Israel and Palestine becoming one nation!"
He said taking the long way around to get
to the facts. While at the same time
dropping a proverbial and political
bombshell. Thus giving the news of a
seeming impossible dream achieved! As if it
was just a passing comment!

"Peace??? No! We'll never know that! As the
holy land is cursed... That land has a
thirst for human blood that can never be
quenched! No one knows peace there! Not
ever!" Said Inari in denial.

"Well they do now!" Uttered Techy speaking
back.

"They, we do?! Whoa? Wait? PEACE! Peace!!!
As in... No? It? Could it?" Exclaimed Inari
in near disbelief, as she now spoke under
her breath in Hebrew.

"One Nation...? God! That is... That's amazing... Peace!" She stated with a slight hint of uncertainty once more and in near complete disbelief?

"Peace! Yeah! Great! It took nearly a hundred years, but you guy's gave up Zionism and decided to DROP THE HATE! Give people the right to return home... Give up the murdering apartheid ways. Knock down that illegal wall of false Judaic prejudiced and fear... And finally recognize them as Human beings... FANTASTIC!" Mocked Jackson back in perfectly spoken Hebrew. "It all worked out in the end!" He said with sarcastic regret. In thinking of all the people, of all the children on both sides and in between. That died for nothing and no-one in the process. Thinking momentarily about his battle in the third temple with "the Impostor" himself!

Surprised at the fact Jackson even spoke Hebrew even better than herself. And having a skin tingling come almost blood boiling reaction to Jackson's comments. Especially on the apartheid thing! Inari now commented back at him with the venom of a cheap shot! That she would later regret!?

"Better a illegal wall, than a illegal WAR, American!" She remarked back in Hebrew,

with a sharp razor blade tongue of extreme.
Yes! Really extreme hypocrisy.

Angrily silent! Never the type of
individual to respond back, with a cheap
shot himself. Even though she had verbally
open the door. Jackson now listened on...
Not letting Inari know what a sore point
her remark really was with him, and his
past. While Liz, knowing that Inari had
said something that had upset Jackson a
little. Now looked at her as if she wanted
to scratch out her eyes...

"Well as I was saying..." Said Techy,
speaking onwards as Jackson himself now
tuned out and switched off?

Five minutes onwards...

"Then the whole concept of it just laid
dormant for decades... Then it mutated,
when time travel was reinvented!"

"Like a cancer!" Remarked Liz.

"Err? Yeah! Like the virus it is! Now it's
being fought through time..."

"By whom?" Asked Inari...

"By... By everyone... That is everyone who wants to rule the world!" Said Techy.

"Don't tell me right, The Jews... Right!?" Uttered Inari, quickly in a mocking sarcastic tone. "We just want to own everything... And are responsible for all the wars in the world, right!" She said, just as Techy was about to speak back...

"NO! You're just the house slaves who work for the people that do!" Mumbled Liz under her breath in Japanese. As Techy now spoke.

"Yeah! You're right!" He voiced answering Inari's first question, accidentally putting his foot in it. While making Jackson. Now back into the conversation, raising a right eyebrow of correction.

"O' no! I didn't mean it like that... I meant to say some Jewish groups do... Well actually it's just a couple... Well about two, actually... And a lot of Christians groups too.

Some Muslims, a few Hindus... Along with a metric tonne of other groups that have cross ties between many ethnicity's, faiths and nations that you haven't even heard of yet."

"While the winning stakes to all..." Said
Jackson. "Being the now... The future to
you!"

"Wait! Re-invented? Well who was the dumb
fuck who did that?" Inari asked! Asking a
very good question.

"Well I?" Techy said getting instantly
interrupted by Jackson himself!

"That's not important!"

"Yeah! There are lots of people who claimed
the credit for laying down the ground
theory work! And someone would have made it
work eventually, just like the atom bomb!"
Said Liz.

"Like whom?" She asked, turning to look at
Jackson.

As saying nothing, not out of rudeness but
out of nearly having a waking dream
flashback to his painful past. Jackson now
looked at Inari as if he was seeing
straight through her!

"What? Cat got your tongue, Hero?" Said
Inari...

"NO!" Remarked Jackson, snapping out of it
instantly. "And I'm NO HERO! No HERO at
all."

"Well you are the good guy aren't you?" She
queried. Taking a moment shaking his head
to himself Jackson now responded.

"I'm not the good guy, I'm not the bad
guy... I'm something else!" He said to a
puzzled looking Inari. "Let's just say that
good's just not my thing, and leave it at
that!"

"Then who are you? What do I call you?"
Inari quizzed.

"I go by many names..." Said Jackson.

"Well like what?" Asked Inari wanting some
answers.

"To some... I'm a nation of one with six
billion to come... To others, I'm the
fastest man on earth." Said Jackson with
super hero like conviction. "But YOU can
call me Jackson! Jackson Carter... I'm The
Planetary Patriot!"

"THE PLANETARY PATRIOT??? Never heard of you!" Said Inari thinking too herself for a moment. "So do you wear blue tights, red boots and a cape with that! Or do you dress up like a flying squirrel... Or do you just have a mask and a decoder ring! CRIME-FIGHTER!" Realizing with self annoyance Inari now knew she had put her foot in it once more!

"Tough crowd!" She mocked. "Look! Jackson. That came out wrong!" She voiced offering out her right hand in friendship. "Let's start over... I'm Officer or rather if you will. Ex-Officer now but that's another story. Inari-Elizabeth Gellar."

Refusing to shake her hand, Jackson now said nothing as Liz now spoke. "Same first name as me!" She stated. "Wait! Elizabeth? I read it was..."

"Yeah great! Small world, Kid!" Remarked Inari brushing her off before she could say her real middle name.

"Look! You're all going too have to forgive me! I'm in a strange place right now... As too me, none of this still seems real... None of this really seems to be the future!"

"Well it is!" Said Liz.

"It's as real as it gets!" Voiced Techy.

"Why don't you tell me more about this time... Like is America still the most powerful nation on Earth?"

"Ha!" Mocked Liz aloud.

"Does, does the UN Actually work in this time...?" Asked Inari.

"Is she for real?" Mocked Liz back in Japanese.

"And, and how long did the Simpsons run for? O' what about those CSI shows? Do they still do them or have they run out of cities now?"

In the know when it came to the popular culture and mass media of the past. Techy was about to say all only to be interrupted... "Well actually CSI is still going in other countries. CSI:Berlin, Beijing, and..."

"You're not here for a lesson in the world of tomorrows mad and bad politics. Or what's on that idiot box they call Television and the know on the movies. Officer Gellar!"

Said Jackson with contempt and a frowning stare. "Although! I can see somebody's been giving you a head start!" He remarked looking at Liz, then looking at Inari's loaned Twilight T-shirt.

"Then what the hell am I here for?" Voiced Inari with attitude.

"You're here because it wanted you here! Officer Gellar!" Said Jackson... "It wanted you alive." He growled, stepping up to her.

"What did?" Said a beyond puzzled, Inari.

STOP THE CLOCK... TO NOW ONCE MORE

Chapter Eight

CARDS CLOSE TOO YOUR CHEST!

"Ten thousand Pharaohs. Six billion slaves!"

Minutes until the afternoon...

PARIS, FRANCE... Thus with morning's end
about to be in ticking effect. That once
before mentioned, unnamed and anonymous
Banking headquarters. Stood cold in the
winter of December. As down below! Keeping
to the orders of "the Committee" Kruger now
entered taking a seat...

"Julius Kruger!" Stated Ran with formal
attitude. "You and the unforthcoming Aryana

are a disgrace to The Order, to our Nation.
Our Aryan Nation!" He voiced shaking his
head to himself Ran now responded. "You
have broken our rules again and again! You
have shown yourself to be truly ungrateful."

"Ungrateful?" Said Kruger, sitting opposite.

"Yes! As have you not forgotten that you
came to us with nothing." Commented Ran.
"Having no identity! Having no past? Coming
out of nowhere as if you'd just fallen out
of the sky!?" He said with increased
annoyance. "We made you. And if you don't
tow the line, we will break you."

CARDS CLOSE TOO YOUR CHEST! That is what
Kruger now did as wanting to speak back.
Wanting to say more to say ALL that he and
Aryana were planning. He stayed quiet!
Taking it on the chin, staying Mum, as in
silent for the moment. Allowing the members
to continue.

"Don't we have enough problems with this
so-called fastest man on earth!" Said the
KKK member.

"Yes... Due to his violent actions we our
now billions into the red. And thanks to
recent events. We will be paying out the
standard one hundred million dollar fine.

And forfeiture of ninety-nine days profit,
to the Machine!" Said Ran sitting up
straight in his chair. "And that will make
us dangerously close of failing to make our
end of year payment." He stated, checking a
number of stock reports, including that of
Avatar Industries.

"Billions in the red?" Said Kruger now
talking back. "Money! Money! Money! Christ!
You all sound like a bunch of Bankers!"
Voiced Kruger, giving a signalling quote
with his hand. Dropping one of the many
coded prejudice terms for Jewish people.

"Do not take the Lords name in vain,
Kruger!" Stated the KKK member with wannabe
false Christian pride.

"The Lord... As in Jesus!" Said Kruger with
extreme sarcasm. "God! You American's
really are the fat loud mouth tourists and
Oil stealing wolves. That history painted
you to be, aren't you..." He mouthed off
half under his breath. "I hate to break it
to you. But he didn't look like that guy,
who they wouldn't even nominate in that
really old Jesus movie! Your Jesus was a
man of black colour. A Terrorist! A A'RAB!

A Palestinian. A cult leader who rose up
against his Roman masters! And he was the

worlds first communist... That's why he was
a JEW!!! That's why they called him KING OF
THE JEWS... For Christ's sake!" Stated
Kruger with contempt. "No! The only white
people in that black and brown Jew book of
worthless Christian propaganda are the
Romans. And they were really off white,
aren't they... Especially the half mud
blooded Sicilians!" Mocked Kruger looking
towards a Italian fascist of the sitting
"Members!" While instantly causing the KKK
member and said Italian fascist to both
take instant offence. Only to be then
simultaneously interrupted by Mr. Ran!

"Bankers? As in..." Said Ran, taking a
moment to get it. "A terrorist! Of... Of
colour! Colour?" He voiced saying it as if
it was a dirty word.

"AN A'RAB? A FUCKIN' SAND-NIGGER! You mock
our Lord Jesus Christ! Saviour to our holy
white race..." He said shaking his head to
himself.

"You can shake your head all you like. You
know what this organization. This order of
the New White World was meant to have
achieved by now... We are third
positionist's time we started acting like
it!" Expressed Kruger with open hostility
to his disgust at all around him...

"O' God no, Kruger! Not this second holocaust thing again." Declared the British fascist with annoyance.

"The last order of the Fuhrer!" Remarked Kruger with disrespect, checking his well groomed finger nails. "Was that plans be made for the final answer to the Jewish question once and for all... For all Jews and other non-Aryans... Russians, Africans, Arabians, Asians, Latin's etc, etc, across the whole world to be fully eliminated. With the results of that order to be found before the end of the century. Now were violently into the next... And non of you are willing to deliver on that promise. None of you seem to want them really gone... I wonder why!?"

"Look, Kruger! There is no way for the once planned second Holocaust to be put into a feasible action... As THE MACHINE would never give us approval again. With Germanic national socialism seen as one of their once approved but failed experiments." Uttered Ran.

"There are many ways to cut a fish!"

"Err? Kruger! Julius. You and Aryana have to get with the programme. This is a new millennium, a new era. We may have racial enemies out there but we don't have to

throw them into box-cars or Gas chambers
anymore... At least not yet anyway!"
Remarked the British fascists!

"No! Just entertain their women and their
rent boys in your beds!" Mumble Kruger
under his breath completely.

"Plus there is a possibility with a false
alliance with the Zionists, both Christian
and Jew alike!"

"With the? O' for crying out loud... Where
are the Cameras? Is this a joke? Are we
being Punked!?" Uttered Kruger in almost
jaw dropping disbelief. "No! You're
serious!"

"Well it is worth looking into as Islam is
a threat to us both. And we..."

"O' bitch, please!" Exclaimed Kruger in
disbelief in what he was hearing.

Ignoring Kruger's insolence for what he
hoped was for the last time Ran now spoke
again. "Gentlemen! And Lady! While a new
nuclear arms race of sky high proportions,
rages across the world..."

"Ka-booooooom!!!!!!!!!!!" Mocked Kruger
with future knowing and interruption...

"And a new version of Nazi nationalism is
continuing to climb quite nicely throughout
many parts of Russia. With them thinking
that their actually part of the group...
Even though our beloved Fuhrer annihilated
more of them than anyone else!"

"Yes! There'll make great pawns and cannon
fodder..." Remarked one Neo-Nazi.

"Is--Islamophia is at a all time record
high! As the war on terror or WAR ON ISLAM,
rages on with no end in sight. That will,
in the end give us the extermination of the
Muslim peoples as a collective whole...
With them now all being the most hated
peoples on Earth... Next to tax
inspectors!" Mocked Ran with a stupid joke,
making the others (With exception of
Kruger! Who acted as if he was watching a
cheesy stage comedian!) smirk and chuckle
slightly! As they all sat onwards enjoying
taking part in the greatest crime against
humanity the modern world has ever seen.

"While with permission given, of course!
Total extermination of the native peoples
of the middle east is moving along quite
nicely. With divide and rule always proving
to be our ultimate weapon of white rule!"

"They are not like those red Indians, or Zulu's... Who let themselves be butchered, you know..." Kruger announced with future knowing. "The Iraqis, The Lebanese... And the rest. They'll wait for the right time, get permission or not. UNITE and take their rightful revenge. The devils army and all that!"

"WHILE! While Islamic governments betray their own people, letting them die of extreme conditions. Leaving them to rot in Earthquake zones... All thinking that they have some kind of alliance with us. As we supply weapons to their nations and groups... Pocketing a kings ransom in arms sales." Uttered Ran with hidden truth. Only to point to the British fascist, to get a progress report!

"Err? O' me... Right... Err? Just a moment..." He said tapping open the files on his screen. "Throughout western Europe wanton vandalism and arson attacks against Muslim and immigrant communities are climbing up nicely... Attacks on Jewish cemeteries our up by eleven percent... And will..."

"Over half that Jew dirt is done by the Mossad, anyway." Uttered Kruger in interruption once more.

"That will... That will hopefully rise within just the first few months of the newly arriving year... With anti Israeli feelings up high and higher, despite what their media is continuing to report." Said Ran with complete contradiction. "Thus altogether generating a new wave of global anti-Semitism that will fuel itself for years."

"Those Bankers got Hollywood. Those celebrities, movies, and the boob tube! They make a tonne of paper and get you everything you want and then some." Uttered Kruger with truth to the power of media and who runs it. "Thus they always get want they want. And then some! They will smooth this all over."

"Showing that the current Prime Minister, and those poodles before. Along with the Whitehouse are indeed Zionist puppets. No offence!?" He voiced turning to the KKK Member...

"None taken. Can't disagree with the truth."

"Err? Our programme to flood U.K urban streets with illegal firearms. And illegal knives are at almost full escalation. Thus increasing black on black and youth crime to higher than high proportions in proceeding ahead, despite recent interference! With U.K society not caring until it becomes black on white crime!"

"Good to hear!" Uttered Ran with a single nod of his head, as the British fascist continued on... "Therefore collectively leading to a sky high increase in Ethnic gang violence, that is escalating nicely. What with Manchester or rather Gang-chester, London and Liverpool leading the way. While the Police form gang units that will fail to make any difference. Thanks to our people on the inside." Stated the British fascist, giving recent project information. "Err? Asians in the U.K! That is Pakistani, Indian and Islamic individuals, NOT Chinese, Japs etc! Are now the most hated ethnic groups collectively! What with the British Government having a secret plan for mass Muslim/Asian containment. With the use of secretly constructed detention centres. Along with the capability to lockdown eight out of ten Islamic communities, as they are mostly centralized in certain areas. If the situation should be needed..."

"It will!" Stated Ran with disturbing certainty. As the British Fascist now quickly voiced almost forgetting just a fragment more of information.

"O' and along with public relations being against them as well. With the media ready to vilify all Muslims as terrorists. In Newspapers and Television News, etc. Whilst TV in the UK, always conveniently has some mad Islamic individual... Acting out." He gestured with a crazy waving of his finger.

"Thus granting a far more openly prejudice society. That will soon be realized." Commented the British fascist with a smile. "While proud to be white, proud to be British. Same thing! Ministers on all sides openly speak out against them. Calling for certain Ethnic groups to be spied upon at Universities and schools by teachers. And for parents to report their children to Police for having views that differ from British, or rather American foreign policy. To as well as getting people hysterically worked up over the veil. And those Hijab headscarf things..."

"O' they just said that veil jibe because if can't see their faces, then they can't hit on Muslim honeys, like they do everyone else. Well not all of them, as most MP's are just... Well you know!"

"While? While at the same time trying to deny just how racist and really intolerant they are to the rest of the world... Forgetting that the British Government has been proud to be joint partners in exterminating countless Arabs, while even trying too deny the body count!"

"Kind of reminds you of somebody!? Doesn't it?" Mumbled Kruger aloud, while everyone else pretended to not hear him...

"Well they were warned... New labour... New danger!" Said Ran.

"How stupid is that! As there is no labour, no conservative parties, no republicans, no democrats they are all just myths. A big joke off the contingency. Of the Machine itself!" Scoffed Kruger with truth. As the British fascist completely ignored Kruger speaking on once more.

"Try as they might the good people of England mostly all know that you have to be white to really be British..."

"Yeah! Right! Over half of their youth don't even act their race!"

"As do the people in Europe, believe that white is right!" Remarked another member joining in as they all still ignored Kruger's comments. Just like a group of bullying school children.

"What with even tolerant, pot smoking,
window whoring, Holland ready to join in...
Banning the veil, with secret plans to ban
the Hijab next. And calls for mass
reduction in the numbers of Mosques
throughout the EU..."

"Quite so! It's good to see that they've
learnt nothing... They might as well just
knock down Anne Frank's house and get on
with it!" Said the British Fascist in
knowing of the same Government plans in the
UK as well. "Although let's be honest we
shouldn't be surprised at these actions
anyway. As most of them were very good at
turning in their neighbours when we
occupied them... Minus that Audrey Hepburn
race traitor and her resistance friends. So
really we shouldn't expect the good people
of the Netherlands or anywhere else in
Europe to act any differently to those they
consider alien. Including Great Britain,
should we..."

"No we should not!" Responded Ran with
glee... "This is all excellent! As from
what I understand a lot of Asians and
Muslims alike got a free pass in the UK,
pre Millennium... with most of them staying
silent at racial injustice. As blacks were
the lowest and worst treated minorities.
Then a staged riot... And the fantastic
event of 9/11 happens. Then those bankers
at the network spread a few rumours of a

rape and got another riot... With too many
Asians not realizing that they should be
allied with blacks, not calling them things
they shouldn't! O' how things have changed.
With the Policeman no longer being their
friend. Despite if they even have a curry
or rucksack!" He mocked with a racist
smirk. As the British fascist gave another
set of facts and racist commentary.

"Yes! Well they should have gone out and
kicked a few footballs around. And played a
lot more sports instead of just wanting to
own a corner shop or have a stethoscope in
hand. Then maybe they could have had the
public on their side more..."

"O' it's too late for that. As they didn't
realize that the waters were being tested
by the Machine back in the late eighties,
with a very literary line of Satanic
attack! That was in itself designed to find
out if they had any effective leaders. Like
Malcolm X, Dr. King... Or anyone else who
would fight for them... And guest what?
They, didn't!"

"Whatever!" Expressed Kruger with his usual
educational racist demeanour.

"Yes! They all failed themselves quite
miserably. Proving they can only take

action against such silly things, like that cartoon. And not protest more important issues! While the blacks, Hindus and Jews once again ignore their plight, when they know what it's like to be treated in such a way! Collectively forgetting... If it's okay to hate all Arabs and Muslims. How long before it's okay to hate, YOU!"

"O' for crying out loud! How cheesy is that!" Mocked Kruger again, as ran spoke onwards...

"No! It's quite amazing how it always happens. They never see it coming... The Jews, the Bosnians, the Rwandans etc, etc. Now it's the Muslims turn... I wonder how many of them will fit into the showers." Ran pondered speaking onwards. "Yes! Give them enough rope and let them hang themselves... Then when the day finally comes when we conveniently get a string of suicide. O' excuse me." He voiced with a friendly smile, a little to friendly to the KKK member. "Homicide bombers that are all black Muslims, we will get real soon. Then move back onto those said blacks again."

"Yes we will." Expressed the British fascist with disturbing glee.

"No! You won't, as the blacks aren't afraid

of us. They got props and then some. Their
only weakness is fighting each other. And
letting the Jews tell them what to do. As
they take a lot of crap all the time.

But if you piss them off enough, they're
throw a brick, they'll riot, they'll throw
down to anyone... That's why the British
government banned that interesting dickey
bow-tie wearing fellow from coming to the
U.K back in the caring nineties. As they
did not want the black youth of England
becoming Muslims... Because if they did,
they wouldn't be taking the crap that
Asians and Arabs do... They'd be fighting
back! As you only have to look at the
actions of that fastest man on earth, to
see that! As he's quite the savage..." Said
Kruger with rhetorical truth. Only to then
turn his head towards the doors... As if he
could hear something that the others
couldn't?

"You know, he's no house boy. Know one who
calls himself Jew tells him what to do!"
Voiced Kruger as if he was a secret
superfan.

"You know on the hush I've heard that
sometimes... He just likes to do things in
the SKI MASK way! Yeah you know, G! You
know money!"

"G? Money?" Mouthed two of the members two each other as he spoke onwards.

"Sometimes he likes to go all Insurgent! Now and again... That means he could come charging through those doors at any second... Screaming blue bloody murder, and yelling kill whitey... Kill those Honkies... As in right, NOW!!!!!" He yelled, only to instantly slam his fist against the table! Thus instantly causing all of "the Members" to almost crap their collective pants, in anticipation of a very violent death!

"Pussy cats!" Mocked Kruger, giving a future talk version of the term.

"Yes! Very amusing, Kruger!" Muttered Ran adjusting his blood red neck-tie. "As I was just saying... Now all of our plans will soon be a living reality! As were doing really well already. With the west and Australia." He said while pointing to a remaining silent member from the Australian Government. "Falling unknowingly into place... As now in this new brave millennium, it's okay to be a bit racist... It's okay to be a lot racist... To racially profile... And not too mention with our friends at The Vatican, and in western governments, along with the press having given us even more ammunition to use

against the culturally backward world of
Islam... And..."

"With the permission of the Machine!"
Mocked Kruger giving a look of you're all
full of it! And then some.

"As I was about to say..." Voiced Ran
giving Kruger a look of given contempt.
"The rumour mill has it. That Al-Qaeda and
the British Government will soon be given
full permission, by the Machine. To
commence with Europe's 9/11! Gaining us a
record breaking amount of support... Far
higher than the far-right trickle that 7/7
generated! That will allow identity
cards... (AKA PLASTIC DIGITAL YELLOW
STARS!) To be enforced throughout all of
the UK! And EU territories that do not have
them yet!" Declared Ran with let's hope so
vile glee to the British fascist and
everyone else. As he then tapped open
another computer file...

"Uncontrolled immigration throughout the
European Union! Allowed by the said Machine
to increase and counter the drop in man
power and child birth rates, that in itself
is allowing us to profit in a underground
slave trade... And..."

"That has extra curricular benefits to boot!" Kruger uttered, with vile yet truthful suggestion!

"OUR Projected investments in the EURO!" Said Ran, giving Kruger a glare of do not interrupt again! "Memory metals and materials. The reconstruction of continued and very conveniently destroyed infrastructures throughout the middle east. And the eventual reconstruction of New Orleans into a white-Christian upper middle class city. With even liberal Hollywood wanting to move in... And thus along with black sea Oil supplies...And our new designs in technology that you have provided us with, Kruger! Will unsure that we have enough capital for our way of life for decades to come. What with the arrival of globalization."

"So no credit crunch for us!" Said the KKK member.

"O' Negro please!" Uttered Kruger back...

"Globalization is a reality... The only question is do we want to be a servant in it or the Master. And as White men, we must always be the latter..."

"Ten thousand Pharaohs. Six billion
slaves!" Interrupted Kruger. As knowing
what was to come in the near and distant
future, Kruger now spoke once more. "Our
way of life? For decades to come?" Said
Kruger shaking with his head to himself.
"God! You really all do sound like the
Zionist's and the Islamist's, don't you.
And just like them you are all Puppets!
Pawns to the whims of the Machine and their
men in Grey lapdogs! Following their rules
of War and Peace at their demands. Gambling
away our natural supremacy for a piece of
the action. For a plum of the pudding!"
Voiced Kruger accidentally saying a phase
from the future.

"What?" Remarked the KKK member. "You mean
a piece of the pie? Don't you? Kruger!?"

"O' whatever!... You are all forgetting who
we are!" Said Kruger one step away from
losing his temper. "Aryan's don't decide
the future... WE ARE THE FUTURE!"

"Strong words, Herr Kruger!" Said the
British fascist. "But what would you have
us do? Dissolve our understanding with the
Machine??? If we break our word with them,
they will make thing's very difficult for
us to say the lease!" He remarked.

"That's putting it mildly." Said Ran. "Let's not forget what happen to a certain very popular Princess some years ago..." He remarked.

"She got herself removed from the equation... Without question or without mercy!" Said the British fascist.

"And all she did was talk about landmine problem and plan a trip to Palestine!" Voiced Ran back in return.

"O' please! That race mixing slut... That traitor to her skin and blood, come Queens of tarts. O' excuse me, hearts! Got exactly what she deserved. And then some! No! The Royals... All Royal families are just actors and prison bitches just like all of the other people in power out there!" Kruger said with truth once more.

"And like the man said. If one lays down with brown, one stays down in the gutter with brown! Mud sticks! And all that and a bag of hamsters!" Announced Kruger with despicable racist quoting future talk spite. "No! That Be'yatch went off script so she got cancelled!" He uttered smirking with poison against one of the last of the "Good people!" (Who could have put a stop to all of today's wrong doings.) Causing "the Members" to take a hypocritical conspicuous look of disdain...

"Both the EU and Congress get permission from them before they act!" Remarked the Neo Nazi female member, who herself had stayed silent to Kruger's traitorous statements. "Even the Freemasons would not go against them... As the Machine are the real reason why the UN is so useless..."

"The UN???" Mocked Kruger rudely with knowing of the future.

"That's right!" Said the KKK member. "Everyone answers to them!"

"They want a WAR they get one... They want PEACE here or there it happens!" Remarked the British fascist. "Everyone asks first before doing anything major... Even Al-Qaeda does!"

"As do we, Kruger! As do we." Voiced Ran.

"Al-Qaeda?" Mocked Kruger with a knowing chuckle. "What a false flag joke!"

"Mock all you like! It's just the price of doing business." Said Ran. "If we make a fuss or push the situation... They will destroy us." He stated giving more excuses. "Just like they did to our beloved, Fuhrer!"

"Your Fuhrer! Not mind!" Said Kruger with contempt. As all eyes instantly fell upon him.

"What exactly is that suppose to mean?" Questioned the British Fascist!

"It means what it means!" Said Kruger. "For countless decades you have all worshipped the Fuhrer as the absolute of racial purity, and greatness. Where you and I all know that he was not!"

With the committee all once again looking at Kruger with the glare of disgust. All offended at the fact that any true White man would ever make such a statement about their beloved spiritual leader. Kruger now continued onwards!

"You all know that he was a disturbed unintelligible individual, of a questionable racial background! Don't ya!!!"

"Questionable background?" Said the British Fascist almost enraged at Kruger.

"Yes! As he was a, Jew! A Gypsy in sheep's clothing. A baggy trousers wearing, stupid little man... Who's idea of a good time was having some party-time with underage girls! Including his Niece!" Kruger said using a future slang term for sex.

Firm faced! Barely holding back, the "Members" listen on! As a few more things were said!

"No! That smack shooting House painter is not my, Fuhrer." He voiced. "I worship a true visionary... The true Fuhrer. Your Fuhrer! The purist of them all..."

Taking out a smaller than small cellphone out of his left breast pocket. Kruger now dialled up an undisclosed number? "Ja! Herr Kruger, here! Transfer funds of one billion dollars, U.S to the assigned accounts..." He said hanging up the cell just as soon as he had just spoken. "ONE BILLION DOLLARS!!! That's your compensation, Gentlemen and Lady. That's your House money! Be'yatches!" He spoke with vigorous slang dropping contempt, with his last word spoken with a Jamaican accent. "You know life's not all Hot-dogs and flowers you know! So don't spend it all at once." He remarked mockingly, as he now got up to leave. Causing the committee "Members" to all look towards his exiting direction! Puzzled once again at his phrases from the future!

As he was now one step away from leaving
the room, Kruger stopped to turn and face
Ran and the others. "Close but no Banana!"
He mocked with fake surrender! Giving a
future version of close but no cigar. That
itself was in mocking reference to a
celebrity sex sandal that would happen in
the years to come and very soon. "When you
race traitors get a BACKBONE... Let me
know!!!" He snarled turning his head with
absolute disgust, storming outwards.

"Close but no Banana?" Quizzed the KKK
member with a whispered mumble to himself.

"Well that said it all, didn't it!"
Remarked Ran. As he now tapped open a file
on the small screen in front of him. "What
do we know about Kruger and his
bodyguard's, undisclosed trips to
Argentina?"

Thirty seconds onwards...

Meanwhile riding a elevator car to the top
of the Bank, Kruger now removed his tiny
cellphone again. That itself now scrambled
the internal CCTV cameras inside the said
elevator car...

"Now is the time!" Said Kruger. Quoting a
famous line from a movie in the future, as

he now pressed the auto-dial button on the
Phone. "You got the GREENLIGHT! You're a
GO!!! O' yeah hail Hitler!" He voiced, now
only to hang up the Phone. As smirking,
knowing that terror and violence were about
to be unleashed on the innocent. Kruger now
spoke again to himself with villainous
glare.

"Let the attack begin!"

Three minutes before...

NEW YORK, NEW YORK... As the morning night
was almost dead and sunrise was one step
away from beginning. A seemingly abandon
warehouse stood drenched in the sound of
distance whispers and false ideals.

Thus containing a number of military grade
Laptop computers. That were all running
displaying maps of the city and battle
plans of attack. The warehouse sat with the
armaments of extreme violence. As a
gathering of KKK member's. Who themselves
all belonged to a renegade division known
as "The Crew!" Stood to attention. All
dressed in the infamous white Klan robes of
hate, cowardice and a unattainable false
racial purity. All now awaiting for their
newly appointed leader to speak!

"I know what you're all wondering! We had
African Americans in the Whitehouse... We
got our troops in the middle east getting
their asses kicked by those fucking rag
head derker! Derker! Darky Hadjis. Those
fuckin' Beltway boy lovers and the Jews
they work for won't let them win! I know
what is being said amongst a few of you."
Said Kyle Walker taking a passing pause,
now removing his hood. "You're saying how
can we complete our mission... How can we
win? How did our surprise attack on the
Christ Killers fail? With the fuckin' sand-
niggers set up to take the blame! All of
our people over there were killed! What
about my cousins capture? What about Club
Hate? And what do we do if this supposed
Planetary Patriot turns up... This fastest
man on earth?" He stated with questioning
rhetoric! "The supposed defender of
NIGGERS, CAMEL JOCKEYS, KIKES and
FAGGOTS... And even Jehovah's witnesses for
fuck's sake too!" Declared Kyle Walker,
with charged violence in his voice. "O' and
not to mention boarder hopping. Lawn
mowing, MEXICAN'S!" He yelled with
contempt. Taking a moment once more as the
others now all looked to each other. Walker
now spoke once more.

"I'll tell you what! There is no Planetary
Patriot! There is no fastest man on earth!
He's a myth, he's fiction! A Ghost... Or
rather a SPOOK!" Stated Walker with racist
intent. "No one... Certainly no Mud hut

dwelling Ape could destroy us... Could defeat us. His creation is just another tool of the left wing liberal controlled media!" Said Walker using another coded prejudiced term. "He does not exist... He's... Just a..." Cut off by the sound of a ringing cellphone. That itself now chimed a digital ring tone tune of Dixieland! Walker and the other villains now looked towards each other, wondering who's phone was ringing?

Realizing just a second later that it was his own cellphone. Walker now answered it. "Understood! Sieg heil!" He said delivering a one worded response, with a cold understanding. "ARE ORDER'S ARE IN!" Walker now exclaimed loudly, as he now hung up the line. "THE GERMAN has spoken and given us our mission. Ra Howa (Racial holy war.) is NOW..."

Thus taking a step forward with hate in his heart and evil in his mind. Walker now continued on giving his speech of real terror. Only for his men to shout back.

"Ra Howa is now!!!"

"Ra Howa is now!!!!!"

"White! Christian! Protestant and pure, is who we are... And even though, those Plane crashing sand nigger ATTA-BOYS did us a favour... It's now our turn to shine in the hellfire of righteous revenge!" Walker said with spiteful wicked reference to 9/11...

"City of dreams... City of Jews... Your time is up!... HEIL HITLER! HEIL HITLER!" He yelled saluting the Nazi call to murder as the others now all joined in again and once more. "HEIL HITLER!!!" Yelled Kyle Walker one last time at the top of his voiced. Only to now remove his Klan robe along with the others.

Revealing that he and everyone else there were wearing the uniforms of... New York City Police Officers!

STOP THE CLOCK! LET'S GO BACK TO THE FUTURE...

Chapter Nine

ON A UNDECLARED MOMENT OF PROBATION?

"If I told you the truth you wouldn't
believe me!"

Ten minutes later...

UNDER THE SEA... Cold and seemingly asleep
just for now, the Alien ship now remained
silent. As a strange looking umbilical
nexus known as "the Tether!" That itself
served as a connection point from the
Island to "The Submarine" and back. Now
seemed to glow with the movement of murky
flashing docking lights. With Liz staying
above on the Island. Jackson, Techy and

Inari had walked through a futuristic looking airlock. Taking a forward elevated trip through "the Tether" itself. Only to now finish their very short journey walking onwards to something amazing. Jackson now walked ahead staying silent. A man of few words and a million actions, as always!

"Some of us are a bit or a lot racist in our own way. And most of us all have a prejudice about something or someone? Either by choice or accident! Most of us fail to correct those thoughts. Or correct others when words that say one group of human beings are less than them are thrown around." That's what Jackson couldn't help but feel. With the judge and jurors of his mind being out for the night so to speak. As with her comments for reasons now not mentioned were truly beyond cutting to Jackson. Deep cutting! He was wondering why he wasn't harder with Inari and her passing prejudice comments against Muslims and Arabs alike! Only to then wonder onwards if there could be just another reason for his lenient actions towards her? As Inari now spoke.

"Are we there yet! Are we there yet?" She exclaimed with a sexy grin. "Where are we going?" Inari quizzed, acting like a annoying kid on a long family drive. Trying and failing to break the ice of silence that surrounded Jackson. As Techy himself

tried to hide his hidden smirk in liking
Inari's current style of humour.

"How deep are we?" She asked. "What about
the bends?" She pestered!

"Things like that don't effect me!" Said
Jackson, breaking his absolute silence.

"O' that's great, Hero! But what about me?"
Moaned Inari. "You're safe!" Responded
Jackson, with a cold faced growl.

"Yep! Were shielded by deep pressure
stabilizing atmospheric generators and
oxygenation matrix fields." Stated Techy
with a round of techno babble that would
have made any Sci-Fi nerd blush.

"Err? Great!" Said Inari, only getting half
of what he meant. "I feel safer already!"
She whispered pretending to know and
understand completely what Techy had just
said. "So where are we going exactly?"

"You'll see, Officer Gellar. You'll see!"
Techy said not wanting to spoil the amazing
and Earth shattering realization that lay
just ahead. Or rather just below...

Now just a few steps away from their
destination. All three of them now walked
down a dimly lit tunnel heading straight
towards the sunken Ship.

"Wait!? I'm sorry." Said Inari remembering
back to what had been said earlier on.
"Peace! But I still don't... Believe it!
Peace! Are you sure!?" She uttered shaking
her head. "How? When?"

"When you stopped dishonouring the memories
of everyone who died at the hands of Nazi-
Germany... When you stopped being slaves to
the GUN and America... When you told the
End-Timers to stick the prophecy! When you
gave up the failed, and just plain STUPID
idea of Zionism... Becoming repulsed in
just the idea of killing children. Of
killing babies! Of the holocaust you. That
you all took part in. That's how... THAT'S
WHEN!" Said Jackson as if his voice was on
fire with truth. Delivering a WAKE-UP call
that needs to be said to every Israeli
today! Right now!!!

"Slaves? We are not slaves to anyone...
We..." Voiced Inari with near anger...

"Yeah! You were... House slaves with
Kryptonian arrogance, to be exact... As the
worst type of slave is one who does not
know that they are one!"

"Kryptonian? As in?" Said Inari with
momentary confusion. Only then getting it.
"As in... Planet Krypton... What the home
of Superman?" Said Inari puzzled by
Jackson's future talk comments as he now
spoke with absolute truth once more...

"As in so overconfident, and over the top!
That no one and I mean no one gets to tell
you, NO! Then you go... BOOM!" Said
Jackson...

"Although don't worry! You're not the only
people who suffer from it!" Shocked to hear
anyone, and I mean anyone be so blunt! As
Jackson was a man who was never afraid to
cut through the bullshit and say what he
actually meant. Inari was a little, if not
quite a lot taken aback. As even if she did
really agree with him. It was and is always
hard too take criticism about the short
coming's. Misdeeds and evil doings when
they are done by your so-called own!

"What the fuck's all that suppose to mean?"
She said with wanton false defence...

"It means that if America and it's flunkies
had really respected you as a people. Who
for centuries had know nothing but
suffering, and no freedom from strife. They
would want to do right by you... They
wouldn't want you to waste your money on

arms and hate your neighbour... They would help you have peace! They would get you, PEACE!"

"I? I didn't think of it like that...?"

"Well think harder!!!" Jackson said, as Inari was about to instantly changed the subject...

"So time travel is real!" Inari spoke thinking for a moment! "The future? Whoa!" She commented to herself, shaking her head. "So how far back have you been... Hero?"

"FAR ENOUGH! Officer Gellar... Far enough!" Said Jackson. Summing up his lengthy and well travelled voyages through time, in just two little words.

"Would it be to much to refer to me as Inari, Hero?" She said wanting Jackson to

at least call her by her first name. Taking a moment to think, acting as if he was going to agree. Jackson now responded.

"NO!" He growled firmly continuing to walk ahead. As Inari now stepped forward trying to keep up with Jackson's long walking strides.

"Well how long have you all been doing
this?" She now asked, increasing her steps
once more. While trying to get a proper
answer.

"O' well, it's been about..." Said Techy
about to say, as he was now interrupted.

"TOO LONG!" Jackson stated, saying so much
with just two average little words.

"You know you must be freezing? Having all
that ice water in your veins?" Said Inari
wanting Jackson to talk too her properly,
looking for a heated response...

"Fucking sub-zero!" She mumbled under her
breath... "Deep space is warmer then you!"

"Get use to it!" Growled Jackson with
force. "You want a conversation!" He
exclaimed! "I'll tell you a truth... And
there's no sugar coating it... Times not a
straight line! Times not an arrow! No! The
world is not nice in this now or yours...
There were no good old days! No good times!
And there are no good guys! As they are
all, dead..." Jackson now declared,
sounding like a man who had no hope! "Thus
leaving only the bad people and scared
people left!"

"So which one am I?" She asked, asking a very good question.

"I haven't decided yet!" Stated Jackson with ice once more. Causing her too not reply? Changing subjects!

"So did you ever try and save anyone famous like? Like James Dean. Joan of Arc, Elvis? Yeah! Elvis. Did you bring the king here too?" She asked getting no answer from Jackson. Just as Techy was about to say something, only for Inari to speak on!

"What about saving Michael Jackson? You know I saw him in concert once. It was the best night of my life! Wait! What about Abraham Lincoln?" She uttered clicking her fingers getting a response she never expected?

"Lincoln?" Voiced Jackson with interruption sporting a contemptuous look! Knowing the real reason to the truth behind the American civil war. "And why would I want to do something like that!"

Instead of having an awkward silence, like most people would have had. In thinking that as a black man, that as a man of so-called colour. Jackson would have automatically wanted to save him, as he freed the slaves. (Even though he didn't consider all so-called white men to be equal, yet alone anyone else!) Inari gave her very own response.

"Okay? That's you're business!" She said with puzzling sexy sarcasm, and a glancing look...

ON A UNDECLARED MOMENT OF PROBATION? Thus now giving him a surprise answer. Inari had accidentally given him half a instant resolution to his own doubts about her. And why he wasn't so hard on her earlier! (With the half other possibly to follow later on?) Setting and laying the foundations for friendship and things more serious to be on the cards...? Well just maybe???? As Inari spoke again...

"Well? What about JFK? Hey! Who shot him anyway? Was it Oswald? Or what?..." She remarked, not realizing that Jackson knew the truth for real! And a whole lot more. As she now went about asking just a few more questions. "Was there a second shooter? You know they say that it was an impossible shot? But I bet I could've of done it! O' not that I ever would!" Inari voiced correcting herself... "O' come on, you can tell me!"

"If I told you the truth you wouldn't believe me!"

"I might!" Exclaimed Inari like a kid.

"You wouldn't!" Said Jackson with confronting forcefulness. "No! The hidden history of this world speaks for itself!" He uttered with the knowledge of a man who had seen too much.

"Hidden history? Like what?" She asked.

"LIVING SPACE, KILLING SPACE..." He voiced in German... "Expand or die! Manifest destiny! Freedom will be redefined. And all that!"

"What?"

"Forget it! Where do I start!" Jackson stated with disdain, speaking back in English. "Throughout my travels I've seen nothing but self-indulgence all throughout! With all roads leading to money... Or rather the love of money... With slavery, genocide, War! Illegal occupation. More wars and all the slaughter houses in between. Nothing but suffering since day one, the norm! With no end in sight!"

"I bet seeing all of this makes you feel that God is out to lunch? Or at very least on a break! Hey?" Voiced Inari saying something that Jackson himself did not agree with. "Although maybe he's not...? Maybe God is helping... Maybe he does care!"

"Like how?" Quizzed Jackson.

"Maybe!? Maybe he sent us you!" Said Inari giving physical food for thought! That only seemed to make Jackson annoyed instead of feeling complemented.

"God help's those who help themselves!" He uttered with knowing nation of one conviction. "And those that cannot have me!"

"So how many people is that?"

"Too many too count, Sister. Too many! As in all, this is a world of a few haves and way to many have not's! Everything has changed and yet everything is still the same. What with the planet officially run by a global mega corporation that's straight out of a sci-fi novel. In the now!"

"Who are they?" She asked.

"Carter-Beck!" Said Techy accidentally nearly putting his foot in it, without realizing?

"Carter-Beck?" Repeated Inari back. "Wait! Any relation?" She asked getting a ignoring no response?

Realizing that she wasn't going to get an answer? Inari now changed the subject, asking more inquisitive, yet frivolous questions... "So! Did you ever think about going back and saving, any other celebrities?"

"Celebrities?!" Mocked Jackson with a near closed mouth snarl. Not commenting on the pure and absolute contempt he had for ninety-nine plus percent of them...

"Yeah! Like... Like... Jimmy Dean! O wait!? I said him already. Buddy Holly? Princess Di? Maybe, Tu-Pac?" Inari questioned. "What about undoing 9/11? Stop this stupid War on terror from ever happening." She said asking a million questions like a inquisitive child.

"Despite the popular belief in this time and yours. That so-called New World War, come false global War on Terror started long before 9/11!" Said Jackson with knowing conviction. "It started the day when the BOMB was dropped on Hiroshima! And the ovens were lit at the death camps... To when the Klan were formed... And the evil British Empire ruled and raped the world, and the seven seas!" Said Jackson like a man who had witnessed all of that, and everything else! "Although too tell you a real truth. It started way back before all of that... On the day when innocent blood was spilt and little children's throats where slit. Just to prove a point or make a quick buck!"

"Yeah! I guest so!" Said Inari in a near sad knowing manor. Thinking of another question to ask.

Quickening up the pace, walking onwards... Not letting Inari know that he had seen a world where "all that" and a whole lot more had happen. Jackson now stayed silent. Knowing and remembering the alternate timelines he had seen played out through History. That themselves lead to the destruction of the world and the extinction of the Human race, every single time! (With the exception of one?)

"So tell me?" Asked Inari, coming up with more questions. "What's with all of this, nation of one. With billions to come? And why call yourself the Planetary Patriot?

Why not call yourself the American Patriot
or something?"

"Why would I want to do a thing like that
for!" Stated Jackson with anti-jingoistic
conviction. As if to say--"Were you even
paying attention too what I have been
saying."

"I'm a Patriot for the Planet... This
Planet! Not to anyone else's false ideals
or tribalism's! My home is Earth!"

Surprised and slightly puzzled, as she had
never heard anyone talk like that. Inari
now enquired as only she could do! "Earth!?
You're not like some hippy U.F.O cult
leader, come comet chaser... Who's gonna go
drink a glass of cyanide lemonade with his
disciples. And go hop a ride on a
spaceship! Are you?" Asked Inari, gesturing
with a you so crazy sign.

"No! Not quite! Or though, I don't have to
wait!" He remarked.

Thus making Inari pulling a you're playing
with me look of disbelief. As she now
stared around...

"This all sounds so amazing! Amazing!" She
exclaimed, raising her hands. "So how do
you travel through time? A giant spinning
clock! A flashing puddle of water! A
Tunnel? A Phone booth? A Police Box with a
blue light on the top? I know..." Said
Inari clicking her fingers. "It's a flying
Delorean isn't it?" Inari voiced going
through the roll call of time travel
devices used in TV shows and Movies.

Getting no answer out of them, with them
both acting as if she had cracked the code
and guessed right. Inari now looked at them
both thinking for a second that she might
be right?

"No it couldn't be? Could it?" Still
getting no answer Inari then talked on. "So
what else is there in the future to know
about?"

"A chair is still a chair, a table is still
a table." Jackson growled giving her an
answer! "And water is still wet!"

"And we are still officially all alone in
the universe..." Said Techy, joining in the
momentary conversation.

"For now." Jackson remarked. "Apart from
that, it's still the same old bullshit as

always. As leading up to this now. Where there was War there was peace..."

"And where there was peace there was War!" Techy stated finishing off Jackson's sentence in knowing agreement!

"With no lessons learnt." Commented Jackson, as they were now about to arrive at the entrance to the Ship. "Although! There is one exception!"

Fifty two seconds later...

THE SUBMARINE... Heavenly, immaculate, amazing, fantastic! All words that one could use to describe that sight and Extraterrestrial spectacle that was the ship, that was "The Submarine" itself. But as she now stood inside it's inner chambers all Inari could do is stare! Wondering if maybe she had been wrong all along. Wondering if this really was all a dream?

"A Spaceship? You weren't joking... You weren't playin'... An Alien, FUCKING Spaceship? A Spaceship." Said Inari without of this world surprise. "This is your time machine?"

"Were you expecting a flying Delorean? Officer Gellar!" Jackson voiced.

"NO! Well! I don't know?" Voiced Inari,
gesturing with a facial expression of how
stupid am I? "Aliens? I always new there
was something OUT THERE! But? FANTASTIC!
FUCKING FANTASTIC!" She stated with a look
of surprise and amazement. Just like a poor
kid getting the must have present they
always wanted for Christmas.

"It's like a dream... Just like a dream!"
Exclaimed Inari touching the side walls of
the ship. Smooth to the touch, as the Ship
now begin to resonate with an impeccable
reverence. Taking a collective moment in
thinking of recent events, she now turned
to Jackson.

"Wait! You're him... The vigilante! At the
School." She stated realizing who Jackson
was and what he had done. "Your the unknown
hero who save the children. The unknown
Israeli?" Said Inari gesturing waving her
hands over her face, as to imply to Jackson
skin colour changing ability.

Taking a second to think over what she
learned about the foiled attack, Inari now
spoke once more. "At the School the crime
scene unit couldn't find any fingerprints,
any trace evidence. And the security
camera's recorded nothing? All the hard
drives were wiped cleaner than clean? But
you were there... God! You saved them. You
saved them all... Thank-You!"

"You're welcome!" Growled Jackson, not wanting to take any credit for just doing what was right.

"So what was it who wanted me here? And when can I go back?" Said Inari wanting to know all and everything.

Not realizing that she had just asked the sixty four million, or rather sixty four billion dollar question. Inari now looked to Jackson expecting an immediate answer!

"The IT! Was this Ship... Or The Submarine as we all call it." Said Jackson. "And to tell you the truth. The whole truth and

nothing but." He voiced keeping Inari guessing on a nervous edge.

"You can't go back... You're here to stay!"

Where the average person would have taken a moment to take it all in. Inari proved that she was anything but average or ordinary. As she now looked Jackson dead in the eye...

"BULLSHIT!" She said stating her opinion. "I have to go back... I have a mission to complete!"

"Your mission is over, Officer Gellar!"
Said Jackson.

"Bull! I have to go back... NOW! Send me
fucking back now!" She cursed with
misplaced anger.

"Like I said... You can't go back."

"Why?... I have to!"

"You can't! Trust me. It's not that simple!"

"WHY???" She voiced loudly.

"Because..." Said Jackson pausing holding
back the hidden truth to Inari.

"Because what?" She uttered with extreme
annoyance. "Cat got your tongue again,
Hero!"

"Because... You're DEAD!" Responded Jackson
giving her the truth and her answer. In
just one single half loudly delivered
sentence.

"That's as far as history is concerned that is! You were K.I.A (Killed In Action!) in the original timeline."

"Dead? Original timeline?" Said a beyond and perplexed Inari.

"How... How did it happen?"

"Escaping from the Château!" Voiced Techy.

As expected not taking any of what she was hearing at all well. And certainly not wanting to believe any and all of it. Inari now slipped in a momentary state of full denial.

"No! No!... It can't be... It can't have happen!" She said trying to wish it all away. "I'm here, I'm alive! I didn't need to be rescued! I don't need some white knight, or some wannabe Superman... Like yourself to save me. I could have escaped by myself!"

"You did! YOU DIED!" Said Jackson, with ice cold non-compassion. "Maybe I was wrong about you... Maybe IT, was wrong about you. I can't see how you can be of any help to me!" He remarked, as Inari was one step away from tears. "No! We don't need to

talk! I'll take you to the mainland... My
Helpers will take care of you from here. A
logo, an I.D! Some money and a place to
stay! I here Baghdad is nice this time of
year!" He said walking away from her by
just a few steps. "You'll be fine!" Stated
Jackson with anti-hero filled
disappointment.

"Baghdad?" Said Inari wiping away the just
formed tears from her eyes. Laughing with a
"that must be the dumbest thing I've ever
heard" smile. "That's not funny... That
place is in ruins... And anyway peace or
not. Someone of my background won't exactly
be welcomed! Not after what we did to them."

"That's where you're wrong..." Said
Jackson, sounding as if he was one step
away from being inexplicably distracted.

"Yeah they have a new record low of
recorded hate crimes against, White
immigrants!" Said Techy about to say more.
"It's practically non-existent! Unlike lots
and lots of other places..."

"Don't worry, Techy. We'll take care of
that too! And then...?" Jackson said only
to now stop as if he was hearing a voice
that no one else could here...

"Look! Please, I need this... You have to
send me back! I have to get, The German! I
have to stop Avatar..." Exclaimed Inari
wanting back into the fight. "We can go
back together... Team up!

Snapping out of his trance like state,
Jackson now responded back."Team up?"

"Yeah! Team... Patriot!" Exclaimed Inari,
making up the name in a thinking instant.

"Team Patriot?" Jackson voiced looking at
her as if to say... "Lady! Can you for once
in your life be serious?"

"Like Team Edward or Team Jacob!"

"Team Edward or Team..."

"Yeah! You know Twilight. Which one were
you?"

"Team grown up!"

"O' be like that!"

"Team acting my age!"

"He was Team Edward!" Techy now mouthed silently behind Jackson's back to Inari!

Knowing instantly what Techy just now said. Jackson now turned around to look at him with a raised eye brow! While Inari herself spoke on. "Yeah! Team Patriot... O' come on! You already got your own gang of Scoobies working for you. What's one more?" She voiced.

"Scoobies?" Said Techy. "As in Scooby Doo? Thanks!" He uttered feeling complemented.

"Yeah! I mean you got that Dog upstairs! You're Shaggy! Hero! Over there is Fred! Liz can be Velma. But not in a dorky way!" Inari voiced trying once again to break the ice that was still completely solid between her and Jackson. "And I can be... Daphne!!!" She stated. "I got the hot bod for it!"

"O' yeah mama! Yeah mami, you hot!" Said Techy checking Inari out. "Smokin'! Flaming! You got it going on... You..."

"You're not Daphne! You're Scrappy!" Said Jackson cutting Techy off. Turning to stare Inari dead in the eyes. Taking a few single steps towards her.

As Inari herself now firmly stood her
ground, folding her arms with the look of
Girl powered attitude.

"Scrappy?" She responded. "As in?"

"As in Scrappy Doo... As in nobody likes
you! And nobody needs you!" Spoke Jackson
with a laced anti-hero grudge. "We aren't
buddies... We aren't friends! Stop
pretending we are!"

"O' please!" Inari exclaimed as if she did
not give a dam. "What I am suppose to back
down just cos you say... C'mon!!!" She said
with an intense frame of mind!

"You can't roll with this! As I work alone,
Officer Gellar... I don't need your help! I
don't have an entourage... And I certainly
don't do SIDEKICKS!" Responded Jackson
back. "As this is not some stupid cartoon
or comic book! Or an even dumber movie
sequel. Were you see me reduced to a two
dimensional character. Forced to team-up
with a gang of goofy College kids... Or
something!" He voiced with absolute
conviction. "This is real life! REAL!" He
stated. "And I have a War on war to win!
Stay out of my way!!!"

"A war on war...? How does that work? What do you go..." Just as Inari was about to make another sharp tongued remark in finishing her sentence. Jackson now touched the side of the Ship uttering three words loudly.

"WORLD CHANGING EVENT!" He exclaimed as if he was possessed by a ghostly spirit!

"What?" Said Inari with an uncertain and very puzzled mumble.

"What does that mean?"

STOP THE CLOCK! TO NOW ONCE MORE...

Chapter Ten

NEO CON PROPAGANDA OFF!

"Sorry about the language remaining
viewers..."

Nine hours and three minutes into Christmas
Eve...

NEW YORK, NEW YORK... City Planet Earth, a
city that never sleeps. A city of Heroes
and a melting pot of humanity. Representing
a hundred cultures, millions of ideas and a
countless infinity of dreams. All set to a
sea of lights that always stay lit
throughout the night itself. As well as
being a great place to have breakfast in
the morning. On any normal day this was the

way "Civilized" false democracy believing people would call it! With it's real declaration being that of the New city of prophecy, of mountains falling from the sky, of proof of the Normans. Of smoke in the garden and so on. A place that has a open wound left in it's skyline. As with the twin towers brought down to their iconic demolition by false flag terrorism. By AmeriKKKa's own lying Zionist occupied government on the orders above those above even the End-Timers themselves. Killing, murdering the last good Americans that the world will probably ever see for a long time to come. The road was still set for a replay of events just a few decades from now. But in this moment things were about to come ahead, in another way...

HISTORY REWRITTEN... On fire! A blaze! Engulfed in the flames of delayed racist rage, anger and misery. Set to the screams of slaughtered innocents. That were themselves drowned out by the collective echoing mix of running gunfire and a thousand ringing alarms... That was the best way to describe what was happening in the city today. As this magnificent Island, that itself was built on stolen land. Blood money! And the evil foundations of racism and fictitious morality (Along with the rest of the whole nation that is America). Stood half dead and defeated, bounced against the ropes for what looked like the very last time. With no away in a manger.

With no crib for a bed... As joy to the
world and MERRY CHRISTMAS to all, and to
all a goodnight. Were on a permanent hold.

"RACE WAR! AMERICA ON FIRE!" Read the on
screen graphic, that served as a prelude to
a live news broadcast. That was itself
telling the truth and whole truth! For
once! With it's unfair and unbalanced, and
frankly institutionally racist. And very
ultra right winged stance seemingly on hold
as well?

"Christmas has been officially cancelled!
Santa Clause is definitely not coming to
town." Said the American newscaster, with
sarcasm. As she wore the look of fatigue...
While the picture quality itself now seemed
to be degrading, as if the TV network
uplinks were losing signal strength
themselves?

NEO CON PROPAGANDA--OFF! Having had no
sleep. The Newscaster now struggled to keep
awake slightly. As a series of race riot
laden TV News images from New York and from
outside the city, now played behind her.

"From our nations capital to Detroit...
From Baltimore to Philadelphia! Riots,
carnage, and destruction stand absolute...
With Chicago, Atlanta, Miami and Los
Angeles following suit. She said, as a

voice from the gallery above now shouted down her ear piece. "In scenes of violence and destruction that out weighed a Katrina ravaged New Orleans, reports of... Err? We?" Voiced the newscaster taking a collective pause. "We now go live to New York and to our eye in the sky..." She stated just keeping up with what was being said down her ear piece. As a fuzzy video image from inside a Helicopter now played on screen, in the top right corner...

"It's like some kind of Zombie movie from up here... The City is dying is... I'm sorry I mean... The City is dying IN a pulse of hate, fire and misery..." Said the Reporter correcting himself, as the he now sighted the patterns of spasmodic and wanton destruction. "O' my God there dragging the bodies of dead Police officers through the streets! That one's still alive...? O' my God there putting want seems to be a rubber tyre around him..." He spoke taking a disturbed pause. "No! No! No!" He exclaimed from the supposed safety of the News Helicopter... "Their setting him on fire... Their burning him alive! God No! Those fuckin' BLACK..." He voiced before he could finish off his heated moment slip of the tongue. Only to be cut off from the sound of incoming gunfire! "SHIT! FUCK! JESUS! JESUS! SHIT! SHIT! We're taking fire, we're taking fire!" He screamed ready to die.

Slight ill-tempered at the fact he had cursed on LIVE Network TV. And getting a second wind, the Newscaster now responded. "That's very interesting Bob! We'll get back to you shortly?" She said with a ice cold if it bleeds it leads mentality. As the picture now for the moment return to a fuller strength.

"Sorry about the language remaining viewers..." She stated with a perfect yet forced fake smile. "But we now have an... Yes exclusive from in side the disaster zone!" Spoke the Newscaster hoping to see more image of carnage. "Can you hear us Tony? Can you hear us?" She said pressing into her ear piece. "And if you can please remember that we are LIVE on Network Television!!! Can you here us Tony?"...

"December 23rd...12/23! A day, just like 9/11 that will be forever remembered!" Said the Reporter as he now appeared on screen in a slightly snow fuzzy image. As if he was reporting from the ends of the Earth. "A day that just yesterday, started with an unexplained heat wave. And then just before noon found itself under attack from... Itself! After...?" Stated the Reporter, cutting himself off from finishing his sentence. As he hid in the remains of an burnt out Iranian restaurant. Along with his Cameraman, who now struggled to stay in focus. Whilst sounds of an incoming howling mob echo outwards.

"The sight before me is unimaginable
madness, hatred! Racial hatred delivered by
all sides, BLACK and white, Gentile and
Jewish and all in between!" Said the
Reporter with a trying whisper.

"Running gun battles! Escaped prisoners?
The Police are no longer a factor! With
most of New York's finest having either
turned coward, or dead! With the latter
being the majority! There's been reports of
rapes and murders in there hundreds,
looting on an apocalyptic scale... It's...
It's like the end of the World here!" He
said wiping the sweat of his brow.

"Get ready I think their moving on." Said
the Reporter as he now readied himself for
a running exit...

"Go! Go!" Yelled the Cameraman.

GONE SUPERDOME... As in left behind because
you don't count! As in gone mad, gone
stupid, ready to rape, to kill, to steal...
Gone zombie flesh eating and blood drinking
crazy. Already to abuse and butcher your
brothers and sisters through and through.
Was the situation at hand and everywhere,
in the city that never sleeps...

As now being in what was know an undeclared war zone. Both of them now ran onwards, with extreme foolhardiness, heading to absolute danger. Cutting through a echoing river of smashed and burnt out concrete streets.

"Love thy Neighbour or Hate thy neighbour! The no longer good people of New York have chosen the latter of the two!" Spoke the Reporter running around the corner of a riot smashed street. Only to now witness a horrific sight. "GOOD CHRIST! ARE WE GETTING THIS... ARE WE GETTING THIS?" He questioned to his Cameraman.

"You're a go! YOU'RE A GO!" Yelled the Cameraman back in quick spoken return...

HEROES ON HOLD... HEROES ON A PERMANENT HOLD... "GET THIS! GET THIS!" Shouted the reporter back... "Now the forgotten heroes of the tragedy, New York City Fire Fighters lay dead! Shot! Stabbed! Clubbed! Even strangled by... By what looks like, piano wire...? We've heard on the lo that gunmen have been shooting dead, doctors and hospital staff of east Indian and Pakistani appearance. While all around the city... And including here... Individuals of a Middle Eastern appearance... And some yeah! Some Hispanics, have all been killed by racial and ethnic misidentification... Lay shot, stabbed, set on fire and hung up on street lamps throughout the City." He yelled one step away from forgetting to take in another breath! "O my God! Even? Even Crucified? Jesus!!! The humanity!" Called out the Reporter, nearly despondent in seeing more dead bodies. "America! Where are you?"

As with his once brilliant white shirt covered in dried blood stains and countless shoe and boot stomping prints. Beaten and shot to death, with nineteen hits. From the head to the torso and even in the legs. FBI Agent Robert Lysander's body now laid out twisted and broken. Along with a number of fellow Agents and Cops. All killed trying to protect the innocent! Murdered by a blood thirsty for payback mob of supposedly good citizens. And good American's!

"Christ! New Orleans times EIGHT million-- all over again... American Baghdad... We were told Never Again... Dam the President to hell!" He voiced breaking the do not question your Government and this administration rules of the network and media outlet!

Five seconds later...

"May God have mercy on their souls..." Stated the Reporter, crossing himself. Just one step away from crying, as he now tried to compose himself. "HARLEM! BLACK and SPANISH..." He voiced clearing his throat, facing back to the camera.

"Along with what was Central Park West. All are no more... The roads outside the city from New Jersey onwards are grid locked in a river of burnt out metal cars... The Holland tunnel is a blazed! Central Park is on fire... And as for the surviving National Guard troops... They are--They are withdrawing... Re-grouping? O' whatever you want to call it. This City is Lost! Escape from the city is now seemingly impossible? NO!" He said pausing... "It is impossible!" He voiced finally realizing that he was trapped there!

As with the way of escape now no more! A single gunshot now rang outwards...

Cutting through the air the said gunshot now delivered instant death to the Reporter in the form of one tap to the back of his head...

"Tony? Tony? Tony?" Called the Newscaster. "TONY???" She called out once more.

As the Cameraman stood frozen to the spot knowing he was next to bite the bullet,

quite literally. In the next few quickening
seconds...

STOP THE CLOCK... CUT TO THE FUTURE...

One minute later...

THE SUBMARINE CONTINUED... Murder!
Destruction! Madness! These were just three
of the words you could use to describe New
York, as the race riot from hell raged
ahead at a full and indifferent pace. In
all and every direction. As witness to
these rewritten events, through projected
images transmitted via "The Submarine!"
Jackson now stood with his hand still
pressed against the wall of the Ship...

"What is it?" Quizzed Inari, wanting to
know.

"Are you going to crank up the TEMPORAL
THREAT MATRIX! Or fire up The Looking
Glass, J.C?" Asked Techy, with the stance
of an obedient soldier and the concern of a
good friend.

"NO TIME!" Said Jackson, with his face
filled with silent anger, as he now turned
to Inari. "You want in...?" He growled
reluctantly. "SO BE IT!!! You stay close!

OBEY orders... And watch you're OWN ass...
Cos I'm not going too!" He growled again,
walking away from her. "UNDERSTOOD!"

"YES, SIR!" Inari said with sarcasm.
Delivering a false salute!

"And another thing!" Snarled Jackson. "This
isn't the Mossad! And all those other
intelligence gathering assassination. Come
baby killing S.S wannabe slaughter crew
squads out there! There's no such thing as
COLLATERAL DAMAGE with me! As I've never
seen an innocent person get hurt when I'm
on the clock! And I won't start now...
UNDERSTAND?"

Tuning out some of Jackson's explosive
comments, Inari now responded.
"Affirmative, Hero! That's a big ten
four!!! Big Daddy!" She announced with
playful mocking and yet serious knowing. As
turning his back on her. Inari now raised
her right middle index finger, flipping him
the proverbial BIRD!

"I SAW THAT!" Growled Jackson, like a
parent having eyes quite literally in the
back of their head.

Playful as always, sticking out her tongue
in a sexy, yet annoyed way. Inari now

looked towards Jackson. As he himself now
walked ahead. Ready for the next coming
battle and ensuing mission of Justice, that
was just about to begin!

**STOP THE CLOCK! REWIND THE TIME, TEMPORAL
RESET...**

T-Minus twenty four hours...

NEW YORK, NEW YORK REVISITED... As a whole
day now begun again without the knowledge
and knowing of the city and the world
itself. Everyone throughout the city of New
York and all around went about their
awaking business. All surprised at the
unexpected and slightly spooky encroaching
heat wave.

"TERROR ALERT! TERROR ALERT! Status is
RED... Status is Red! Attack is imminent!
Over! The Airports are to go on Lockdown...
With exception of VIP traffic.

The FAA (Federal Aviation Administration)
are grounding all commercial and civilian
air travel over the entire state..." Said a
Secret Service Agent into his radio-link.
"The Principle is aboard Angel One and is
en route to the assigned Evac point!

Fighter escorts are on approach! Over... We are now moving to the assigned evacuation point. Over!" He stated as a motorcade of black Limos now raced to escape the potential arrival of an attack on the city. Only to now pass a fleet of police cars heading in the complete opposite direction? As nearly every Cop from City Hall to Times Square and beyond the city limits now raced to the Financial District. A fleet of marked yet newly looking Police patrol cars now seemed to head away from the supposed destination, only to take turn after turn, heading towards Harlem instead?

Elsewhere...

WALL STREET... "If you ain't got no money take your broke ass home! Winner takes all! Pull up the ladder jack and forget the rest. Cash money dreams of making a fast buck at the expense of some unsuspecting sucker, who was hoping for a free lunch!" These were just a few of the countless examples to describe the twisted nexus, and central power point to the decadent. "Greed is good!"

Yet supposedly working cancerous capitalism that is the nation of AmeriKKKa, and the rest of the world. As with this palace of poison and namesake of a great movie built on the broken bones of what was one of the

biggest slave markets, in all of the
Americas. This casino of fixed numbers was
laced with nothing but lies all throughout!

Thus called into action once more, given
only the passing break of a long Plane
journey. Agent Robert Lysander now found
himself once more press-ganged into the
back of the helicopter. Sitting amongst of
group of fellow FBI Agents. All heading to
the heart of Wall street itself.

As the Helicopter now travelled inwards.
Heading for it's respective landing pad.
Lysander now sat firmed face trying to
displace his very own memories of his past
encounters with Jackson! Remembering how
they first met? And just how many times he
came close to catching him?

Same time different place...

UNITED NATIONS HEADQUARTERS... Magnanimous
landmark! 39 floors! Uniting Nations... (O'
Please!) The United Nations, that was the
failing goal and pointless mission
statement of the never listen too. Or
acknowledged joke that went by the name of
the U.N. That itself was wide open to
beyond obvious corruption and Nuclear
selective racist hypocrisy. As well as many
other crimes against humanity... But for

now all of that was on hold, with the
building and whole complex readying itself
for a possible evacuation... As just below
in the buildings main underground car park.
Ten armed UN security guards now escorted a
VIP towards an awaiting Limo. That itself
was ready for a speedy trip to a secret
place of escape.

Carrying an Aluminium briefcase chained to
his wrist. With two more guards in tow. The
said VIP, was none other than Kruger's
party guest UN Ambassador Dr. Victor. "The
package is secure! Even though it's
useless." He responded, having a two way
conversation. "NO! There was nothing on THE
CALENDAR... No permission was given! No...
They would know better than that! This is
someone else?" He voiced with cryptic
suggestion. "I'm now heading for the
extraction and hand over point now... I'll
reach the secure location thereafter! As I
said the item is secure!!!"

Now seeming as if she had come out of
nowhere! A young and mysterious raven jet
black haired woman. Now leapt upon their
collective positions!

"BOUDICCA LIGHTENING CHARGE!!!" She
exclaimed with an echoing feminine power
grunt! Thus knocking down and out all of
the guards with one power move!

With all this happening within just two
violently charged seconds. A surprised Dr.
Victor stood frozen to the spot, as the
woman. A disguised and black wig wearing,
Aryana! Now took instant aim with Inari's
stolen handgun. Only to fire one single
shot to the Doctor's chest, not killing him
outright?

"Guns! How vulgar!" She exclaimed, as to
all masters and practitioners of the
Martial Art of Murder. Guns and use of all
firearms in themselves represented the tool
of the weak and cowardly.

Thus treating the stolen weapon as a throw-
down, just like a dirty Cop who had gone
too far. Aryana dropped the gun. Only to
turn around in a spinning instance,
snapping into a running sprint, faster than
an Olympic athlete. As more security guards
now entered!

Once a place falsely dedicated to the
preservation of peace and Human dignity.
The UN was now tainted with the splatter of
violence. As Dr. Victor lay half dead in a
pool of his own blood. That itself looked
more like a black oil slick against the
grey and blacken concreted surface of the
car park...

Springing into action too late, the just
arrived guards reacted with caution! "Shots
fired! Shots Fired!" They yelled
collectively, as they now drew their guns.
"Where's the shooter... Where's the
shooter." Shouted one of the guards, as the
other now checked for Dr. Victor's possible
vitals?

"LOCKDOWN! LOCKDOWN!!!" Yelled another
guard into his shoulder strapped radio.
"Bravo two! Bravo two! The Ambassador is
down, repeat DOWN! We need EMS... Repeat
EMS report top level, OVER!"Said the guard,
ordering the standby Emergency Medical
Service Ambulance, based at the UN in the
lower levels to respond!

"Bravo two! Over... On our way!" Exclaimed
a violently toned South African voice, back
over the radio!

Four second onwards...

Escaping the murderous actions with beyond
lightening speed, Aryana now exited the
bottom of a lower stairwell. Dressed up I
the cunning disguise of a New York EMS
technician. "The Plan is in motion..." She
said speaking into her own modified Red-
Cell. "Cry havoc and let slip the Dogs of
War!" Aryana gloated, now putting on a pair
of plain glassed nerdy spectacles?

Same time... Different place...

A HYPER WI-FI CONNECTION OF THE FUTURE IN THE NOW... Receiving her message instantaneously, on the other side of the World. Kruger now sat in his study typing away at his computer screen. As a digital manifest of Water, Power, and Communications systems of the greater Manhattan Island area now displayed itself...

"Go! Shorty! It's you're birthday... It's you're birthday!" Sang Kruger to himself, with a hypocritical love of early twenty-first century Hip-Hop. As he now typed at an even quicker eye blinking pace than before.

Thus causing his computer to just barely keep up with his command override protocol's! Instantly displaying multiple digital blueprint images of the city's financial district! As well as real time satellite imagery? And CCTV traffic cameras...?

One minute later...

BACK TO NEW YORK... Back to the jungle, the concrete jungle that is! Thus with the

NYPD's very own Hercules teams. The Bomb Squad! Nuclear N.E.S.T! Sniper sharpshooters! Along with Troops! Cops on duty and off, detectives as well. Countless scores of Fire trucks and EMS buses, Police patrol Cars and Support vehicles and Mobile Command centres. All now arrived into the district. Storming towards all of the Banks and financial buildings around. Showing that the whole area was now on official LOCKDOWN!

As this scary, yet impressive roll called sight of might and aid now unfolded. One could only wonder if everyone was here to protect the innocent workers inside. Or the billions and countless billions to the trillions, in main-framed money and top dollar investments. That the financial district represented! That being the given life blood of the Nation and capitalist World that followed the lead of America, at every seeming turn... As the Government and local Administration had dispatched nearly every single division of Law Enforcement. That was to be found in the city and just beyond. As if it was Harlem coming under suspected attack, would they have responded with such force???

Countless in number. Teams of Cops, SWAT and Government Agents now stormed through every single building awaiting the worst! Whilst Lysander, commanding a unit of

Agents. Now entered a sub level computer server main-frame hub, of an undisclosed Bank.

Twenty five seconds onwards...

"Something's not, right!" Said Lysander to a fellow Agent. "Why would Al-Qaeda send out E-mails, telling us of an attack... They didn't with Madrid or London! Or? Why tell us where they were going to strike? It doesn't make any sense?"

"I know, but the coded message was deemed authentic by Home-Sec and Washington! It had all the right phrases and dialogue and code words!" Said one of the Agents in response.

"It's got to be a trick..." Remarked Lysander to himself... "A diversion!" He stated as now without warning the imposed LOCKDOWN now became an enforced reality... As without warning all of the power now cut out! Thus accidentally tripping all of the buildings new and improved, post 9/11 security systems and protocol's. Thus sealing every single door. Window and every exit in every building, throughout the whole financial district. Including the building Lysander was searching...

"Jesus, Al-Qaeda! we're under attack!"
Yelled one of the Agents, pulling his
weapon taking off it's safety!

"Holster that weapon!" Ordered Lysander,
annoyed at the Agents rushed judgement!

"My radio's dead!" Called one Agent, not
getting a signal.

"Hey! So is mine?" Exclaimed another.

"This is it?" Said an Agent, in thinking
that an all out attack was imminent!

With seconds ticking by as the emergency
lights of red now activated, throughout
every single blacked-out building. Lysander
now readied himself to take charge of the
situation. "Diversion!" He said looking
down with ominous knowing! As his radio now
too was silent!

Same time... Different place...

HARLEM... "Good Morning America!" Exclaimed
the DJ over the Radio, that was placed on
the counter of a grocery store. As children
of all ages ran inwards, already to buy ice
creams and soda pop.

"HEAT WAVE! That's today's special word for this morning of December 23rd!" Said the DJ. "I know what you are all thinking. How come there was snow everywhere two days ago? And now it's one step away from being ninety-nine degrees in the shade... Is it Global warming? I think the facts are speaking for themselves people!" He uttered as the young children now exited, with ice creams in melting hand. Heading for the playground across the street.

"We have a lot of calls coming in... Stuff about the Cops and Soldiers heading to Wall street... Fire and EMS services are being put on stand-by... Some are already on the move? Is the Terror Alert being raised from Orange to Red? Is an attack imminent? The answer is, NO! Absolutely NO!!! It's staying where it is people!" Voiced the DJ in a serious tone. "The NYPD and the Mayor's Office are just calling it a drill, as the Al-Qaeda E-Mail was a hoax! Just a hoax folks!" He said reading a written on-line statement. "Now let's have some music!!!" Said the DJ, as radios and boom boxes now played on every corner. With Harlem itself standing drenched in the sweat of the unexplained heat wave...

Thus with the scene set for the cold blooded murder of the innocent. Who were all wearing summer clothes, that were until early this morning put away. Jump ropes! B-

ball and said ice cream were the call of
the day on this Playground...

As given a break! With a little secret help
from a 6'3 tall man. Who was faster than a
speeding bullet and nearly as fast as light
itself! Come momentary stay. (Real
momentary!) Just for one night only. And a
heartbreaking sunrise that followed. With a
super high body count of bangers, pushers
and child prostitution ring traffickers.

But now all was back to reality. All was
real, too real. All was "ghetto" but not in
the cool false way of hip hop songs. But of
blood stains on the concrete. On the
playground! Of used crack vials and smashed
crack pipes along with dirty needles, used
condoms and 9mm spent shell casings. As now
without warning a rumbling of near and
distant thunder now rang outwards...

Ignored as just business as usual by the
children and adults alike. A squadron of
Fighter jets, now stormed through the
morning sky... Heading away from the city.
Travelling upwards to a higher altitude, to
patrol the east coast boarder of a
supposedly grateful nation.

While her friends continued to play jump-
rope. One little girl now looked up, seeing

the planes speedy exit. As a fleet of Cop cars now slowly approached the Playground from both sides!

"The sound of da Police, the sound of da beast!" Was now at hand! As entering the undeclared Plantations that way too many poor communities, Black, Hispanic and poor White and all in between seem to be. With a screeching halt, and thud tapping click!

Stopping and exiting the cars all at once. The Cops, with fully automatic silenced weapons by their sides. Now walked straight towards the playground... All remaining unnoticed by the Adults and children alike! Except for the little girl who had just been watching the planes go by...

"TEAM TWO! Attack from opposite position! Said the lead Cop into his radio. As the officers now approached!

COPS IN THE KKK--COPS IN THE KLAN... Dunkin' doughnuts and officers of the peace, these Cops, these killers were not. Filth! With a capital F, come a bloodthirsty slaughter Crew with a following and total dedication to murder they were! As two faced like a snake getting ready to bite you in the neck. The Lead Officer, Kyle Walker. Now looked the little girl directly in the eye! Giving a false and you are perfectly safe smile of reassurance. Only to then pull his gun, taking off it's safety. Taking instant aim for the aforementioned as cute as buttons little girls head...

Frozen in one imminent violent moment, as the rest of the would-be Cops aka "The Crew!" Now took aim with their assault weapons, ready to murder every single person of so-called colour who was there.

One second onwards...

And thus with the words "Abandon all hope!" Seeming the appropriate thing to say. A miracle happen!

Chapter Eleven

THE RACE AGAINST THE DEVIL IS UNLEASHED!

"In a New York Minute... Everything can
change!"

ENTER THE FASTEST MAN ON EARTH! PLUS ONE...

SHOCK! SURPRISE AND ABSOLUTE AMAZEMENT...
These were all the ways of describing the
seat jumping excitement of what happen
next! As an automatic spray of bullets
screamed near silently outwards. A speeding
truck now stormed into harms way. Taking
every single bullet strike! Thus deflecting
the bullets away from any person or person
nearby, or otherwise! As if it was
magnetized!?

Now exiting the truck in one single slow motion moment. Bangkok dangerous! Taking this city by storm, and expecting to leave all enemies dead on arrival. Jackson Carter! Aka the fastest man on earth, was ready for battle and murder! As standing now bullet empty! Kyle Walker and all of the other Cops, were one step away from shock!

"Jesus! He's real!!!" Exclaimed Kyle Walker.

"No! He can't be! You said..." Exclaimed another.

"FUCK NO! It's him? He's real!" Whispered one more!

"He can't get us all. Kill 'em! Kill them all!" Ordered walker with a turning running yell. As he himself now cowardly ran back towards his Patrol car.

Running and taking cover as this all now unfolded. The Adults and children now tried to escaped to nearby safety.

THAT'S THE NAME OF THE GAME... That was the theme, the title track and event to be described. As with extra curricula activities on blacks by the Police. Was now

the factor at hand! As three quarters of
the Cops now charged towards Jackson. The
other Cops, who remained on the opposite
side. Now reloaded, taking instant aim
towards the escaping Children and Adults...

"Bang! Bang! Bang! Duck! Duck! Duck!" Would
have been the things to call out and holla!
If there was time to step back and write
lyrical notes... (But there wasn't!) As
just as the first child was about to be
shot in the back. Sniper fire now rang out
from above, from a housing tenement. With
the solo shooter being Inari!

Who now put her said sharp shooter skills
to maximum use. Killing all of the taking
aim Cops in just a few well timed seconds.
With multiple quick fired lethal one tap,
one kill, shots! Making the term--"Ya run
ya still dyin'!" The best and only way to
describe what was happening.

Thus with the innocent people now on the
way to safety. And as the Cops drew out
their Nightsticks, that were themselves a
modern representation of the overseers
whips. All thinking in some way they could
win! "Motherfucker, you gone!!!" Was now
the business of the day, from "The
Planetary Patriot!" As the said Cops! In
high number, stood ahead!

"BLOOD DRINKING JACKALS, YOUR TIME HAS
COME!" Jackson growled aloud... Cracking
his knuckles into fists!!! With the look
of--"Fire FIFTY SHOTS at me and see what
you'll get!" In his eyes...

And thus being a man of a "FUCK THE POLICE"
mentality. And by that I mean a Person who
was ready to Murder Cops. White, black and
blue all alike where they stood. If they
were doing evil things to the non-guilty...
Or on the flip-side ready to do battle to
save them. On any given "honest" day on the
street and beat! Jackson now snapped into
action! Primed to engage every single Cop
nearly at once.

**BROWN SHIRTS IN BLUE YOU AIN'T GOT A
CLUE**... With ten seconds or far less, being
all it would have taken to defeat them.
Jackson now made sure that it took at least
twice or thrice as along. Slowing his moves
and skills down a couple of levels out of
sheer anger. Jackson now went about
murdering all of these evil men quite
literally where they were standing! Cutting
through them all with just two or one
punches, kicks, or elbows.

"GET THAT, NIGGER! GET HIM!!! WHAT ARE YOU
WAITING FOR?" Screamed Walker! "GET IN
THERE! GET IN THERE!"

187 IN MOTION AND IN PROGRESS... By way of zero respect! Unleashing a hidden and wanton sadism! Showing them that they were temporary like baby teeth. Jackson now used their very own tools of oppression against them. Busting and breaking them down with their very own Nightsticks!

"GET IN THERE... GET IN THERE!" Walker continued to scream aloud.

"GO! GO! KICK AND BEAT HIS BLACK PORCH MONKEY ASS... FOR GOD'S SAKE, WHAT ARE YOU ALL WAITING FOR! HE'S JUST ONE MAN... GET HIM! GET IN THERE!!!" He ordered only to then turn, jumping into his car.

"Change! Change! Shit ain't changed! Rodney King I'm not! Officer equals Overseer! Glad to be a Cop Killer! I'm not seventeen and afraid! Eight times out of ten a Policeman is not your friend!... And why can't we all just get along?"

At least one of these many thoughts and statements were on the mind of Jackson Carter. As he now went about slaying half of them within moments. Kicking one of the Cops forward straight into a nearby lamp post, thus bending it in half and killing the thug instantly. Only to then knock one incoming cop down. Stomping his face and head into the ground, with a quick impacting kick!

N.H.I... Aka NO HUMANS INVOLVED! Was something that a lot and a few more Police Officers liked to use in secret or in loud mouth openness. (Along with many other comments!) Used as a coded term for the Murders of Gang Bangers. Drug dealers, enslaved Prostitutes, the Homeless, immigrants, black or Hispanic people. Or anyone else unfortunate enough not to be missed by anybody!

Thus with intense irony this term was now applied to the incoming Cops. To these incoming Crooks On Patrol. With extreme destructive prejudice!

Two bloody seconds later...

"Proud to be an American where at least I know I'm free? Where the Cops can shoot a broke black man nineteen times plus... Or beat his ass on TV!" That was the anti-hero theme tune given to the beat-down situation at hand... With--"This little Piggy went to market and got his head smashed in! And with this little Piggy won't be getting roast beef, as he's DEAD!" Being the scene of events. With instant FLATLINES handed out to all of the human filth concerned!

Now pushing forward, cutting through the last of them. Jackson slammed a stolen Nightstick straight into the eye socket of one Cop. Only to then rip off another Cops NYPD shoulder insignia patch. Pressing it hard into the said Officers cheek, with a sledgehammer hitting bitch slap to the face. Instantly killing him!

"Officer down! Officer down and he's not getting back up again! EVER!!!" Was the fact in hand. As then taking hold of the just dead Cops Nightstick!

Turning the table's as the next Cop that came towards him. Jackson now violently applied a quickly delivered choke hold! A move and manoeuvre that ironically and in itself had been used by Police Officers. Or racial profiling overseers! As some would say unfairly!? To murder countless individuals of colour like Jackson himself.

Consequently crushing the wicked Cops throat into a twisted windpipe mush. Snapping his neck nearly off from his shoulders. Jackson now cut through the remaining rest, breaking them apart with his bare hands. Finishing off one Cop by slamming his fist into his chest! Driving the Cops badge right into his very own heart. Killing him with a blood impaling thumb!

Now nearly the last man standing. Not wanting to die! Trying to run away! The last remaining Cop, fled away like a true blue cowardly bully. Sporting a face filled up with the look of pure terror and absolute disturbed fear! That in itself nearly, just nearly made you feel sorry for him. (Well just nearly!)

"GOD! No!!!!!!!!!!!!!!!" He screamed, as he now realized he had failed to escape Jackson's long reaching arms. "PLEASE!!!" Squealed the swine with a plea for mercy. Only to now find himself grabbed by his belt and shirt collar. Hoisted completely upwards. As Jackson from behind, now lifted him off the ground!

"TEMPORAL SPINE BUSTING-SLAM!!!" He yelled! Bending over backwards like a wrestler, quite literally slamming the Cop into the concrete...

Thus with the last thing on Earth he tasted being the dirty asphalt. The would-be evil doer come overseer. Now died with a skull and spine busting crunch.

"He fought the Law and... He won!" That was what Jackson had done, afraid of no man or no one! As he now instantly sprung backwards ready to deal out even more destruction!

Seeing that all this had happen in just under thirty seconds or just less, Kyle walker. Who was one step away from crapping his pants. Now tried to make a desperate and speedy getaway!

As the Patrol car screeched down the road, trying to rev up it's engine. Jackson's face stood cold... With him now snapping into a instant ZERO to SIXTY charge as he stormed down the adjoining road...

In consequence, heading him off at the pass. Jackson now ran at super speed straight towards a incoming Walker... Revving up the engine once more, with his shaking foot against the pedal. Walker now increased his speed! Thus making it seem that all was lost! As to the unknowing it now looked like Jackson himself could not win against the weight, and metal of the speeding patrol Car?

"NIGGER! Let's see you survive this!" Said Walker with expected racist fear...

"TEMPORAL BODY OF STEEL!" Jackson yelled, solid as a rock. As he now stood his ground, just a second away from being hit by the Car!

"Man Versus Car! Car always wins!" This was always the quote to be used. If anyone was stupid or unfortunate enough to step out in front of a speeding vehicle. But as always and every time when it came to Jackson. The rules of the moment and rules of the game did not apply! As now a would-be Angel of Death! Extending his arms outwards in a respectfully charged crucifix like manor. Jackson now won the battle at hand! As the incoming Patrol Car SMASHED and CRASHED straight into his person. Just as if it had surely crashed into a super concrete steel girder!

Stepping away from the damage without a single scratch or mark on him. Jackson now walked calmly over to the drivers side of the Car. While with half of his face and teeth, bloody and broken by a second too late to deploy air bag. Kyle Walker now exited the said smashed Car.

In pain with internal bleeding, that was unknown to him. Walker now just managed to stand himself up! "YOU! JEW YORKER, FAGGOT, DAGO AND MICK LOVING BLACK COON BASTARD!" He yelled with blood pouring from his filthy speaking, trash talking cut mouth.

"YOU THINK YOU'RE ONE OF THE CLEVER ONES, DON'T YOU! YOU MAY BE FAST! BUT LET'S SEE YOU DODGE A BULLET, NIG...!!!" He yelled

Walker half a second away from pulling out his side arm!

"FUCK YOU PIG!!! FUCK--YOU!!!!" Was the look in his rhythm and gangsta eye. As unlike those microphone no commanding, NO SPINE consenting house slaves. Proving as always why he was worthy of the title fastest man on earth! Jackson now took hold of Walker's Nightstick! Thus removing it in one quick, and eye blinking continuous motion. Before Walker himself could even pull out his weapon. Or finish his last spoken word...

Therefore SLAMMING IT! Straight into Kyle Walker's vile and hateful mouth! Only to turn around in spinning motion. Like some Sword wielding Asian movie hero, acting as if what he had just done was nothing at all.

Thus neutralizing him without delay! DEAD!!! Murdered quite literally where he stood, Kyle Walker now slumped down to the ground. As taking a few steps away from the scene of destruction, Jackson now stood still. Looking straight ahead and seemingly straight through the city itself...

TEMPORAL FLASH FORWARD... As time and space were now ripped apart all around him, in a pool of waking light! Jackson now found

himself standing amongst the ruins of a
smashed and destroyed New York!

Drenched in black clouds, with falling
white like snow. The entire city stood
broken and dead! As with a change of
location, Jackson now found himself
standing in Rockefeller Centre...

Normally one of the most impressive sights
in the City at Christmas. The view was now
anything but. As melted glass, scorched and
blacken buildings were now seen throughout.
Along with the remains of ice angel
statues. Now all metal skeletons. And one
charred to a crisp giant Christmas tree!
Taking it all in just for a few disturbing
seconds... Turning his head! Jackson now
saw a group of children. From different
neighbourhoods, from all around the City.
Looking like a poster for "We are the
world! Children are the future," etc and so
on!

Left behind to die "Katrina" style. Left
behind and left for dead... Standing in
grey and soot blacken and very much blood
soaked clothing. The children all seemed to
have what looked like radiation burns on
their faces... As one of them now stepped
forward, looking Jackson dead in the eye.

"SAVE US!" She said. Said the little girl.
The same little girl from the playground.
As she now pointed towards the sky?
Following disturbing suit, all of the other
children now pointed towards the same
direction. As a down pouring of BLACK RAIN
now covered their position!

THE RACE AGAINST THE DEVIL IS UNLEASHED...

"I predict a riot!" A race riot from hell
would have been the aftermath and events of
destruction. If not for his and Inari's
actions! As now instantly snapping out of
the Temporal Flash Forward. Jackson stood
still as if he was hearing voices?

"Hey! Hero?" Yelled an approaching Inari
with charge.

Thus now with her rifle slung over her
shoulder. Having herself just completed
policing her brass as always. Thus leaving
NO trace evidence of sniper shell case
activity behind. Inari stood with her side-
arm weapon now in hand...

"In a New York Minute... Everything can
change!" Stated Jackson with obscure and
whispered suggestion.

"Yeah! I know I love that song... Are you okay???" Responded Inari with increased concern.

"I'm fine!" He responded back, knowing what he had to do next!

"Well that was easy. We won! The bad guys are all dead. Fuck po-po and all that!" She declared in slang reference to the word police.

"You know, I gotta say, they had a pretty good idea of dressing up as fake Cops! And..."

"Who said that they were fake!" Stated Jackson with interrupting truth. Showing that NO one or NO institution was beyond his reach of attack or justice...

"Okay!" Expressed Inari in surprise, almost rolling her eyes.

"What's next? Do we go take the Truck and the stuff back to that Candy girl, or what?" She voiced, giving a mention to one of Jackson's Helpers in this present time.

Not answering at first as they now walked
back to the parked truck, Jackson now
spoke. "It was too easy! They were just
Cannon fodder... We have to get to the
Airport..."

"Which one? This cities got three or more!"

"John F Kennedy to be precise!"

"Why?" She asked.

"To protect the future... That's why!" He
stated with conviction! Not telling Inari
the rest.

"That's good enough for me, Hero!" Said
Inari, with a sexy grin, as they now
reached the Truck. As inside the back of
the said truck, weapons and two
motorcycle's stood ready for use....

MADE IN THE U.S.A--AMERICAN MADE... With
all the parts, apart from one coming from
Japan. Sporting a dream team design of a
supercharge custom job from heaven.
Jackson's bike. A concept Harley Davidson.
Sat immaculate with a perfect polished
chrome look! All thanks to one of his
countless Helpers, the already mentioned
"Candy!"

Jumping onto his bike, as Inari grabbed a few more ammunition clips and another weapon. Jackson now ready himself for the chase!

"Agent, Gellar!" He said taking hold of a crash helmet. "Safety first!" Voiced Jackson with cool concern, throwing her the helmet.

As she herself was now putting on a pair of sunglasses. That was a perfect match to her short leather jacket and I love New York T-Shirt! "Message!" She exclaimed, throwing the Helmet aside. Taking Jackson's safety advice with a sarcastic smile! As if he was a over cautious Dad on a TV show. Giving out gee wiz golly, "You know son" advice!

A 357 Desert Eagle and Black Mack 10, were now the weapons of choice for Inari. As she now jumped onto her Japanese motorcycle.

"Try to keep up!" He spoke, revving up his custom Job Harley Davidson's engine.

"What about the truck?" She asked. "Are you just gonna leave it here?"

"It's taken care off!" He exclaimed with a cool growl! "Computer! ALPHA ONE! AUTO

DESTRUCT!!!" He voiced, only to one second
later speed out of the Truck.

"Wait! AUTO-DESTRUCT?!" Exclaimed Inari as
she now revved up her bike, making a quick
and speedy exit herself...

As they both now sped away on a path to
exit Harlem. A swirling vortex of
superheated fire now instantly and yet
safely engulfed the Truck. Destroying every
single piece of any traceable evidence
inside. Only to then put itself out...

Elsewhere and ten seconds later...

With Jackson and Inari's race against the
Devil through the city now beginning...
Lysander! Along with nearly every Cop and
Law Enforcement officer in the city. Now
still remained trapped at Wall Street! As
unknown to them Kruger now sent a signal to
reverse the lockdown and radio blackout!
Just as a number of SWAT Team members, were
about to try and cut open a blast door with
welding torches.

Thus with blue now turned white hot light
flashing across the Bank's lobby. All of
the Cops and Government Agents inside
waited nervously. As without warning the

red emergency lights deactivated, switching back to normal.

"The lights! There back on..." Yelled a Police Captain as his radio now also activated?

Fifty seconds before...

While down below in the Banks underground car park's top level. Now drenched in fluorescent false light. Lysander! Split from his Team, now walked onwards. Working something out in his head?

"Diversion! Diversion... Attack!" He said getting a gut feeling. "Enter the Planetary...!" Said Lysander to himself, only to now be interrupted by the sound of a loud and rude business man. As two uniformed Cops stood next to a luxury and customized sports car, admiring it.

"Hey! Cagney & Lacey!" Said the Broker with complacent rudeness towards the two male Officers. "I've just spent what seemed like an hour trapped inside an elevator. Ergo! I don't care what Pissed off Goldberg hating, sand castle building Camel Jockey is planning to do!" He exclaimed with uncaring racist incenses. "This is my Car... My fuckin' Car!" Voiced the man flashing his lucky rabbits foot key chain. "This is a piece of technology that you two Doughnut dunkers couldn't afford if you were reincarnated as someone like me a billion... No scratch that a zillion times over... Understood? Beyatches... So don't touch what you can't afford!"

"I bet your wife tells you the same thing every night!" Said one of the Cops back.

"O' that's funny... That's funny, guys. But I don't think you realize who you are talking too...? Do you?"

"O' yeah we understand!" Said the other Cop mockingly.

"Yeah! I understand perfectly!" Voiced the first Cop, one step away from putting the New York frighteners on him. As too the two Cops, the Stockbrokers. "I'm a rich white man, I can talk to you how I like. And people like me don't go to Jail pass." Was invalid in the present situation of a monumental attack! Getting and strange feeling, one step away from it being quite spooky. Lysander now took out his PDA. Tapping open a highly detained map of New York City... "If this is a diversion the place of att... Will be the... The Airport?

Which one which one...? JFK!" He said
pausing, playing hunch. As the blast doors
now opened and full main power now came
back on-line. Thus looking up and all
around only to see the Stockbrokers
customized, and illegally supercharged
classic Ferrari. Lysander now broke into a
quickly performed jog.

"Great the powers back-on." Said one of the
Cops. "Now Sir! May I suggest you..."

"Agent Lysander, FBI!" He said flashing his
I.D! "I need to commandeer this vehicle!"

"You and the rest of this City, fuck face!"
Voiced the Broker.

"F--face...?" Said Lysander, as he snatched
hold of the Broker's key chain. "Officers!
Arrest this man!" He stated with false

conviction, as he now slammed the door
shut! Starting up the Car's engine.

"Yes, Sir!" Said both Cops at once. "What
charge?" One questioned as he put on the
cuffs!

"Being an, ASSHOLE!" Said Lysander, revving
up the cars engine. Only to now instantly

burn rubber, making a shrieking speedy exit...

"O' Jesus no, my Car... my Fucking Car!" Said the Broker nearly crying. As one Cop now spoke to the other.

"Err? Can we make that charge stick?"

"???! Yeah!" Said both Cops turning to each other.

A second later... A different place!

BACK TO THE UN... With the United Nations now fading into the distance. Aryana's EMS Buses sped ahead, sirens screaming! Breaking the speed limits. On a supposed errant of mercy... While inside on the front dashboard a rolling 3D video road map. That itself now pictured a live action feed of the clearest route of escape? Now displayed on the buses G.P.S monitor. Showing corrective after corrective turn!

Thirty seconds later...

Wearing a pair of safety goggles. Snapping on a pair of white latex gloves. Sitting in the back of the Bus, dressed as a E.M.T as

well. Brutus! Lucky to be alive after
getting bitch slapped by Jackson. Now
looked like he had just called the
heavyweight Champion a sissy, sporting one
bruised and black eye of a shiner from hell.

"The packages self destruct system is still
activated!" He said placing a PDA type
device over it. "Outer auto-destruct...
Deactivated! Inner systems still on-line!"
Voiced Brutus, as the said PDA device now
hacked into the cases security system.

Sat in the front passenger seat next to one
of her many anonymous Henchmen, who was
driving. Aryana now spoke over the sound of
the shrieking sirens.

"Cut away, Brutus!" She stated with polite
loudness. "And remember... If you break it,
you bought it!" Remarked Aryana letting
Brutus know that failure was not an option!
As he now cut away the still just alive
Doctor's arm!

Ten second before...

Now reaching the nearest Bridge, Aryana's
Ambulance now cut a quick speedy path
through traffic. Using it's sirens as a
free pass. As just one or two steps away

from the bridge itself. Zooming down the lengthy drive, and therefore nearly catching up! Jackson now revved up his bike once more, performing a perfect back wheeled wheelie...

Holding her respective own, looking the part. With her wavy raven jet black hair blowing back in the wind. Inari now performed a wheelie herself, in playful response. Sporting a cheeky smile! With aforementioned ice water in his veins. Thus not giving an inch in silent return, taking no notice. Jackson carried onwards!

Focused in complete and total dedication to his mission at hand. As now reaching end of the Bridge, exiting ahead at an ever increasing speed. It now seemed that Aryana was going to indeed make her escape!

"O' Hell no!" That was the expression on Jackson's masculine cool face, as he and Inari now sped onto the Bridge in full pursuit!

Made to supercharged performance and perfection! Giving him higher than high speed and acceleration. Jackson's bike could only be described as the fastest bike in the world! As thus sweeping ahead in one continuous moment, cutting a line through on going traffic.

Still playing catch-up, both he and Inari now cleared the said Bridge. Seemingly in a quick rolling instant!

Now on the Expressway, charging forwards thanks to her Ambulances improved and modified engine. Aryana's escape now almost seemed to be inevitable! But all was not lost, as Jackson and Inari now entered onto the said Expressway. That in itself stood lengthy in sculpted concrete. With reinforced barriers to match. All serving as a highway to speed and freedom of travel. As a sea of countless vehicles travelled in opposite directions. All mostly obeying the speed limit.

"ROLL'IN! ROLL'IN! ROLL'IN!... KEEP ON ROLL'IN!!!" This was the theme and movement of the moment, as commanding the road as the ultimate easy riders, with absolute attitude. Jackson and Inari powered forward over the seemingly forever stretching, Expressway!

LIVING LIFE IN THE FASTLANE... Is how he lived his everyday, with nearly every second counted! Put to use to help and protect the innocent peoples of the world. As thus taking charge, already to catch-up! Jackson now pulled along side Inari.

"FOLLOW ME!!!" He shouted with a extremely loud snarl.

"O' shit! He's not serious!" Said Inari to herself, as if to say that he's one crazy Motherfucker. Therefore realizing what he was now about to do.

As Jackson now fearlessly jumped straight into a stream of incoming traffic! With the chase and the race against the Devil now to be continued!!!

Chapter Twelve

THIS IS YOUR CAPTAIN SPEAKING!

"Bomb Voyage... Future Boy!"

Ninety-Nine seconds later...

NEW YORK, NEW YORK CONTINUED... Seek and
destroy! That was his plan of action, and
just like a scene stealing moment in a
movie. Jackson now just cut through a
caravan of cars and trucks and anything in
between... Thus following in reluctant
suit, with an officious need for speed
herself! Inari without even thinking, just
doing. Now cut her way through the said
incoming traffic. Just missing certain
death at every single fast blinking, full
throttled turn!!!

While still just in front. On a head on
course for the Airport, Aryana's Ambulance
continued onwards. Not realizing that the
game was nearly up!

"The package is secure!" Said Brutus
holding up the Doctor's now blood soaked
case.

"I hoped you doubled gloved?" Expressed
Aryana with a cold smile.

"As you know statistically, of colour
Africans are most likely to have that dirty
VIRUS!" She remarked with racially charged
suggestion and reference to HIV. Thus
causing him to quickly wipe clean the case.

"Excellent, Brutus!" Remarked Aryana. "Take
our..." She said only to be interrupted by
a now yelling Brutus.

"NEIN!!! He's found us!" He voiced with a
violent quake in his voice. "THE FASTEST
MAN ON EARTH--IS HERE!"

"Impressive! All is going to Plan!"
Exclaimed Aryana, unflinching to the just
given news. "As I expected! Future Boy,
will not quit... Back-up Support...
Engage!" She ordered into her Red-Cell.

Speeding inwards from both sides, while at the same time hitting their sirens... FOUR more Ambulances, that were of the same make and model. Now instantly joined up to Aryana's bus.

"He's not alone!" Shouted Brutus, loading his M-4 sub-machine gun plus grenade launcher.

"O' I see he's slumming it!" Said Aryana with cold offence towards Inari, as she now stared into a wing mirror.

"Ja! The Juden is just behind him." Brutus voiced, taking a near fearful peak out the Buses back window.

"Hold you're fire for now, Brutus. Your job is to protect the contents of that case... With your life!" Said Aryana, turning her head towards him with a cold ominous stare. "Let's BLACKEN his name shall we..." She said to herself aloud rhetorically, pressing into her Red-Cell! "1013! 1013! Officers down... Officers down... Shots fired in Harlem! Repeat! Shots fired in Harlem!" Voiced Aryana, breaking into a very convincing New York accent, posing as a radio operator. "Suspects are one African American male, one white, possibly MIDDLE EASTERN female... Both suspects are ARMED and DANGEROUS, escaping via..."

Eight minutes later...

Therefore and elsewhere, and not that far away. Knowing that his hunch was right after picking up Aryana's false radio message. And having himself just requested back-up on his radio. Lysander raced ahead at a fast yet skilled pace. Turning corners, completing laps through out going and incoming traffic with the skill of a Stuntman come NASCAR driver. Making sure he saved the turbo boosted use of Nitrous Oxide for later. While breaking about at least thirty public safety codes. With his stolen vehicle containing a mini tank of NOS. And a illegally modified supercharged engine. Lysander now took caution, as a group of kids played around a open fire hydrant, cooling off amongst the spraying water. Causing him in a passing instant to reduce his speed to a turning crawl...

Smiling at him with cheeky grins, the children now stared with "Wow's!" At his borrowed Car. As Lysander now smiled back quickly in response. Only to rev up once more now reaching the start of the Expressway to see...

CHAOS! CARNAGE! SMOKE RISING! And Death on the Highway or Expressway. For all except the last statement this is now what could be seen. As pursuing Police Officers in

Patrol Cars and a couple on Bikes. Who were themselves heading for Wall Street! Had all failed to arrest and apprehend Jackson and Inari.

CALLIN' ALL CARS--CALLIN' ALL CARS... As their Patrol Cars and bikes lay smashed or crushed. The Police officers acted in the way of men and women who lived up to the meaning of the word Hero. Acting the way every officer should act. As they all were ready to protect and serve. Calling in Fire and EMS support. They all now went about checking and helping the civilians who's vehicles had been destroyed, and wrecked in the ensuing chase. While entering the Expressway, cutting a path through the destruction. Lysander could now see that zero fatalities was an absolute throughout, as he then raced ahead...

Elsewhere and further on...

Just minutes away from the Airport and not far away from exiting the Expressway. With perfect formation with precision driving. From place to place and from new position to new position, again and again. The Ambulances, completely identical in colour and design. Now took up speeding positions, with two in front and two behind. Allowing Aryana to play an undeclared game of piggy in the middle... As racing towards the said

Ambulances, travelling ahead! Jackson now
focused on the leader, not fooled at all by
her cheap trick.

As the EMS Buses now continued to dash
forward. Jackson Carter with Inari by his
speeding side. Now was just one step away
from catching up to their speeding
positions. When the rear Ambulances back
doors now swung opened...

Thinking that they had got the better of
them, two Henchmen in the rear ambulance
now opened fire! Only to see that Jackson
and Inari were now not behind them?

"Where are they?" Yelled a thug, to the
driver, trying to reload!

"I Don't see them?" Hollered the driver
back. "Wait?" He then yelled taking in a
quick breath... "In front! In front! Shit
No!"

One second before...

Thus racing instantly in front, with a dip
to her right. Inari charged between the
last two Ambulances. Just as the pulse of
Semi-Auto weapons fire now rang outwards
from the EMS bus in front. That missed her,

but killed the driver of the bus behind
instead... While at the same time the said
Bus in front's driver now looked to their
left, in seeing Jackson speed past him...

"He's speeding ahead..." Voiced the driver,
as one of the henchmen in the back jumped
into the passenger seat.

"Where's the other one?" He asked
reloading, only to get no answer as the
driver turned to his right. To witness
Inari taking instant aim for them from the
other side!

With a cold killer look of--"Dodge THIS
Motherfucker!" Firing just one shot from
her Desert Eagle, Inari now HIT the driver
and passenger. With the single fired
bullet! That itself passed instantly
through both their bigoted heads. Thus
blowing their collective racist brains all
over the front windscreen. Causing the
Ambulance to rev out of control in full
reverse, slamming into the bus behind.

"Brutus! Take out the trash!" Ordered
Aryana. Now seeing the two buses the were
leading the rear, crashing upwards and
smashing straight into the express ways
concrete barrier.

Responding to her command with haste.
Brutus now pushed out Dr. Victor who was
still half dead on the stretcher... As his
body nearly bounced of the rolling said
stretcher. Brutus took aim firing a single
grenade at it!

Therefore hitting the crashed stretcher
within a popping and propelled instant. The
grenade detonated on target! Engulfing and
blowing apart the stretcher. Ejecting Dr.
Victor's dead, yet now burning corpse
through the air...

Simultaneously dodging the Doctors engulfed
and charred body, swerving to opposite
sides. As the corpse now landed on the
road. Now with the monstrous car crashing,
fender bending pile up of traffic far
behind them. Jackson and Inari collectively
sped ahead. Staying on target travelling
onwards. Luckily missing the impacting
explosion! While Aryana's bus now took the
unexpected lead, leaving two buses in
protective cover behind...

Five seconds onwards...

Hot on his arch enemies seated
acceleration. Jackson seemed to have left
Inari behind as the rear buses back doors
were thrown open, with two Henchmen now
opening fire!

Swerving in what seemed like a miracle to herself, Inari just missed the incoming gunfire. Only to now return fire herself, between heartbeats! Killing the two henchmen dead within four quick fired shots! As thus DEAD, the thugs bodies now tumbled out of the back of the Ambulance. Slamming to the ground with a hard hitting thump!

Pivoting from left to right, dodging the incoming bodies. Inari just kept up with the pursuit. As Jackson now increased his speed!

"He's gaining!!!" Yelled Brutus, as he now pushed open the back door of the EMS Bus once more! Firing a thunderous blast of gunfire!

Dodging the incoming shots as well with quick ease. Jackson zoomed from left to right and back again. Making it almost seem like he knew the path of every single incoming bullet! As he now surprisingly reduced his speed? Cutting a reverse path directly in front of the Ambulance behind him? Only to then push-off his Bike backwards, delivering a high impact stomping slam! Smashing the Ambulances engine apart and inwards on itself. Thus causing it to flip upwards and crash on it's back! Just like a sea swept turtle... Impacting into the bus just behind it.

While jumping forward as all of this now
happen, from the metal mashed crash site.
Jackson landed back on his Bike, acting as
if he hadn't even been off it!

Zooming past the crashed Ambulance herself,
and having a bullet in the chamber. Not
afraid to dice with death or danger! Inari
now fired a rapid multitude of shots behind
her, with herself not even taking aim...

BANG! BOOM! Plus and swirling SWOOSH! These
were the sounds heard as the bullets hit
the fuel tank, exploding the EMS Buses into
fiery pieces. As after now reloading her
weapon. Leaving behind a crashed and
crushed composition of carnage. Inari
revved up ahead...

"Two more down! One to go!!!" Stated Inari
with ice cool conviction as the image of
Aryana's Ambulance reflected off her
sunglasses.

"Risk everything! Never give up (NEVER!!!)
never lay down your arms, and whatever you
do... Don't let the bastards grind you
down!" These were the thoughts and
convictions of Jackson Carter. As he raced
at a frightening pace in pursuit of Aryana.
While Brutis now was ready to open fire
again...

Two seconds later...

Pounding through three tightly controlled
shots! Inari now skilfully knocked Brutus'
weapon out of his hand with just one tap.
Just before he could shoot back. Thus
giving him a fresh bullet burn scar on the
side of his head. Knocking him down and
nearly out. As the next shot now set off an
Oxygen cylinder in the back of the speeding
Ambulance as well...

Blasting itself forward like a Rocket
Propelled Grenade. The cylinder now
rocketed ahead slamming straight into the
front of the Ambulance. Killing it's driver
instantly! Turning his head into a exploded
water melon of bloody destruction.

"NEIN!!!" Screamed Aryana, with blood on
her face. With blood on her hands. Looking
as if she had been within the vicinity of
an exploding ketchup bottle! As she now
pushed out the dead Henchman's headless
torso, taking the wheel herself.

Taking advantage of the situation, emptying
the remaining clip of her Desert Eagle.
Inari now filled the Bus with numerous
bullet holes! Just missing Aryana's and
Brutus' fallen positions!

Thus reloading in a quick restoring moment!
Inari now tried and failed to take out the
Ambulances back tyres. As they were
designed to take countless hits of
punishment! Even from a tyre shredder.

Now swerving and taking full control of the
wheel. Covered in chips and fragments of
crystallized safety glass. Aryana revved up
the Buses engine. Speeding forwards... Just
a single minute away from the Airport!

Thirty seconds later...

THE AIRPORT... Planes, Planes and more
parked Planes, that was the sight of the
Airport. As armed security patrols and
spotters now kept watch around the
outskirts! And crowds in the hundreds, and
near thousands lined up into countless
queues on the opposite side of the Airport!
All with plastic see through bags in hand.
Having their I.D's checked and double
checked! With most dressed for winter and
not for this very, very unexpected and
almost unbelievable heat wave. Causing a
collective uncomfortable condition to be in
effect...

**PASSENGER PROFILING AKA CRIMINAL
PROFILING**... A return to the good old days.
A fantastic way to give the disturbingly
nine times out of ten, and always proven

right! Al-Qaeda (Aka CIA!) what they want.
A great way to give white supremacist want
they use to have... And lastly both safe
ways of saying that it's okay to be a
racist! Thus not surprisingly endorsed by
MOST of the AmeriKKKan majority. And Europe
as well! (Who then later and years on, will
of no doubt deny that they ever did so!
Like they do with almost everything!) And
given the green light by media outlets
across both sides of the Atlantic. That
collectively and all together begged the
very disturbing question--"If racially
segregated flights were next on the cards?
How many people would be for it!???"

Thus being made to feel like common
criminals as it now seems to be the thing
to do. Individuals of Arabian and Asian
ethnic extraction had just been taken out
of line, and placed onboard a row of parked
airport buses. That now all moved away,
taking seemingly forever to pass the lines
of people. With even the excuse of
nationalistic privilege--"We're Israeli,
we're Israeli..." Not cutting it today.

As with a sea of violence coming in the
air. A young olive skinned couple were now
strange bed fellows with their middle
eastern counterparts. As they were made
also to go onto one of the buses.

"They all know something or someone who is a terrorist! They hate America and the west, they oppress and beat their women! Fuckin' Arabs, fuckin' ragheads and sand Niggers, fuckin' Hadjis. We should do to them what Hitler did to the Jews! We should holocaust them!" They were the half of the hidden mental thoughts present.

As thus just like a instant moving picture in the style of old school Polaroid days... A moving image of collective glares, mixed with self accusing stares now played out. As with a sigh of relief from half of the people in line, and a eyes down look of shame from the other half. (Who were from ethnic groups that will remain nameless in their collective shame!) A beyond awkward moment of discomfort was in full effect... Making you wonder if you were really in the twenty first century, or were rather back in the nineteen fifties. Or back in apartheid South Africa.

Thus now doing something that too many Police Officers have always done, with pride anyway! Now doing something that most of us do whether we mean too or not! Racial profiling was in full effect. While onboard the slow moving buses. Teary eyed mothers consoled their children and young adults felt rightfully consumed by anger and injustice... As at the same time escorting the buses, walking along side. Some nervous guards were almost trigger itching to shoot someone dead.

Only then for two other guards too now stare at each other. As if to say--"God! Has it really come down to this?" About to here a sound they hoped too never here?

"Suspects! Err? Scratch that... Arabs and others removed..." Said a Guard into his radio walkie-talkie, as the buses now drove into a secure section that was immediately locked down by a high security barrier... "Gate secure! Will...? What the... O' no!"

Six seconds before....

"Shots fired! Shots fired! EMS Transport from UN under attack!" Aryana yelled with a perfect American accent once again into her radio. As she now zoomed into the grounds of the Airport.

Setting of a stream of Alarms... Aryana surged inwards. As Jackson and Inari now made a speeding rendezvous towards danger.

"MOVE! MOVE!" Shouted a lead guard, as he and nineteen armed Airport security guards. Ran into the Checkpoint entry bay.

"HEY! HERO! WHAT NOW?" Yelled Inari!
Wanting to know whether they were going to
have to treat the Airport guards, as
friendly or hostile? As all Twenty guards
stood ready too shoot to kill...

"IT'S ALREADY HANDLED!!!" Growled Jackson,
as he now revved up his Bike performing a
back spinning wheelie! Using his Temporal
Abilities, Jackson now locked on. Noting
every single standing position of all of
the guards! Thus jumping forward countless
metres ahead. With a spinning, leaping
somersault. Clearing the checkpoint barrier
like an Olympic hurdler. Jackson snapped
instantly into a faster than motion assault.

"TEMPORAL IMPACTING SLAM!!!" He yelled.
Leaping downwards! Stomping his left foot
into the ground. Setting off a concussion
impacting wave. That ripped out the
concrete beneath and around his millisecond
standing position... And was in itself non-
lethal. Causing all of the guards to be
ejected upwards and thrown back in all
directions. Thus knocking them down and out
for the count. Not allowing them to even
see their attackers unbelievable assault.
All looking like they were struck down by
some unseen force or would-be poltergeist!

Now jumping backwards, knowing the exact
still nearly two second later speed reduced

position of his Bike. Jackson now landed
perfectly. Once again looking almost as if
he hadn't even got off.

"WHAT? HOW?!" Exclaimed Inari to herself
aloud. With it looking like Jackson had not
even left his Bike at all.

Revving up at full throttle! Speeding just
a bit forward. Inari now wore a sexy
knowing smile on her face... As they now
raced into the grounds of the half
evacuated Airport. And heading straight for
and into the central terminals. Both
looking the very part of action and danger!
Laced with a volatile mixture of sex and
death! All rolled up into one violent
reverberating force...

Finally seemingly breaking the ice between
them. Inari now just for a second made
direct eye contact with Jackson! As they
both now charged ahead... Straight into the
first terminal. Using it as a short cut,
Jackson and Inari now zoomed inwards.

Both cutting a black rubber streak that
marked the cleaner than clean white floors.
As a SWAT Team now stormed towards them,
from an upper level!

"THERE THEY ARE!" Yelled the SWAT Team leader, as his squad moved into position.

"I'll take care of them, Hero! You push on!" Shouted Inari as they were now taking fire from above.

Saying nothing, only giving Inari a firm "I hear you nod!" Jackson coolly sped forward in response.

Now taking instant aim with her Black Mack 10, Inari let rip... Proving herself as always to be an expert marksman at all and any time. Missing on purpose, shattering shop windows and glass walk way panels all around the SWAT Team!

Thus zooming ahead and making an apparent quick getaway. Speeding around an incoming corner. All now went wrong for Inari. As one SWAT Team member got in two lucky bursts of return, select-fire! That instantly blew out her Bike's back tyre, sending Inari crashing forwards and upwards off her said Bike. And right into and through a clothes shop window!

Lay down! Stay down! That and more was now the order of the day. As Inari was now cut and unconscious...

Leave no man, leave no one behind could not be applied to this impending situation, as Jackson now pushed onwards... Passing by high hung flags of the stars and stripes! Now racing up a switched off escalator.

"One hostile in custody! Pursuing remaining other!" Shouted the lead SWAT leader. Wondering in the back of his mind why had the female "terrorist" missed them? As they now moved in on Jackson.

"There he is... OPEN FIRE, OPEN FIRE!!!" He ordered as he and the others, now unleashed a continuous blast of now fully automatic gunfire!

Heading downwards into a long stretching terminal junction. Jackson once more swerved from side to side. Just before the bullets could strike him in the back. Allowing the just fired shots to break and shatter countless windows just ahead of his speeding position!

Turning to his right not taking the path you might have expected him too. Jackson now cut a path towards and into the adjoining skywalk.

"He's on the skywalk! He's on the skywalk!" Yelled the SWAT team leader, reloading. As

he and his officers now took aim, firing a
countless volley of gunfire!

Breaking through all obstacles that lay
ahead, taking no prisoners. Jackson pushed
onwards through the narrow, unoccupied Jet
way tunnel that lay disconnected to any
aircraft! As a river of bullets cut
countless holes just behind his speeding
position.

With sunbeams projected through each and
every single bullet behind him. And
reaching the end of the line nearly fast as
he had entered... Now took his Bike
airborne! Stuntin'!!! Landing onto the
Airports grounds, leaving SWAT for dust!

Elsewhere in the Airport...

"Your Plane is fuelled and ready, and
you're cleared with the tower for a VIP
special exception passage of flight!" Said
the lead Henchmen.

"Excellent!" Exclaimed Aryana driving
forward. "Brutus! Ya still alive?"

"Ja!" He snarled, as he now nursed another
bullet burnt hand and head.

"Good man!" Remarked Aryana, as she now drove straight towards a Hanger Bay. Pressing into her Red-Cell... "Time to takedown, Future Boy. Alabama style!" She mocked with an over the top southern bell accent.

As now driving into a large hanger bay, that itself housed a large Cargo Plane. Aryana's bullet ridden and battle damaged EMS bus now stopped! As herself and Brutus were now greeted by six fully armed Henchmen.

Six seconds later...

Turning a corner, just seconds after Aryana had turned her respective corner into the Hanger bay far ahead. Jackson now viewed two Airport Fire trucks blocking his path ahead!

"He's here! Get ready!" Shouted one of Aryana's Henchmen.

As half of them now took aim with automatic weapons! While the other half now took aim, holding three fire hoses... "GO! GO!" Called the lead Henchmen, ordering them all to attack...

Powerful! Projecting a near concrete stream of pressurized water. The hoses now released their collective payload straight towards a fast approaching Jackson! As the water was now forced forwards, and it seemed that he would be overpowered... All Jackson could say was his favourite three words in the world!

"TEMPORAL NOVA CYCLONE!!!" He screamed with abundant charge. As Jackson now leapt upwards of his bike, snapping into his unbeatable Power Move!

A VORTEX OF WET SILENCE... Sculpted and thus remoulded into a encircled swirling whirlpool. Shaped in the form of a spinning cyclone! The projected water was now corrupted by gravity itself. Shattering all of the glass window's of the Fire Truck! Only to now break apart, dissipating in all directions with a thinly intense skinned wave of water! That on impact now knocked every single thug from their respective standing positions!

Thus smacked down to the ground as if they themselves had been sprayed by the said hoses. The Henchmen wet! And near battered by the wave, now struggled too regain ground. As jumping back down to Earth, Jackson now stormed forwards... Just as half of the thugs stood up, trying to take aim!

Jackson now reacted to danger by killing
half of the thugs in just two seconds flat!
Only to now turn around and unleash one
single and instantaneously delivered uppercut! That broke and destroyed the thugs
lower face. Lifting him upwards of the
ground, dead before he could even land!
Seeing that the last of the Henchmen now
regained their footing. Jackson snapped
into continued combat, as he now ran up to
and instantly spun lose a tightly clamped
fire hose!

Empty of it's contents, the fire hose had
now become a weapon of demolition. As
Jackson wielded it as a whip! Just like a
evil Slave Master himself! Spinning and
turning it over his head in one fast quick
twisting motion! Striking dead one, two,
three, four, no five more thugs! As the
last three now approached from behind!

Snapping the hose now come whip behind his
solid position. Jackson now cracked it
tightly together in his strong hands.
Murdered! Standing together in a straight
line, the Henchmen now all sported cold and
voided expressions on their faces. As it
could now be seen that the said hose had
penetrated their bodies, cutting through
their upper torsos!

Now snapping the hose back, dropping down.
Thus causing all of the dead, yet still

standing Henchmen to fall down like the would-be Toy Soldiers they were. Jackson now walked back over to his bike...

Coolly composed after just dispatching Aryana's thugs. Acting and looking as if he'd just finished doing a daily work-out! Jackson picked up his Bike, kick starting it... Thus revving it up and speeding away once more. Signalling that the chase was now on again!

Chapter Thirteen

THE KABOOM OF SYMBOLIC DETONATIONS!!!

"Bitch I'm gone! Later! Motherfucker..."

Same time and same place...

PEDDLE TO THE METAL... Revving up his
engine as well. Lysander now sped into the
grounds of the Airport, looking for Jackson?

"DAM IT! NOT THIS TIME! NOT THIS TIME!!!"
He shouted to himself aloud, trying to get
more speed out of his stolen vehicle.
Sighting a faint distant dot that was
Jackson himself...

"TURBO BOOST!!!" He yelled, like a kid who
had watched to many repeated reruns of
Knight Rider on TV. Using his lucky wild-
card of Nitrous oxide. As his borrowed car
now screamed forward at a supercharged,
super quaking pace.

Too fast and nearly uncontrollable, the
Nitrous Oxide now sent up a pulse of flames
from the Car's engine. As Lysander just
manage to keep control. Just one step away
from catching up!

In another place...

While changed into flight suits, that were
strange in design and colour. Aryana and
Brutus now both looked more like futuristic
NASA Moon shot test pilots. Taking up
positions as pilot and Co-pilot, readying
the Plane for take-off.

"The Cargo bay is secure! Back-Up JATO
system on-line..." Voiced Brutus checking
the aft instruments.

"And the package?" Asked Aryana, talking
about their stolen case.

"Ready for transport!" Stated Brutus, as he
now shut the cockpit's armoured vault door!

"It's all good!" Remarked Aryana as she now begun to move the Plane forward and out of the Hanger bay.

Taxiing itself forward, weighting tonnes in steel and raw power. The Cargo Plane now travelled towards the main strip of the outer runaways. A master and ace pilot with skills and moves not yet dreamt up. Aryana now steered the massive Plane with complete ease. Powering forwards picking up speed!

"HE'S HERE!" Said Brutus with a slight fearful snarl. As he now saw a distant and yet speedy Jackson heading towards them.

"Don't worry Brutus. Not even he can stop me now!" Remarked Aryana with total over confidence. "Detonate the BOMBS!" She said as Brutus now obeyed!

Two seconds before...

Heading towards two countless rows of parked and empty commercial Jetliners. Jackson with Lysander just behind him, now made a storming progression ahead. As he now sped underneath the said Planes...

Cutting the air between and under the Planes apart with his speeding

acceleration. That instantly made a
rumbling swoosh! Jackson now stormed
onwards. As Lysander using all of his
driving skill to a cool usage. From the
opposite side, now followed suit zooming
under the Jetliners underbellies. Sending
ripping currents of air outwards and above
from his speeding position!

With Jackson just ahead opposite and
Lysander just behind from his position.
Disaster now struck! As the Jetliners had
all been booby trapped with countless
blocks of explosives!!!

THE KABOOM OF SYMBOLIC DETONATIONS!!! That
was now the scene of events. As the bombs
now began to detonate. Thus causing the row
of parked unoccupied Jetliners, one by one
to explode in a cascading super rally
domino effect.

"Escape!" That was now the single word on
both Jackson's and Lysander's mind. As a
river of fire molten and broken debris now
ripped it's way from burning Plane to
Plane! Provoking them both to
simultaneously push forwards, avoiding a
instant and fiery death! With a raging wave
of destruction increasing behind them...

As the said built up wave of the last explosion rained inwards. Jackson now found himself to be first to clear the field of parked and exploding Planes. Coolly pushing ahead, at near full throttle!

While just in behind, at a near deadly second place. Lysander now found himself nearly ejected forwards. As the blasts concussion now lifted the Car's back wheels off the ground for just two single seconds...

But with his expert and would-be wheel man skills. Lysander just managed to regain control. As the thunderous raw of the just detonated aircraft, that themselves now lay destroyed and ablaze!

Screamed outwards in all and every single direction. Thus causing an army of Airport security personnel, SWAT and just arriving Police Officers to race towards the scene of devastation!

Driving forwards just seconds behind. With his white shirt sweat stained, and with a look of sheer determination. And the impulsion of maybe, just maybe finally catching him! Lysander matched Jackson's moves and course. Heading unknowingly straight towards Aryana's Plane.

"The harder they come, the harder they
fall." That was Jackson's philosophy to any
and all evil doers. As he knew already that
Lysander was hot on his tail. That he'd had
to leave Inari behind. And that nearly
every Cop in this city would soon arrive.

Thus with failure not being an option.
Continuing ahead, unstoppable and beyond
indefatigable. Jackson travelled onwards...
Knowing that he would not let Aryana
escape. Or see this city of dreams. This
city of tragedy destroyed!

"He's still on our tail!" Said Brutus, as
Aryana now increased the Planes speed and
power.

Consequently almost racing nearly side by
side. Not believing his luck, as he was now
so close to Jackson! Lysander now felt
amazed at the fact that victory of getting
his man was nearly at hand! As Jackson!
Disobediently dangerous and defiant in all
things. Turned to his right looking
directly at him. Therefore giving Lysander
a quick turning perfect carefree grin!

"NOT FUNNY, PATRIOT! NOT FUNNY!" He said,
annoyed at the fact that Jackson was
seemingly not taking him or the situation
serious.

As still continuing to keep one eye on the sprawling runway strip and the other on Jackson. Lysander now revved up his engine storming forward. As Jackson himself now gestured towards him with a pointed, turning finger!

"What the???" He exclaimed as a violent volley of gunfire now rained on his speeding position. Shattering half of his windscreen. Thus sending safety glass up and around his person!

Now under fire from two armed Henchmen, who were standing next to a half dropped Cargo ramp. At the back of the Plane. Jackson was just about to take action as one of them now took aim for Lysander with a super sleek shoulder mounted Rocket Launcher!

"R.P.G!!! (Rocket Propelled Grenade!)" Shouted Jackson very aloud with "combat" recall.

"Bitch I'm gone! Later! Motherfucker..." That's what Jackson's cool and composed face now expressed. As he now sped straight towards Lysander's acquired Car. kicking it with one light tap. Thus sending it crashing upwards and over on itself. Saving his would-be Javert from a violent burning death.

Tossed and turned over countless times like a salad in a tornado. Lysander's Ferrari now landed upside down... As ten security vehicles raced onto the scene heading straight for Jackson.

Therefore with time nearly up! And Aryana's Plane now just less than thirty seconds away from take-off speed. Jackson put his plan of action, (That he just made up about two seconds ago!) into completing effect! As snapping into his focused Temporal Ability, he now looked ahead... Seeing a narrow gap through the thermal current Jet-stream of the Plane's engines!

WAY 2 FAST, WAY 2 FURIOUS... This was now the moment of truth and the would-be hour of the blood drinking Wolf. As just as Jackson now made his move, cutting straight and safely through. All Ten Security Vehicles raced inward just behind...

Instantly trying and failing to follow Jackson's cutting safe path. The quaking reverberations of the said Jet engines. Now shattered all of the windows of the approaching vehicles. Lifting up every single one of them. Sending them flipping and turning through the heat waved winters day!

Now just regaining his sensors with only
his pride wounded. Lysander jumped as the
lifted up vehicles now rained down just
missing his crashed position. "Christ!" He
yelled! Pulling himself upwards, climbing
outwards.

Standing by the smashed Car. As the smell
of burnt rubber and burning jet fuel hung
thick in the air! Thinking he had safely
escaped... Lysander thanked God, the Virgin
Mary, the Holy Ghost and his lucky stars
all at once. "Nine Cars!" He said counting
the smashed vehicles all around him.

"Wait?! There were?" Lysander stated as
without total warning the tenth Car now
dropped out of the Sky. Falling straight
onto and on top off his borrowed Ferrari!
Popping all four of it's tyres like party
balloons!

Diving for cover out of sheer instinct.
Lysander laid stretched outwards, as the
Ferrari's Alarm system now activated! Only
to be drowned out by the sound of the
Airport's sirens and the deafening sound of
the Cargo Planes Jet shrieking engines...

STUNT 101! That was the business and action
of the day. As with time up! And all
seeming lost!? Jackson now sped nearly in

front of the Plane! Turning to look Aryana
dead in the eye. Letting her know the her
ass was about to be grass! And that she
would be burning in Hell... Very soon! As
he now applied on the breaks, while
simultaneously performing a hand standing
move. Lifting his person up from the Bike.

Thus now doing the seemingly impossible.
Jackson now lifted up the aforementioned
Bike! Throwing it straight into one of the
monstrously rotating Jet engines...

Airborne! Leaping upwards high in what
seemed like slow motion, delivering another
MONEY-SHOT moment! Jackson flew backwards,
performing a crane position just above the
still speeding Plane. As it's impacted
engine now cut itself to pieces catching
fire! Just a handful of seconds away from
engulfing and blowing apart the whole Plane
in a Jet fuelled explosion!!!

"Warning! Warning! Engine..." Voiced the
cockpit's computer system, only to be
interrupted by a near panic stricken Brutus!

"NEIN! Were done for..." He yelled.

"Hold your tongue!" Snapped Aryana, one
step away from losing her cool composure!
Like a Mother in a Supermarket checkout

line. As she now shut down the effected engine!

"Were losing speed! If we stay were finished!" Voiced Brutus with instant defeatism.

"All is at hand, Brutus... All is at hand!" Mocked Aryana. "JATO! System... Engaged!" She voiced, flicking a switch.

"CODE BLACK! CODE BLACK! IT'S AN ALERT! AL-QAEDA... WERE UNDER ATTACK! WERE UNDER ATTACK!!!" These were the things yelled across the whole runway and grounds of the Airport. As countless upon countless guards, SWAT Teams, Cops and just arrived National Guard troops in the background. Moved onto the scene of carnage...

While standing up to his just defeated feet. Dusting himself off. As he'd done nearly a Hundred times before. Lysander now took in a until next time, breath! Only to instantly duck down to his knees, as a beyond deafening blast of a rocket propelled escape now echoed outwards. Cutting across the whole of JFK.

J.A.T.O (JET ASSISTED TAKE-OFF)... This piece of aerospace technology is what had made Aryana's getaway possible. Sending her

Plane up high skywards like a rocket to the Moon, travelling over an unsuspecting City below. As hundreds and a few hundred more Guards, Cops, Agents and Soldiers all now looked upwards at the escaping Plane!

Turning! Standing to his feet once again. Lysander now looked upwards. Just one, repeat, just one single step away from waving his fist at the sky! As he now snatched a radio out of an Agents hand.

"This is Agent Lysander! Get me--AIR SUPPORT!!! GET ME AIR SUPPORT NOW!!!" He yelled, only to now turn. Once again looking upward to the sky wondering where Jackson was?

One single minute later...

ABOVE NEW YORK... TWENTY THOUSAND FEET AND CLIMBING... That was now the situation at hand. As Aryana, ever the clever villainous individual and one step ahead Lady Boss! Now planned to commit mass murder, just to cover her tracks and protect the theft of what she had stolen?

"TIME TO GO!" Exclaimed Aryana strangely, feeling that they were not alone? As Brutus opened a strange looking airlock like hatch at the back of the cockpit. "Climbing up to

Sixty thousand feet. Auto-Pilot...
Engaged!" She said getting out of her seat.

Now without warning one of her thugs in the
back Cargo bay, now yelled into his radio-
link. "THERE'S SOMETHING ON THE WING?" He
screamed loudly with exclamation! As he now
looked out of a window.

Instantly as this was said only Aryana
understood. As Brutus looked on puzzled?

"Always IMPRESSIVE!" Was the silent thought
in her head, one step away from grinding
her teeth with annoyance!

As a massive loss of Cabin pressure was now
signalled by the Plane's on board systems.
And the screams of dying Henchmen now
screamed outwards over the cockpits
speakers!

"HE'S BACK!" Remarked Aryana, like a six
year old, as if she didn't have a care in
the World!

LIKE AN 80'S TV SHOW IN MOTION... "Get on
the Plane, Jackson! Jackson get on that
Motherfucking Plane!" That's what you would
have been yelling and shouting to yourself
or aloud. If all of this was just a movie

or a TV show. And just like you would have
expected! Jackson coolly jumped onto the
Planes wing just a split second before the
JATO system was activated!

Thus with two dead Henchmen's bodies laying
just behind him, broken and bloody! Feeling
that something familiar, that he had dealt
with before? Lay not far ahead in the
Plane's sealed up cockpit cabin? Jackson
now moved ahead towards a strange looking
black cargo container. That itself was
extremely weird in shape and design?

Continuing to walk forward through the
dimly lit Cargo bay. And with his Temporal
Abilities shielding from the elements and
drop in cabin pressure. Jackson was about
to now used his skills of improved sight to
scan it's contents! When...

"TICK TOCK! This is your Captain
speaking..." Exclaimed Aryana mimicking a
Airline Captains voice! "You're too late...
The Big Apples about to be baked! This
GAMES about to be OVER!"

Now taking instant cover, as a swirling
swoosh of ice white gas now gushed outwards
from the container. Jackson now too his
absolute KNOWING horror now sighted the
inside contents. Which was a fully armed

thirty Mega tonne Nuclear Bomb! While elsewhere on the plane. That is through the upper airlock and sitting inside a strange and very futuristic looking cockpit. Which in itself looked more like the inside to a Flying Saucer. Aryana now powered up her very own Mini Space Plane. Readying to make a quick exit!

"You've been an excellent opponent." She voiced, watching Jackson on a inboard monitor. "But now it's time for you to just shut up and face it. You lose!!!" Aryana mocked with a sexy grin pressing the release button. "Bomb Voyage... Future Boy!"

Now dropping open the lower cargo bay hatch popped apart. Sending the Bomb sailing instantly downwards. On an altitude timed detonation of five thousand feet!!!

Game over was indeed what it looked to the average person. But as always he was anything but... As on a wing and a Hail Mary pass and prayer. Jackson leapt forward! Calm like a bomb! Like the falling bomb below! Diving without a Parachute! Straight out of the Plane on a downward freefall to destruction!

"What?! He jumped!" Exclaimed a shocked and slightly surprised, Aryana. "No matter...

He's no Superman, he can't fly!" She
mocked!

As she now fired up her Space Planes
engines. Using the planned Nuclear
destruction of the city below. As a cover
for escape and to keep hidden the theft of
the priceless item she had stolen. As well
as hoping for the death of the fastest man
on earth also! Aryana now put the final
step of her murderous plot into action...

Thus detonating with an explosive bolt
wake, the Planes nose cone now fell away.
As Aryana's said Space Plane now made an
instantaneous exit. Sailing! No! ZOOMING
upwards into the high heavens just beneath
the void of Space. Heading to places or
rather a place unknown? Engulfing the still
airborne Cargo plane into flames...

With it now looking that all was indeed
truly lost! And that Aryana would now
succeed in getting away with mass Murder.
As was the usual norm for Nazis in the
past! Jackson now flew through the air...

Falling or flying which ever way you wanted
to look at it. And a man truly without
fear! He now refused to quit or too die.
Fixing his body into one long straight and
solid descending form! On a path to catch
up with the Bomb!!!

Thirty thousand feet and falling...

GO!--GO!--GO!--GO!--GO!--GO!... "GO!
JACKSON! GO! JACKSON!!!"

That's what you would have said if you had
seen Jackson pushing himself forward....

Twenty thousand feet and falling...

"Never give up! Never surrender!" A line
from an old movie and the thought on
Jackson's mind. As he continued downwards
now almost catching up to the falling Bomb!

Thus riding the eye of the storm and about
too try and thread the eye of a falling
needle, he now caught up...

Fifteen thousand feet and falling...

"If you don't succeed try, try, and try
again!" This would usually have been the
case. But this was anything but usual or
normal, as Jackson twice failed to grab on?

Ten thousand feet and failing...

"I DON'T KNOW HOW TO LOSE!!!" This was now
the thought and belief on his mind. As he

now with perfect focus grabbed onto the
Bomb.

Seconds to go...

"How do you dismantle an Atomic Bomb at T-
minus ten thousand feet?" Was the
questioned at hand! As now with time about
to run out Jackson did what was the only
choice left too him. Using his Temporal
Abilities to interface with technology...
Deactivating the Bombs Nuclear triggers and
distorting the Bombs core panels. As to not
allow Nuclear fission to take place.

Five thousand feet...

Now with the Bombs nuclear mechanisms
switched off. Disaster struck, as the said
Bombs plastic explosives. Which were in
place to create and focus the shockwaves
into the Nuclear core of the device. Now
detonated!

BOOM!!
!!!!!!!!!!!!!!!!!! Thrown! Blasted outwards
from the cutting explosion. Jackson now
tumbled through the depleting, falling
sky...

HISTORY RESTORED... Thus with his mission to save the world again and again, whether it was in the today, the tomorrow or even yesterday! If it took him a billion times... Failure! Defeat! And Death! Now seemed like an absolute. As Jackson fell to the Earth like a Angel who had lost his wings? Crashing straight downwards below into the Hudson. Into the river below. Without a parachute, and maybe... Just maybe, without a prayer as well?

Chapter Fourteen

ESCAPE FROM BUILDING 13!

"Don't worry! I'll meet you at the top!"

Nine hours and nine minutes after the Airport...

NEW YORK, NEW YORK CONCLUDED... A fortress! A vault! The most secure Government building in all of the City. This was and is the place codenamed as Building 13! A secret headquarters to the FBI and numerous Law enforcement/Government divisions. Building 13 stood occupied by countless Agents and an army of SWAT and security guards. As in a half lit no windows office, alone in the near dark! With a dim lit

whiteboard in front of him again. And a TV
NEWS Pod cast playing on his laptop.
Lysander now tried to complete a working
profile of the day's very violent and very
action packed events...

*Who is the unknown female captured at the
airport?*

Why did she miss hitting SWAT?

Where did Patriot get his bike from?

*Who hacked into the Wall Street security
system???*

*Why did the unknown terrorist? Murder the
UN Ambassador?*

*Was "The German" on the plane? Did Patriot
escape from the plane...?*

These were the collective questions that
had been scanning through his mind, looking
for answers... As representing a would-be
Dragon in the cave and a in completed
challenge to him. Lysander would be now
doing a furious workout! Lifting weights!
Doing press-ups, sit-ups. And knocking
seven bells out of a punch bag. If this was

all just another spineless Hollywood movie
with nothing to say...

As nearly always. But this wasn't! As thus
having once more nearly his ticket punched
by a breakneck pursuit of Jackson.
Lysander!

With a few facial cuts. A stitched cut just
above his right eyebrow and scrapes along
with a killer headache. Could now barely
focus, knowing that once more Jackson had
escaped. Leaving a trail of bloody and
broken dead bodies in his wake, as always.

"Good evening viewers! And all loyal
American's! Everywhere!" Exclaimed the
newscaster with over the top and frankly
smug, invalid xenophobic Patriotism. As
Lysander tried to view his laptop...

Now with the look of fresh spring time and
morning daisies! The very same newscaster
from the alternate and very much extinct
timeline, of a race war destroyed New York.
Spoke politely with an update on the events
of the day!

"With night now fallen inwards on the City
of New York. The Presidents approval rating
is sky rocketing this evening. As ALL--New
Yorker's themselves stand proud and united!

As with NO civilians dead or injured! The
FBI and Home-Sec with National Guard troops
in support. Foiled an all out attack on JFK
International today! Leaving only a number
of terrorists dead and a single hijacked
Cargo Plane shot down by air support in the
form of F-18's." Stated the newscaster in
one near seemingly one breath moment. As
images of F-18A Hornets with afterburners
flaming through the sun setting sky. And
Military Helicopters landing at JFK
Airport. Now played on screen behind her.
"With two or three unconfirmed reports of
dead bodies falling from the sky, that
still remain to be identified!"

"O' we have two of the bodies, but some how
I don't think that they were working for
Al-Qaeda!" Mocked Lysander aloud and to
himself!

"As this evil Al-Qaeda plot of mass
destruction unfolds, news of a joint
multiple task force operation of Law
Enforcement. That was designed to secure
and protect our Nations banking districts
and financial institutions. Is quickly
becoming know to us!" Spoke the newscaster
taking a momentary pause.

"While reports of what exactly took place
at JFK International have been extremely
sketchy at this time... With reports of

controlled explosions of booby trapped
Jetliners... And authorities still refusing
to confirm or deny, whether that they do
indeed have a terrorist suspect, alive and
in custody!"

"Yeah! We have her! But she isn't talking!
And somehow I don't think she in Al-Qaeda
operative either?" Spoke Lysander to
himself again with sarcasm, as the
newscaster now went into the next story!

"In a unrelated incident today zero
fatalities rained throughout the expressway
after two ambulances. Crashed! Causing a
massive traffic accident! For more on this
we now go to our reporter on scene." Stated
the newscaster, turning to her plasma
screen TV monitor.

Unknowingly lucky to be alive, as was every
single soul in the City. The reporter now
counted himself in, ready to make his
report! "Tony! What do you have for us?"
Said the newscaster looking to her right.
As a live feed of the damaged Expressway
played on screen.

"Well, what can I say...?" He said taking a
strange deja vu like pause. "It is a season
of miracles today, as..."

"Lies, lies and more lies!" Remarked
Lysander, taking off his

shoes. With a near defeatist attitude?

Same time, Same place...

With the night kicking fully inwards. A
shift change of personnel was just about to
be on the cards. As a single white shirt
wearing security guard, who stood at a
familiar 6'3 in height. And was of apparent
Hispanic descent? Now entered the building.
Thus setting the scene for action. Wanton
destruction and the most spectacular rescue
mission that anyone could ever witness.
That would all be taking place in a number
of arriving minutes...

Five minutes and five seconds later...

Now having splashed cold water on his face
in the bathroom next to the office.
Lysander, wearing only a white vest and
black trousers. Was about to put on his
black socks and black shoes. As his Cell
now rang!

"Ring! Ring! Ring! Ring!" Chiming with a
standard store brought demo ring tone. The
Cell beeped for just a few seconds, as a
wet handed Lysander now quickly answered it.

"Agent Lysander!" He stated with a polite and respectful phone voice. Even though he had a dry bad taste in his mouth...

"Hey, Rob!" Spoke the Chief Pathologist over the line. "Assistant Director Langford was just here!" She said, calling from the department of forensics Morgue. That was located in the lower sub levels of the same building.

"He was! What did he want?" Asked Lysander taking hold of a dry towel.

"Everything! Even the remains of the Jane Does Bike?" She said dressed in the standard white Doctors coat, with a collective whisper. As apparent FBI Agents. Four in all, now collected and boxed pieces of just recorded evidence from the days events...

"Remains?"

"Yeah the bike burst into flames as the tech guys tried to examine it? Add that to your own wall of Weird, hey?"

"Wall of what? Never mind!" He said wiping his forehead dry. "When you said everything? You meant--?"

"Everything! Well everything from today..."
She voiced as a collection of digital X-Ray
photos, depicting high impacting injures,
all fatal. Were displayed on the x-ray
screens monitors.

"You've really pissed him off this time.
Hey! I just..." She said breaking
conversation, yelling at one of the Agents.

"Look! There's more...!" Uttered the
Pathologist, turning away from the agents
lowering her voice. "Your prisoner is about
to be moved."

"But she's..."

"Yeah I know..."

"No! I'm not having this! There be NO
renditions to rape rooms or water-boarding
torture cells on my watch!"

"I don't think their sending her to those
git-mo styled black sites that we're not
suppose to have anymore!" She said lowering
her voice once more. "As there are a group
of agents from the Mossad on their way up
to her now... Their going to take her into
their protective custody!"

"Like I said they'll be absolutely NO
renditions on my watch!" Remarked Lysander
in repeat. Disgusted at the very "human
rights" violating idea of rendition (Which
itself was a polite word for racist
presidential approved all around torture,
gang rape and cold blooded murder.) Saying
it as if he had personally seen one in
progress once before? "She's my prisoner...
And I'm heading up this..."

"Sorry Rob! You might not be for long. As
Langford said that he's going to have you
up on review, and that you... What the?"
She paused, as a security alert alarm now
rang out!

Hanging up the his Cell instantly as the
alarm activated, grabbing his gun! Lysander
snapped into a knowing realization that
"The Planetary Patriot" was making a house
call. "Okay, Patriot!" He said to himself,
slipping a live round into his gun's
chamber.

"Let's see you get out of this one!"

One minute before...

Back from the set and covering all bets as
always. Having survived his one way free
falling descent without a prayer and a

parachute! Jackson now moved through the lower corridors, unmolested and seemingly invisible! As without warning a single lone woman pounced upon his position!

Thus instantly reacting to this impending assault between the single rhythm of a heartbeat. Jackson blocked the incoming strikes. Spinning the raven haired woman into his arms... While the said woman herself, one Inari Gellar. Could now be seen to be sporting a number of freshly acquired cuts, having just beaten down all five Mossad agents... Instantly after being forced out of her medically induced coma.

RIGHT BETWEEN THE EYES... Playing dirty, dropping back. Delivering one quick kicking high knee right between Jackson's legs and proverbial eyes! Inari instantly thought that this would win her the ensuing fight. Only to get the opposite... As not reacting in the way any other man in the world would have. Jackson did indeed prove that he did in fact have Balls of steel... As he stood tall and unmoved at this low blow and violent action.

"What? Wait?" Inari remarked with a instantaneous realization of who she had just tried to injure. "Whoa!!!" She voiced looking him dead in the eyes. As they both now took a single step towards each other.

AYE PAPI!!! HEY MAMI... Was the collective cool Spanish language exclamation of the moment. As Inari had a face of-- "O' shut up!" Amazement in seeing that Jackson was alive! While Jackson in return, had a look that was happy to see her as well! As he now placed his right hand against the side of her face.

Driving through the pain of her window crashing fall. Having stolen the outfit of a one kick, knocked unconscious infirmary nurse. Inari! Did not realize that she would not have escaped all the way. As she would have died from internal head injuries, within just a few minutes of making it onto the city streets...

Now standing around for what seemed way to long, as if they were about to finish a date with a goodnight kiss! Both now paused just for a moment, staring at each other. Looking as if they hadn't seen one another in years! As Jackson, having a flash forward vision of her second death earlier. Now used his temporal Ability.

Healing up her superficial cuts, scrapes, slight concussion and head injury! Thus touching the side of her face and healed up cut lip. A second later, Inari now spoke.

"I'm glad to see that you're okay, Officer
E. Lopez!?" She said reading Jackson's
named badge alias.

"That's Officer Edward Lopez, to be
precise!" Remarked Jackson back in a
surprisingly, it's dam good to see you
playful response.

"Time to..." He said taking a knowing
pause.

"What is it?" She asked with concern.

"Foothold Alarm!" Said Jackson with a
spooky sixth-sense a' la Temporal ability.

As just a second later the said security
alarm now revved outwards through the whole
of building. Thus signalling an escape and
security breech!

Slightly nervous in thinking of a plan of
escape, Inari now looked from left to
right, as Jackson stood not bothered at all
by the screaming alarm!

"This way!" He said with collective cool
pointing towards the right direction.

ESCAPE FROM BUILDING 13...

Having an instant exit strategy. Jackson
with Inari next to him now walked with
powering forward steps. Straight towards an
elevator located at the end of the corridor.

Lockdown and secured! All of the doors and
elevators remained sealed shut. As Jackson
now extended his right hand, placing it
next on to the elevator's control panel?

Cracking the code and breaking the lockdown
on the elevators and doors. In a Temporal
Ability charge nano second. He now stood
back as the doors to the elevators now slid
open!

"Ladies first!" He stated and gestured with
a cool growl!

Stepping into the said elevator car, Inari
now turned to look at Jackson. Suspecting
that he knew something that she didn't? As
the security alarms continued to ring out,
Inari's hunch now came instantly true. As
countless security guards now stormed
towards their position from the opposite
end of the corridor.

Looking at him with a caring, some would even say, loving concern of a girlfriend or Wife! Inari spoke silently with her eyes. Giving the look of "Be careful! And come back to me alive!" In one single second glance!

"FREEZE!" Yelled a lead Guard with his weapon drawn.

Thus as this was said Jackson acted as if he didn't have a care in the World once more... "Don't worry! I'll meet you at the top!" He said to Inari with a caring stare, as the elevator doors slid shut!

COP! GUARD! AGENT OR OTHERWISE... If he had too Jackson would have destroyed and killed every single person in this building. In Building 13! If they were oppressing and raping the innocent or torturing the indifferent! If they were doing medieval come Nazi come Zionist! Come Neo Con or Democrat wickedness. As in say Abu Ghraib or Guantanamo bay... They would have all been ghosts by now!

"FREEZE! Let me see your hands!" Screamed and yelled the guards, all pointing their weapons! "Show me your hands!..."

Turning! Raising his hands coolly upwards, with a sense of here we go again! Jackson now followed their orders to the letter?

"Identify yourself!" Called out the lead guard! "Identify yourself!" He repeated with a loud howl!

With Guards, SWAT and all of the Agents, even Lysander! Jackson did not for this time view any of them as Enemy Combatants! But instead viewed them all as just a would-be bump in the carpet! Just people in his way. Yet rightly doing they job! And it was with this thought and knowing, he was now about to respond!

Thus having two choices given to him. ONE! Which was to either bluff his way out of trouble. Or TWO! Storm a path right through the building in an act of sheer bravado! Jackson as always, well nine times out of ten at least. Chose the latter!!!

"I go by many names..." Jackson growled with almost cocky arrogant confidence! "But you can call me... The fastest man on earth!" He stated with mocking conviction!

And thus with his hands still up in the air, Jackson now snapped into battle.

Performing a quickly delivered SLIDE
ATTACK! Cutting a path straight through all
of the Guards! Knocking every single one
down and out for the count! Taking a posing
and self praising expressionist stance,
just like a champion Toreador!

Now with the Guards unconscious as the
alarms still screamed! Jackson jumped into
a faster than fast running assault storming
down one long corridor after another.
Turning down and up each single corridor
with a slipstream cutting wake...

"FOOTHOLD!"

"FOOTHOLD!"

"Foothold! We're under attack!"

"Send back-up from the Sky Lobby!" Screamed
countless Agents all occupying rooms and
offices adjoined to the corridors. As they
all, with weapons drawn. Now rushed for
their doors and collective exit points...

FLIP THE TRAPS... Thus cut down! And thus
knocked downwards. As well as being thrown
across their rooms and offices by Jackson
slip-streamed escape! All of the Agents
involved found themselves eating fitted

carpet and cold tiled floors. As a sea of
paperwork was now blown upwards, sailing
across and downwards. Drifting in multiple
directions through the climate controlled
air inside!

SWAT! Above! Guards below! Agents in
between. Actions On! Action stations!
Intruder alert etc. Code Black and
Foothold! These and more were all the facts
of this moment! As Jackson powered forward
at an Humanly impossible speed!

Thus coming to the end of one corridor.
Jackson now came to an instant dead stop on
reaching a stairwell entry door. Taking a
moment as if he already knew what was
behind the said door. He now opened it to
instantly find countless armed Guards
racing up one stairwell. As even countless
more now ran down the adjoining stairwell.
All heading straight for him!

Entering inwards and thus jumping upwards
straight into the air. Jackson now quickly
delivered two kicks. Knocking every single
Guard downwards or upwards, depending on
their collective positions. As the Guards
all now tumbled upwards and downwards
Jackson instantly snapped into a fast high
corkscrew jump! Bouncing straight up, just
like a high dropped rubber ball. Leaping up
and up passing countless flights of
stairs...

Landing at the top of the stairwell in
seemingly one twisting motion. Jackson! Now
arose from a knee crouching position. Once
more snapping into a fast pace, almost
slip-streamed run... Quaking! Waking the
air apart just behind him.

Now reaching the end of a corridor as soon
as he had entered it. Jackson stopped!
Welded to the spot as an army of fully
armed, pistol holding SWAT Commandos. Now
took aim from both right and left
directions.

Looking straight ahead. Jackson now thrust
out his strong muscular arms instantly
ejecting all of the SWAT. Twenty on both
sides, forward and against each other. Thus
enforcing a domino rally effect!

As more pistol aiming SWAT now took aim!
Jackson spun around turning his back on
them. Only to now jump upwards and
backwards over them all...

Giving a slight and I mean slight tap to a
SWAT Commando, who was taking up the rear.
Jackson now once bought about another
domino effect. Sending all of the SWAT
forward in a cascading ripple!

Just as more SWAT took aim and firing
positions down a long and seemingly forever
stretching corridor. That itself looked
like that it had been exacerbated or rather
exaggerated by an infinity of fun house
mirrors.

Thus with their fully automatic weapons
locked and loaded for murder! SWAT now
readied themselves to quickly put down
Jackson's speeding and mistakenly appeared
terrorist assault to bed. With countless
bullets ready to strike him dead in the
head, and everywhere else!

Speeding straight towards danger not afraid
of the murderous weaponry that lay just
ahead. Jackson once more uttered his three
most favourite words in the whole World!
"TEMPORAL NOVA CYCLONE!!!" He screamed with
yelling focus! Unleashing a raging vortex
of concussive and projected wind. Come
temporal energy against all of the gun
holding, corridor dwelling SWAT!

Knocked back instantly from all of their
standing positions. One after the other!
All of the SWAT Commandos now found
themselves instantly and spontaneously
ejected backwards. Each slammed in unison
through a shut and closed office door!

Splintered! As well as being ripped of their hinges! All of the office doors were smashed to pieces. As every single Commando now hit the ground, unconscious! With the swirling atmospheric rage that was The "Temporal Nova Cyclone." Now shattered every single pain of armoured glass, inside each door smashed office! Sending more paperwork through the air and out of the window like giant confetti!

Thus with all of this taking place within ticking seconds. Completing his Power Move with violent ease. Jackson now landed, twisting over onto his feet! Just as the still upward travelling elevator now reached it's destination!

With the elevator ride taking what seemed like a long, long time. And with a cheesy tune playing inside. That was in itself cheesier than an metric tonne of Edam that had been left on the Moon for a million years. Inari now looked ahead as the doors open!

"Hey! Hero... I..." She voiced, only to find herself forcibly ejected from the said elevator car.

"MOVE!" Snarled Jackson with a passionate--"woman I'm trying to save you," yell!

Spun out of the elevator in one fast quick
motion. Inari found herself avoiding
instant death! As a volley of high powered
automatic gunfire just missed her standing
position! Filling the elevators back steel
walls with high amounts of metal cutting
bullet holes... Whilst far downward from
the open elevator. A newly arriving on
scene unit of SWAT Commandos now pushed
forward, with weapons just freshly fired.
All just steps and seconds away from both
Jackson and Inari! Who themselves both now
ran around the next and nearby corner, only
to bump into six more Commandos. That were
this time armed with 9mm Pistols, carrying
armoured shields.

Snapping instantly into his Temporal
Ability! Slamming his solid fists into the
Bullet-proof armoured shields. Breaking
them apart! (All by one!?) Jackson now
knocked down and out all six Commandos in
just one continuous frozen moment! While
Inari herself stood fixed to the spot
inside the said frozen second. She now saw
all of the Commandos bounced up and back to
the ground.

Knocked out! All of the SWAT now laid
outwards in a straight piled heap. As
Jackson now coolly took hold of the one
remaining armoured shield?

"SURF'S UP!" Said Jackson with cool! Only to have Inari give him a look of...

"If you're thinking what I'm thinking... you're one crazy, Motherfu..."

Six seconds ahead...

SKY LOBBY... Near and next to the top of the building and built out of sculptured steel and armoured, bullet resistant glass. The Sky Lobby stood cold and seemingly empty. As the sound of clunking navy blue boots that belonged to an army of SWAT, now approached from both sides. Armed with automatic weapons of German and Austrian named variety. That each held a hundred plus rounds of ammo in plastic clear blue, bullet bulb magazines. The Commandos now took up firing positions!

Just as four of them now moved up closer to a top entry door, all said four now found themselves knocked backwards...

"Drop it like it's hot... Drop it like it's hot!" That would have been Jackson's theme of the moment as he, with Inari scooped up in his arms. Now bounced through the lobby surfing his way down flight after flight of stairs...

"OPEN FIRE! OPEN FIRE!" Yelled the lead
Commando! "SHOOT TO KILL! SHOOT TO KILL!"

As the armour piercing rounds just missed
their surfing position. The bullets now
shattered half the supposed bullet
resistant glass. Sending jagged and failed
pieces of apparent safety glass downwards
throughout the lobby!

Flipping the shield now come surfboard
upwards, Jackson now cut-jumped! Performing
a cork screwing spin through the air as
more bullets just missed. Thus landing back
down, with Inari still in his arms holding
on for dear life. Only to now slide down
the side of a long and lengthy stretching,
metallic grey hand stair rail!

Now bouncing up once more. Jackson threw
Inari up across the remaining space of the
lobby. Only to now jump forward stepping
off the shield, reaching the end of the
lobby himself.

Standing frozen to the spot. With his arms
extended outwards, looking ahead? Jackson
now remained cooler than cool. As a falling
yet flying Inari now fell from high above,
just like an angel falling from heaven!

"O' SHIT!!!" She screamed to the sound of incoming gunfire. As her perfect body twisted through the air.

Thus landing safely into his strong and solid arms. Inari looked slightly surprise and even shocked. As she had quite literally had her breath taken away from her! Whilst Jackson, now not even letting her compose herself. Now forcibly frogmarched Inari out of the sky lobby and onto the roof.

Just as a running, barefoot Lysander stormed inwards. Cutting his feet on the glass...

"PATRIOT!" He screamed as blood poured from his feet. As the Commando's now turned toward him.

"HOLD IT!"

"FREEZE!"

"Identify yourself!" All these things and more were yelled at Agent Lysander, as he now spoke.

"AGENT LYSANDER FBI! I'm FBI!" He screamed at the top of his voice, with his ID firmly held up in front of him and his gun lowered!

Nineteen seconds later...

THE ROOF... With just under twenty seconds of time expired. Lysander with SWAT in support now stormed the Roof top. "Check the Helo!" Yelled the lead Commando to his subordinates, as a Helicopter now sat apparently empty on it's Pad!

"Relax John! Have a few laughs!" Said Lysander with movie quoting sarcasm. "Have a few laughs!!!" He uttered completing his would-be Die Hard a' la, John MacClane impression.

Now with his feet bloody, cut! Bruised and nearly blistered! Lysander now reached the end of the line. As Jackson and Inari had seemed to have vanished without a trace?

Thus looking downwards at a higher than high multi countless storey drop to the bottom. He now lowered his weapon! Barely holding back his pain, anger and near raging posture. As all he could do was look across the bright lit city.

Drenched in sweat, with his shower clean
look now a memory. And his white vest
sticking to his body... Wanting to scream!
Lysander, knowing that he was not alone, as
the Commandos secured the scene. Now stayed
silent! Stayed serious as always. Standing
in a slowly forming wet patch of his own
blood. Biting his tongue proverbially and
nearly literally! As he now took a passing
glance at his watch, that surprise,
surprise now ticked backwards???

Chapter Fifteen

WHAT IS THE BLOOD LIBEL?

"You can't be serious, Avatar?"

One hour and fifty five seconds to Christmas eve...

PARIS, FRANCE... Covered in falling snow, thus signalling the near arrival of Christmas. As the UN of White supremacy was in another meeting again...

"Not learning nothing, with a body count of thousands of dead soldiers. And thousands to a few thousand more that are physically, or mentally handicapped. Or both! Pre-emptive war is still unbelievably on the cards for both Britain and America. With them using the policy of FORCED WAR to gain control of the planets dwindling resources... Giving us, the white race a new wave of undeclared colonization! That will... O' what's this?" Said Ran as a E-mailed report popped up on the front of his monitor... "O' dear... Not him again..."

"What is it?" Remarked the British Fascist in return.

"Ten eastern European vice gangs, murdered! Last week in Romania... All of their teenage sex slaves that were being held for transport. Missing from the scene of the blood soaked crimes?"

"Weren't we suppose to take delivery of them in two days?" Voice the female Neo Nazi member.

"Yes! They were to be sent onto our people in Moscow, then onto... O' wait...? Now take the lost in profit of that... Add three hundred million plus in losses this week alone..." Voiced Ran taking an account of losses generated by Jackson's mission's of Justice in the past month. "Add to the 1.3 Billion in lost slave labour. Narcotics trafficking and distribution. Prostitution and... Child..."

"And a Partridge in a pear tree!!!!!!!!!!!" Exclaimed a polite cold feminine voice that belonged to...?

Entering the conference room, with doom as her ally. Dressed looking like an ice princess and wannabe Snow Queen, wannabe white Queen. Wearing a fashionable Techno folk styled white trouser power suit. Aryana! With a bleached white fur coat, made from Polar bear. (Yes Polar bear!) That in all, collectively reflected her Great White Shark appearance and Ethnic stance. Stood tall and alone, wearing a platinum icy blood diamond vial necklace...

"Take a seat!" Ran voiced, turning his head to the right viewing a now entering Aryana. "We'll be done shortly!"

Taking a said seat sporting a grin that would have frightened the Devil himself. Aryana now took a seat opposite, facing Ran. Who himself now continued on with his speech...

"Ladies and Gentlemen our steps to completing the Fuhrers dreams are coming to ahead." He voiced raising his hands upwards. As a 3D holo image of the European continent now swirled into construction, just above the centre of the table.

"World Jewry is too reliant on the false help of the Neo Cons, and those monster raving loony End-Timers... What with countless Christian groups for the holy land playing both and all sides under the counter. While giving false support to Israel above... As most of them still rightly blame the Jews for murdering our lord Jesus Christ! Thus lulling those Jews into a false sense of security. With them not realizing that they should make peace with the Arabs, and take care of us! Therefore now said Jewry will have no where further to go. With Israel surrounded by soon to be Nuclear enemies..." Said Ran, as he now opened up another computer file in front of him. "Our drug trafficking alliances our allowing the streets of Europe to be washed with cheap Heroin from the liberated nation of Afghanistan. Giving drug crime a high boost! But we must be vigilant as Europe must be kept white. With no more other racially inferior eastern European nations being allowed to join up. Only then can a fully united Europe including that of Great Britain... Be one day soon realized!"

"United!? How amusing!" Exclaimed Aryana with rude interruption.

"What exactly is that suppose to mean?"
Responded Ran with charged annoyance.

"It means exactly what it means..."
Remarked Aryana quickly in return. Taking a
moment to look at all of the members.

"For years... No! For decades you have all
ruined your chance to achieve an effective
take over of the world. And instead what do
you let happen?" Remarked Aryana with
venom! "The Zionists cry Holocaust,
forgetting about the other sixty million
slaughtered in what was World war two. And
get a nation! Stolen from Muslim vermin!
The peoples of black colour get their civil
rights in America..." She uttered with
contempt. "O' sure they can't get a cab or
a good Job. Or expect a rescue in a
Hurricane! But they thrive... Without none
of you getting even a little offended. And
now--And now as long as their willing to be
a Pro-Zionist and House of Saudi puppet to
the contingency. Now they can be President!
God dam their goes the neighbourhood!"
Aryana uttered with a glance of wickedness.

"Then South Africa! On the hush... The only
bastion of true civilization on the whole
AIDS infected continent. And what happens,
they did not have the protection of
Hollywood. Like Israel does. NO! So they
failed, and you surrendered once more!

Caring more about your suits and your bling ring, jewellery... God! It feels like there are more Jews present here than at Oscar night!" Voiced Aryana...

"How dare you question our racial purity!" Said the KKK representative, slamming his fist against the solid black desk.

"How dare I? How dare you!!!" Said Aryana with a mocking grin. "American's!!! The good old U.S. of A... And the worlds biggest melting pot... You people haven't been pure since day one!" She mocked speaking onwards! "You see that's the problem with putting you white men in charge. You can never keep it in your pants. From your founding fathers to all of you today. Always whoring around with Beasts of colour, at every turn! Creating all of those different sub-races and divisions, that threaten my ethnic Germanic stance today..." She expressed giving her own bigoted views. "O' plus, not forgetting those of you who engage in even more foul acts of sexual dysfunction!" Said Aryana looking directly at both Ran and the British fascist. Who themselves were both really gay, and both firmly in the closet.

"You've gone to far this time, Aryana!" Said the British Fascist with imminent fear of being outted!

"Gone to far? Gone to far? O' boyfriend...
Please! I haven't said nearly enough!"
Spoke Aryana.

"O' but I think you have..." Said Ran
tapping the screen in front of him.
Displaying classified UN in house security
reports. "A UN Ambassador was shot and
killed yesterday by a disavowed Israeli
Assassin... Posing as an Ambulance driver.
Who apparently stole his body setting fire
to it, on the Expressway... While at the
same time stealing an item that belongs to
very important people!"

"You mean... The Machine!" Mocked Aryana
once more!

"Don't play games with us Avatar... We know
you had a JEW Agent steal the item..."

"That was very clever using a racial enemy
to do your dirty work!" Remarked the
British Fascist. "I guest all it cost you
was thirty pieces of silver!"

"We know that you now have it in your
possession!" Said Ran.

As sitting like a high school kid facing
three months of detention! Who did not give
a shit! Aryana now sat listening on...

"What did you think you were doing Avatar?
There is no way the Machine would let you
keep it. No one is allowed to own it a
anymore..." Remarked the female Neo Nazis.
"The only person who did was our beloved
Fuhrer, and even he had it taken off him!"

With a knowledge true and undisclosed to
the public history! Aryana now responded.
"Don't you mean stolen? Stolen by a Tarot
card playing little traitor, slash double
agent. Slash plane stealing defector!"

"Save your history lessons for those who
are interested!" Snapped Ran with
disapproval.

"Forgetting your history! Our history!"
Said Aryana stepping out of her seat. "It's
because of race traitors like yourself we
lost our rightful place as rulers of this
world!"

Looking at each other the "Members", all
wonder what exactly was it Aryana was
saying or talking about? As she now
continued...

"I was born in a time where because of weak
men like you... All pure Aryans are a true
minority! Having no surviving culture, no
racial pride!"

"Born in a time? What are you talking about?" Asked Ran with a puzzling stance. "Now is not the time for you too have a mental episode, Aryana!"

"Maybe you're a little too pure? A little too inbred? O' I'm sorry I mean pure bred!" Said the KKK member with a smirk!

"Yes! What exactly is your relationship to or with, Kruger." Exclaimed the British Fascist with a hinting to something improper smile. As the rest of the "Members" all smirked.

Making the worst mistake of their lives. Like telling a Mafia "Godfather" that his Wife, daughter and late mother were all good in the sack! "The Committee" all looked to Aryana for an instant answer. As the KKK member now mumbled the famous or rather infamous Banjo tune to the movie Deliverance. Thus causing the other members to smirk in hinting agreement. All thinking that they have got the better of her.

"Look! Aryana! We have more pressing problems than too worry about your mental health and your little PET PROJECTS..." Said Ran with conviction.

"Pet projects?" Responded Aryana.

"Yes! The private army you've been training in Argentina? The aforementioned item you stole from the Machine. The other item you brought from Gideon. That was itself stolen! The fact that you already secretly own, forty seven percent of South Africa's development holdings unofficially."

"Fiddy two actually... But who's counting!" Mocked Aryana not giving a dam that they were on to her secret plans.

"What are you planning?" Spoke Ran tapping open his computer files in front of him. "Why would you want to own so much... As countless areas of which contain little or no mineral wealth? And are not even developed at all? Just wide stretches of jungle, valley, desert and dust? Everywhere as far as the eye can see?"

"Well I was thinking about building a house... Putting in a pool, a tennis court, maybe a golf course. Who knows?" Said Aryana with a mocking smile. "I might install a mobile weapons platform, capable of launching ICBM's with a biological genetic payload?" She mumbled under her breath with a sarcastic grin...

"Mock! Joke and make fun of things all you like, Avatar. You're dangerous, and at

worst... You're stupid!" Said Ran causing
Aryana to look in his direction, with that
of a stare of wanton murder.

"Your illegal activities must stop now...
Your army is to be disbanded. You will hand
over a penalizing sum that will be in the
higher than..."

"Higher than the figures that you and this
committee are making. With your trade in
white sex slaves to the Asian markets..."
Snapped Aryana. "Plus not to mention
turning my Pure blooded Germanic Sisters
into whores. With the Legalization of
Prostitution in the Fatherland! Where they
get the vile opportunity to be raped, and
raped. And face painted by knuckle dragging
Non-Aryan soccer fans and blood drinking
tourists... Again, and again and a million
times a year, again... As if they were in
enslaved Bangkok!" She expressed with
racist yet pro feminist commentary!?

"As I was saying..." Declared Ran. "You
will pay an higher than high figured sum
and..."

"And?" Mocked Aryana in return.

"And your Doctor's studies at our black site HIV experimentation clinics in South Africa... Will not continue once they are rebuilt!" Stated Ran, with Father knows best styled like rhetoric. Not knowing that Dr. Soap was already deceased! "I mean trying to complete that GM virus... Don't you know how dangerous that is?"

"Yes! There's a very good reason why the Apartheid government didn't use it!" Voice the female Neo Nazi member.

"Maybe if they had, they would still be in charge!" Said Aryana with passion.

"That's foolish talk, Avatar! As you know that GM virus is unsafe and would kill just as many whites as it would blacks. And everyone else in between!" Remarked the Australian member speaking for the first time...

"It wouldn't kill those of noble true Aryan blood!" Voiced Aryana with knowing. "Say, someone who was the purist of them all! Would it!"

Laughing at her with straight face grins, the "Members" all now shook their heads collectively. Not believing what they were hearing.

"My goodness. Why don't you and your daddy or boyfriend. Just get into your Area 51 borrowed flying saucer. And go find Atlantis or the Ark. Or something!" Said the British fascist with a mocking chuckle. In reference to mythical places and objects...

"I've got one better. Why don't you go out and just find the Tower of Hell. And get it over with!" Said the KKK member, trying not to laugh.

"Don't forget to find Santa and the Easter bunny while you're looking!" Mocked the British Fascist.

Laughing with a light giggle all of the "Members" now mocked her. In thinking that she was being sarcastic! With the exception of Ran, who now looked Aryana dead in the eye!

"I nearly have!!!" Said Aryana with conviction!

Stepping up and out of his seat slowly. Ran's face was now filled with fear. As just like the movie line "Solyent Green is people!" Knowing! Even searching for the Tower of Hell would get you killed. Dead! Shot! Buried without a grave, or a care!

"The Tower of Hell is just a myth. It is not to be explored or discussed in great detail in anyway. The Machine kill anyone who even tries to look for it, or discusses it in the open." Remarked Ran with upsetting concern, that all of the others now instantly shared.

"You people are pathetic, you know... The Tower is our history, our future. As Aryans! As the White Race. And all you can do is stand and sit there in fear... In fear of the truth! In fear of yourselves and the Machine! In fear of the Blood Libel that will make me immortal! That will make me a God... THE GOD!"

WHAT IS THE BLOOD LIBEL...? A myth to enforce bigotry, to enforce Anti-Jewish prejudice. A myth spread and used by the End-Timers and their "unknown" masters to maximum efficiency. To get Hitler's Germany, to get an Israel, to get 9/11 and their rapture. A myth and blood soaked lie that was used to murder, and lynch innocent individuals of the Jewish faith. Young and old, and all in between alike for centuries. While the world as always turned a blind eye! With it still being foolishly and almost unbelievably, still falsely claimed that it is widely practised by all Jewish people today! That is what was being discussed and debated by them both...

"Blood Libel?" Whispered Ran as if she had said a dirty word... That's not been practised in a millennia. With it's only use being that of casting hatred against The Jews... On the orders of the End-Timers, so they could get want they want!"

"The Blood Libel is real! The Tower is real... It's just been forgotten! But soon it will be remembered and claimed by me, as my fortress of purity..." Voiced Aryana with a cold and absolute degree of I'm going to rule the world evil!

"You can't be serious, Avatar?" Remarked the KKK Member, shaking his head to himself. "Only damnation awaits those who would go against God and perform the Libel! Avatar don't!" He exclaimed just like a preacher giving a Sunday sermon.

"You hypocritical Bible thumping fools." Snapped Aryana calmly. "With your cuckoo bananas constitution. Idiotic founding fathers. And disturbed flag worshipping, pro miscegenation ways..." She remarked, in reference to so-called multi Ethnic/so-called interracial genealogy. Only to then gesture with her right hand, signalling that she found the whole idea of America to be a joke! "You know I don't remember reading anything about you good old boys, and your United States! In that black Arab

JEW Book of lies! That book of half truths
and fairy tales... You all just can't stand
the fact that the Libel is more powerful
than your conveniently invisible God! Your
Hebrew God!" She voiced with contempt!

"Do not mock our Holy White God! The Flag!
Or the righteous founding fathers, Avatar!"
Uttered the Klan member back with

quick answered reverence.

"Righteous!? More like tax dodging
terrorist!" She mocked again going for a
lower blow. "And how old was the VIRGIN
Mary?" She mocked once more and again,
shaking her head to herself!

"You FUCKIN' GERMAN WHORE! HOW DARE YOU!!!
You..." Yelled the KKK member. Forgetting
his fake polite Southern "well I do
declare" accent, for that of an enraged
hill billy.

Thus ignoring his impoliteness just for the
passing moments. Aryana now spoke onwards,
seemingly not offended or unmoved?

"Here we go again, American's... With your
so-called free speech! You people think you
get to rule the world... You think that you
can do anything!" She snarled with quick

spoken spite! "Steal oil, bomb nations!
Make war on the word of an hillbilly, vote
stealing, impure mud blooded President!
Sowing the seeds of democracy by giving the
Iraqi and Afghan people the wonderful gift
of HIV, syphilis and countless other
Sexually transmitted diseases. By going all
Vietnam! Raping the local women, little
girls, little boys and a few men... A lot
of men! And not to mention killing little
vermin Muslim babies! To infinity and
beyond! With your drugged up troops and
corporate mercenaries!" She voiced stating
facts and horrors about the War in Iraq,
Afghanistan and beyond (Including
Pakistan!) That for some reason are mostly
denied or not admitted too!

"We are just pursuing our white Christian
right of manifest destiny. That will lead
us too a return of absolute white rule
across the globe... Taking whatever or
whomever we see fit!" Declared the Klan
member with a loud church like vibration.

"Keep lying to yourselves... You Jew
puppets! You End-Timer afraid prison
bitches!" Aryana remarked. "You really
don't realize that you only get to be
number one, for as long as the Machine say
you are!" She said, about to state knowing
information on the world of Tomorrow! "And
in the not to distant future you won't be!
Hell by the end of this century. You oil

junkie crack whores, will be lucky to stay in the top twenty! Once your Jew money, and that Pope and his Mafia jump ship!"

"And how the hell do you know this? Do you have a crystal ball or something?" Voiced the Klan member in anger. As Aryana continued on...

"All the warning signs were given to you by history and the future itself. But none of you would listen... The Protocols of the elders of Zion! Was a warning from tomorrow and..."

"From tomorrow? As in the future? The bitch has lost her mind!" Mumbled the Klan member speaking again... "The book was a Russian fake!"

"O' really!? So why do you think that idiot Hitler, or rather his backers really wanted them gone? Why give up six million slaves?"

"It was because they were bleeding the white race dry..."

"Pod-cast!" She exclaimed with future talk slang. "They where mostly all poor back then... The Jews had no money! It was a stereotype."

"They killed the baby Jesus! It was their punishment, by God himself!" Declared the Klan member as if he was a bigoted false preacher on a Sunday.

"The baby Jesus? God!" Mocked Aryana shaking her head. "What is it's with you lot and that black Arab commie, Jew! Who even stood up for tax inspectors. God! Was the guy giving him a tax-break for head, or carpentry lessons? Or what!? No they wanted them gone to thus undo the evangelical End-Timers prophecy, once and for all." She voiced given some disturbing facts and truths. "No Jews equals no Israel. No war within the war, in the summer of 2006. They don't unlock the gates of hell and bring about the third and final anti-Christ. Thus saving the world from the battle of Armageddon, so we whites could rule it for a thousand and then some years."

"The final anti-Christ? Are you off your head you crazy Bitch!"

"O' I see! You only believe in some parts of that Jew bible. That's cool, Homie. That's cool!"

"They were destroying our lines of racial purity!" Remarked the British fascists sounding down Aryana's comments...

"Please! What are you talking about? You
know your God is a Jew too! And you look
like a Jew to me. No! It was because he
knew of the future... Via Nostradamus. Or
rather Nostradamned-us, if you knew the
truth! And that the said Protocols were a
fake within the truth. As that's how you
get away with it. Like Bush and his CIA did
with that Iraqi porno thing on the net. And
the U.K Press did with that fake torture
photo!" Said Aryana still speaking on with
more to say. "You tell the truth making it
look fake. Even though it is the truth.
That's how the Zionists tried to use
America to wipe out all of the Arabs, and
Persians to rule the world, but failed to
do so. That's how the Russians tried to
rule again after that! As the truth is
always the deadliest weapon!" She voiced
telling more on the facts on the history of
tomorrow.

"The truth? The truth!" Said Ran taking
charge of the situation. As if he was the
President or Prime Minister of a Nation,
about to take a firm stance. "The item you
acquired from Gideon just before his
stunning demise. The other item you had
stolen from the UN, killing an ambassador
in the process. Betraying your oath to
us... To our Aryan Nation! To our Order of
the New White World!" He voiced reading out
a set of invisible charges, as if he was
reading them off a piece of paper. "Plus

the fact that you were ready to destroy New
York! Just to hide your crime. That could
in itself have lead to Nuclear destruction
across the globe!?"

Once again taking absolutely no notice
whatsoever, Aryana now decided to respond!
"Your just a joke... A bunch of busters!
Ballers and lame name callers... Cowards
through and through... All unworthy of
being WHITE! All unworthy of being
ARYAN!!!" She said with a hit of venom
laced spite. "Ya feel me!"

"I've heard enough of this... Himoe,
Hommie. Or whatever!" Ran voiced with a
mumble! "The Machine will be demanding
answers!" He said taking a pause, never
intending to let Aryana get away with what
she had done... "And I intend to give it to
them... GUARDS!"

Clicking his right fingers. Ran now stood
short yet resolved, folding his arms
together. As the doors to the conference
room now slammed open! Revealing a unit of
armed guards... Twenty in all. Dressed in
full body armour, that in itself looked
like a throwback to a futuristic 70's sci-
fi movie. The said guards each now carried
a taser like stun baton...

"Well! I guest you've got me guys." Said
Aryana, with a glare of extreme and nearly
over the top sarcasm! As standing ready,
the guards batons now tingled with the hum
of stunning high voltage electricity...

Defeat! Time to give up! O' and let's go
and get some coffee! These things and more
were not on Aryana's mind. As she now stood
up, removing her coat. Taking a step back
standing just behind the guards collective
positions. "Well I guest you can't win them
all!" She remarked with a smile?

"No you can't!" Stated Ran wondering what
the hell Aryana was up too?

"Well! The Game is up!" Said Aryana,
raising her hands up into the air! "I'm
busted!!! It's a fair cop! I give up... You
got me bang to rights Governor! I am not
the ripper!" She mocked once more, with a
London cockney accent! "You know I guest? I
could sum all of this up in just three
little, yet lengthy words..." Remarked
Aryana with her voice now back to normal!

"And what exactly would they be?" Enquired
Ran, asking a question that he would wish
that he hadn't.

"O' just something simple like..."
Responded Aryana.

"Like what?" Asked Ran!

"O' like..." Aryana voiced taking a false
pause, as she now jumped into a backwards
performed somersault!

"BOUDICCA THUNDER STRIKE!!!!!!!!!!!!!!!!!!"
She screamed snapping into a lethal power
move...

Thus instantaneously and in all directions,
the conference room now almost shook itself
apart. Just as if a Bomb had been
detonated! With the said power moves wake
sending outwards a single projected
shockwave. Killing all of the guards. With
the exact cause of death being that their
bones and skulls where cracked apart. Into
countless fractured pieces. Along with the
walls, floor and ceiling to the room
cracked apart as well.

Thus with all of the "Members" now all
sporting the look of Earthquake survivors.
Clasping against the long black table,
still in their respective positions. With
the exception of Ran who was now knocked to
the floor. Coolly snapping out of her Power

Move stance. Almost as quickly as she had
taken to it. Aryana now snatched away her
own necklace! Throwing it down and away as
if it was nothing. Just like a super rich
Zionist Hollywood trash movie star...

As bouncing along the table, the three
million dollar Platinum blood diamond vial
necklace now smashed into a million glass
crystal pieces. Just as Ran tried to gain
his stance!

Stepping up to his feet, as the others now
sat back up into their chairs. Ran now
looked strange? As if he had just received
bad news? Or had a case of the Flu?

"You don't look so good!" Mocked Aryana!
"In fact all of you don't look so good!"

STOP THE CLOCK... THE FUTURE IS CALLING!

Chapter Sixteen

NO MAN IS AN ISLAND!

"Make yourself welcome My home is your home!"

Forty six minutes after leaving...

PROMISE ISLAND... Cloaked and hidden away from the world. Drenched in the high distant light of the midday noon sun. The Islands now sat quiet from a distance, as an infinity of calm and far stretching seas stood throughout...

THE SUBMARINE... Alien! Mysterious! Who built you? Where do you come from? Why are

you and Jackson connected? There were a
hundred, a thousand, a million unanswered
questions you could ask? But all that
really mattered now is that Jackson was
about to return...

TEMPORAL FLASHBACK... Where did Jackson and
Inari go!? That's what you would have asked
yourself if you'd been there. And how did
they escape from Building 13!? Was it by
Helicopter, concealed parachute, or a Jet
pack from the future? Or just something
else?

Therefore pushing through the exit doors of
the sky lobby. Jackson and Inari now ran
onto the roof of Building 13...

"The Helo! I can fly us out of here!"
Stated Inari loudly, pointing at the parked
Helicopter. As the wind of the cold
arriving late night blew inwards.

"O' we're flying out of here. Just not the
way you think!" Said Jackson with an
instant plan of action!

Giving a look of "what are you talking
about?" Inari now stared as changing his
skin colour and ethnic appearance back to
normal. And placing one hand on her waist,
and the other against her right shoulder.

As if they were about to perform some kind
of steamy hot Latin dance. Jackson now
spoke... "Don't be afraid!" He whispered
into Inari's ear, softly like a devoted
lover. "I'll catch you!!!"

"Catch me???" Snapped Inari realizing what
Jackson meant! As just a second later.
Inari found herself thrown upwards and
across the roof top. Heading straight over
the edge!!!

With his Temporal Ability in effect!
Splitting a single second apart, charging!
Running forward reaching the edge of the
roof top. Seemingly in one instantaneous
motion. Jackson now jumped! Sailing over
the said edge without a care. Just as if he
was a cliff jumping champ diving into a
lagoon!

"When you get caught between the Moon and
New York city" was now the view in sight!
As a sea of traffic and an infinite river
of lit and illuminated glass windows,
rained across everywhere and throughout!
And thus with a concrete slamming death
imminent for her. Inari now viewed the most
beautiful sight, seeing the city descending
at night.

Silent! Without a scream! With Zen like reaction and composure! Feeling more alive than she had ever felt in her life. Free falling for just a few seconds. That in themselves seemed like minutes as the ground got closer and closer...

One second later...

Caught! Saved! Scooped up from the jaws and bloody clawed clutches of death! Jackson now took Inari into his arms... Activating a path back to the world of tomorrow! Back to the future! And...

BACK TO THE SUBMARINE... Pushing forwards passing through the fabric of space and time, without breaking it apart. Jackson and Inari now made their returning entry back to the future, through the now opened portal.

"Wow... Ya hew! Ride 'em cowboy! What a rush... I'd never get tired of that!" Yelled Inari, just like a kid just getting off the fastest and best roller coaster in the park! "It's better than sex!" She stated.

"I would not go that far!" Said Jackson causing Inari to smirk. Thus fantasizing with wonder for just a passing second.

"WORLD CHANGING EVENT! Undone, J.C! History restored!" Said Techy entering the portal chambers.

"Err? Hello! He had a little help..." Said Inari, gesturing towards herself. Turning to Jackson. "See I told you, TEAM PATRIOT was a winner!"

"Don't spoil it, Officer Gellar!" Said Jackson, walking up to Techy. Pretending that he did not care, sporting a hidden smile. Feeling that he was just a few steps away from getting too close to her.

"Did he just smile then?" Was the look on Techy's face and silent thought in his head. "He never smiles?" As out of earshot whispering into his ear. Jackson now spoke to him, as Inari looked on, feeling as she was not being let in on what was next!

Now with just nearly a minute passing. Inari continued to look at Jackson, annoyed that he was still giving her the cold shoulder. Which in itself was highly unusual, as if it had been anyone else. She would have normally just told them to get lost, or said something else that was more ruder. But with Jackson things were different! Was it Love? Was it lust? Maybe it was a bit of both!

"Hey, you know it's rude to whisper!" She called out.

"It's for your own good, Officer Gellar!" Said Jackson back in return, quite rudely continuing on. Telling Techy what exactly he sensed on the Plane and what the item Aryana had stolen!"

"No way!? Are you sure?" Stated Techy with surprise! "O' course you are!" He said already knowing the answer! "I didn't think we ever see that..."

"Bullshit!" Inari shouted with rude in return interruption... "I guest you don't really want me here after all! Baghdad? I'll take it!" Said Inari turning her back on them both! "Well it's better than being stuck in Nazi Germany, or the dark ages!" She stated with sarcasm! "Or..."

"NO MAN IS AN ISLAND!" This fact was true for everyone, no matter how alone or lost in the world you might feel. As Jackson, giving some what of an unusual apology. Well unusual for him that is. Now spoke!

"I'm sorry! You've got the wrong end of the stick, Officer Gellar!" He voiced! "Make yourself welcome... My home is your home!"

"What?" Remarked a slightly puzzled Inari, expecting Jackson to get angry with her?

"You're in! But the question is do you want in all the way?" He asked with cryptic questioning?

As looking him dead and directly in the eye. Inari paused just for a single moment! "You bet ya!" She responded with cool and sexy absolution and knowing!

"J.C?" Asked Techy. Surprised and slightly taken a back just a little. Wondering if Inari could handle the Earth shattering secret she was about to be let in on?

Thus taking a single step forward with commanding reverence. Jackson coolly addressed, Techy. "You heard the lady!" He voiced with she's on the team for now conviction! "Let's go down to the lower level..."

STOP THE CLOCK... BACK TO NOW...

One minute to Christmas eve...

PARIS, FRANCE CONCLUDED... Empty and completely quiet of sound. The conference

room hung silent all throughout, with the
exception of a single pair of foot steps...

"MIRROR MIRROR ON THE WALL! Who's the
purist of them all???" Questioned Aryana!
Standing! Walking around the room.
Retracing and retracing her footsteps again
and again, enjoying the moment to the
extreme.

"Well it's certainly not none of you!" She
mocked circling the "Members" like a great
white shark! As a download of information,
records and monetary funds from the banks
fire walled computers now took place.

"I smell JEW! I smell Gipsy. I smell Polish
and just a hint of... Homer--sexual!"
Remarked Aryana, continuing to walk around
the table. "Australians! Mixed half breed
convicts... Italians? Why are you people on
our side? You're not white... Even though
you think you are! Neither are you British,
as half of you are Jews anyway! As for the
rest? Well!!!" Said Aryana, looking at all
of the "Members." Who themselves all now
sat dead in their chairs! As the plasma
screen monitors flicked with hundreds of
flash imagery, signalling that the download
was continuing...

All victims of Aryana's newly acquired GM virus. All having gone through a most painful and blood choking death. That was too disturbing to describe! With the only safe details being that all of their bodies had been destroyed from the inside out, by the said unknown GM virus. "Gentleman, Gentleman, Gentleman and lady! And I use that term loosely!" She said mockingly, breaking into a overtly masculine toned voice. Placing her Red-Cell device into her left ear.

Strange and seemingly disturbed? Aryana now looked around the room. Only to now turn, looking straight towards the now very much deceased Ran! "You stupid individuals! You race traitor sell-outs, you... Degenerates!" She mocked back to her regular accent. "You think you were so clever, so smart... That's what you get for worshipping that stupid illegitimate little House painter! Who was only tough enough to make a little Dutch girl hide up in her attic doing a dear diary... Who thought he was so big for killing SIX million... And six million plus more... That history keeps forgetting to count!" She continued to mock. Only now stopping, in taking sight of the Hitler bust!

"What do we have here!" Aryana remarked! Walking up to it. Studying the said statue from all angles and directions, as if she was going to buy it at an auction!

Now switching to black without warning, the Computer screens were filled up with indecipherable code. As Kruger now spoke... "Download complete!" He remarked over her Red-Cell. "Brutus is on his way... Extraction in ninety seconds..." He voiced giving the time and command for Aryana to make her escape!

Smouldering with sexual disgust! Moving up closer... Aryana now gave the bust of Hitler a peck on the cheek! "Amateur!" She exclaimed with an collective whisper. Knocking it of the stand and smashing it to countless cracked pieces! Giving a one worded cryptic hint to what plans she had in store for all non-blonde, non-blue eyed. And non-Caucasians and the world itself!

Same time different place...

AUSTRIA REVISITED... "What's in the case? What's in the case? What's in the box? What the hell could it be??? Etc! Etc!" These were the things on your mind if you were there. If you had witness the scene stealing events of the day. As after just hanging up the line, standing inside his study. Kruger! Now walked up to the sterilized clean stolen case.

"Many men have killed for you over the ages, not understanding or knowing what to do with you. While countless races and peoples are extinct because of you." He voiced to himself, gently touching the said case as if he was in love with it's inner contents.

Thus now having a near holy moment of victory, and feeling like a kid in a locked closed sweet shop. Kruger felt like jumping for joy... "TV on!" He said now as the flat screen hyper 3D TV. That was disguised as a walled mounted mirror. Instantly switched to a classic movie channel. That itself was playing the motion picture, THE SOUND OF MUSIC...

"Traitors!" Exclaimed Kruger, shaking his head to himself. "Change channel... O' my favourite! O' wait! Change channel." As both Platinum and Strawberry now rushed into the room.

"Mein Herr!" They exclaimed simultaneously. "We have company, attack teams incoming from all directions!"

"How quaint! The Machine send in their silent assassins to do their dirty work!" He said. Not afraid of what he had just heard. "It's too bad... I kind of like this

place!" He remarked typing just a few keys
on his Computer? "Ladies! Time to go! O'
wait! Me almost forgot!" Said Kruger, as he
now stopped. Only to then take hold of a
signed autographed and frame picture of his
two new favourite celebrities.

Walking as if he didn't have a care or gave
a dam. Kruger with Strawberry and Platinum
in tow, now walked towards a secret escape
exit! That in itself was in the form of an
elevator hidden behind of large book case.
Located at the back of the study!

"The game is indeed afoot..." He remarked
taking a moment, as the elevators door now
slid shut! "Play on, playa!!!"

STOP THE CLOCK! BACK TO THE FUTURE...

Chapter Seventeen

ENTER THE LOOKING GLASS...

"Whoa! This room is huge. Echo, Echo, Echo?"

One minute, seven seconds later...

THE SUBMARINE CONTINUED... Cold and crystal calm in perfect serenity. Jackson's ship of destiny. Ship of tears and doorway to the past and yesterday stood asleep. Awaiting the next world changing event to history.

"You know I got to ask, why do you do all of this?" Exclaimed Inari wanting to ask the why, what and everything? As all three of them now walked through a network of connecting crystal chambers...

"To quote an old movie. Let's just say that, here's a Man who stood up! That's all!"

"I know that one! You talkin' to me! You talkin' to me!" Said Inari giving a very good Deniro impression. "So who did you stand up against?"

"Against everyone!" He said with a silent lead pause. "Especially those who would terrorize the innocent and abuse the different." Stated Jackson with nation of one conviction!

"Can...? Why? What happen to you?" She asked, asking one question too many!

"That's my business! Officer Gellar!" Snapped Jackson keeping his personal cards to his solid chest. "But I'll let you know this for free..." He said about to tell her more information on the world of tomorrow! "In this future that is your home now... Life moves at an even quicker selfish pace! With money and power still infecting men's and women's souls like a cancer. With no lessons learn. As the rich get even richer

and the poor get even poorer... With
economic slavery raging ahead, with neo-
globalization in play... Walled off nation
plots against nation and it's own. While
the said poor, and all in between alike
know only hunger and misery."

"Soylent Green! That's what it's like,
Inari!" Said Techy jumping into the
conversation.

"Soylent Green? Not as in...???"

"No minus that!" Remarked Techy correcting
her.

"For now! Who know's the way things are
going."

"You're joking right? Hero?"

Giving no answer Jackson walked onwards as
Techy talked on. "While with the light-
switch effect a reality, the effects of
global warming have long ago kicked fully
inwards!" He voiced. Putting in a word.
With Jackson not minding the interruption,
rather welcoming it. Showing their
friendship was strong. "And time travel
technology a hidden reality!"

"Thus giving us all a guaranteed one way ticket to the sixth extinction. With the hope of a tomorrow, a today... And worst of all a yesterday now gone!" Said Jackson in his very own misanthropic way. That itself could have made anyone want to slash their wrists in suicidal depression!

"Whoa! Try not to make it sound too depressing will you." Inari said. "So I know you're not a fan of the Whitehouse... O' I'm sorry. Plantation House, and all that... But who funds all of this?" She asked with nosy neighbour like intrigue. "Congress!? Some US Government, secret Time Police Enforcement Agency? Or something? All fighting for the good old red, white and blue!!!"

"Old red, white and?" Voiced Jackson with an I don't think so stance.

"Yeah!" She exclaimed with a smile. "You know... For truth! Justice! In the American way!" She voiced mockingly like a superhero.

"In the AmeriKKKan way? Fuck that! FUCK AMERICA!" Questioned Jackson wanting to laugh. As if to say what the hell are you talking about? And once again thinking--"Where you even paying attention to what was said before, and even before that?"

"Yeah! Well by your accent you're American? Aren't you?" She asked. Only to get a look from him as if she had called him a dirty word.

"American! As in the beast! The great Satan!" Uttered Jackson with rightful revulsion.

Now not even getting a bit slightly nervous as most "civilized" people do. Whenever America is ever rightly criticised. Inari now looked towards Jackson as if she was his girlfriend. With a look everyone in love gives without realizing they are doing so.

"Yeah the Romans with iPods! An American?" Said Inari asking again.

"An American?" He spoke with a knowing smirk, of blatant pure contempt! "I stopped being one of those a long time ago! Inari." Jackson now remarked with missing poignant regret? Mixed together with a deep seated loathing as well. Trying not to bring up his past. Accidentally calling her by her first name! "No! Like I said before. I'm just a nation of one with six billion to come... Although in this time frame it's more like twelve billion plus."

"So who's side are you on then?" She said,
asking a very good question! A very
important question. As Jackson now stopped,
looking her dead and directly in the eye!

"MY SIDE!!!!" He stated with firm
conviction.

Thus with this just said! Looking towards
Jackson with concern. Wanting to know about
his life, and his pain... Asking herself
the question. "What happen to make you do
what you do and the rest of it!?" Inari
stared onwards, as they were all about to
reach the lower levels...

Three minutes and nine seconds later...

ENTER THE LOOKING GLASS... A window to the
world of today, tomorrow! And most
importantly a window that could look onto
all of the countless yesterdays that have
past and gone by.

All the way back to? Well a long way back!
That's what could be said of the this
mysterious centre piece of technology. As
strange looking and seemingly not like
anything that anyone alive or dead had ever
seen or imagined. This Alien window on time
sat switched off! Just for a fleeting

moment as Jackson, Inari and Techy now all
entered inward...

Impressed with the incredible and nearly
unbelievable to say the least. Inari now
looked up, down and all around! Taken all
quite aback!

"Whoa! This room is huge. Echo, Echo,
Echo?" She shouted out! Only not to hear
her voice reverberate outwards. "What?"
Said Inari, surprise at the fact that her
voice did not echo as it should have. "Now
that's spooky? What is all of this?" She
exclaimed aloud, as Jackson now walked
forward.

"Over here!" He stated not answering her
question. Walking around the said Looking
Glass, towards the other side of the
room... Towards a solid wall?

"Err? Hello?" Called out Inari walking up
to Jackson. Only not to get an answer!?

Hidden and concealed like a closed off room
in an old Mansion or a secret level in a
video game. An adjoining chamber containing
more secrets inside... Now swirled opened!

"What's in there?" Inari asked, only to
have Jackson not answer her.

Thus walking inwards Jackson and Inari entered, to see a hidden wonder... To see another time portal?

Permanently fixed to the spot and enveloped in a eerie wake of hard, yet soft looking light! The single portal stood alone in the backdrop of the large echoing sized hidden chamber...

"This is the what and why to everything... This is the reason I do what I do!" Voiced Jackson taking Inari by the hand softly like a boyfriend, like a husband! "For what it's worth... I'm sorry!"

"What? Why would you be..." Said Inari only to now turn and stare directly into the would-be void that was the portal!

A TEMPORAL WAKE IN EFFECT... Feeling as if she was really there. Inari! With Jackson by her side still holding her hand, now witnessed what was through the said portal...

"Sorry for what!" She exclaimed. Finding herself standing in the biggest wide stretching path of greenness of green meadows. "This place is lovely... The air is so clean, so fresh... There's nature everywhere... What?"

All Inari could do is look perplexed. Not
getting what she was supposed to be seeing?
"Can you give me a clue!?"

"There's nature everywhere except her most
dangerous creation!"

"Man?"

"Human beings... Their are none here or
anywhere else on the planet!" Signalled
Jackson as the ground seemed to move on
it's own beneath their collective feet.
Flashing! Rolling! Sliding along showing
Inari the whole Planet Earth. That did
indeed have not one single person. One
single soul left alive or even dead on it!

Looking forwards and seemingly beyond all
the horizons. Inari stared with a look of?
Well a look of a person who was about to
either wet themselves, scream! Cry! Or just
collapse downwards, slipping into a
permanent catatonic state. Only to now
instantly respond with just a few words...
As only she could do!

"O' FUCK NO!" She cursed giving just three
words to sum up what she had seen.

"No! It can't end like this... Can it???"
Uttered Inari as Jackson now brought her
safely out of the portals flash forwarding
Temporal wake!

"The apocalypse! The End!" Said Jackson
with concern. "The day of mutually assured
destruction?" Voiced Inari, strangely as if
she had already knew what laid ahead?

"We've seen this happen before, with the
world ending by fire." Said Techy. "Then
ice... But both times J.C prevented it from
happening. Pushing the end of days back...
All the way back to this. The first day of
the twenty second century."

"The catastrophe, this day of reckoning..."
Uttered Inari, as if she was momentarily
eclipsed by time and space itself.

"Or as we like to call it. The Conclusion!
The day of judgement!" Voiced Jackson with
monumental conviction! "The conclusion of
Humanity... The conclusion of you all!"

"Conclusion? How???" Question a puzzled
Inari. "You all?"

"We don't know!" Stated Jackson. "All we
know is that in just over seven years from

now. Some event that as of yet we can't
undo, will destroy all Human life on Earth!"

"No life anywhere." Voiced Techy, taking a
step forward. "On Earth, on the Moon! Heck
even on..."

"Can't you go through it? Stop all of this
from happening?" Inari said interrupting,
one step away from tears...

"No! I can only go where the ship wants me
to go!"

"And that's never in the future, that is
from the point of 2092!" Voiced Techy,
giving a set of quick answers.

"There must be a way?" Inari asked.

"No Inari, it's shielded!" Voiced Jackson
flicking his right fingers against the
shields humming ping!

"A fucking force field?" Cursed Inari with
annoyance. "Look! You have to stop this! We
have to stop this... Team Patriot! Like I
said before. I want in all the way. I'll
see this through with you, to the very
end!" She remarked with a falling in love
look towards Jackson!

"Okay Officer Gellar!" Said Jackson, as
Inari now turned to look at him, with
hidden attraction! Giving the glare of say
my name, say my name! "Okay, Inari! You're
in all the way... To the end!"

"To the end!" Said Inari, with a collective
sexy whisper.

"O' heck yeah, Team Patriot!" Exclaimed
Techy. "I like the sound of that!" He said,
as giving him a friendly look off shut the
fuck up. Jackson now stared at Techy as
both him and Inari smiled back in return at
Jackson!

"O' wait... What's that!" Said Inari in
viewing a large quite gigantic American
flag that hung suspended in the background.

"See I knew you were still burning a candle
for your homeland, Hero!"

"No I don't!"

"So what's the flag for then?" Asked Inari
in confusion. Getting no answer at first!

"Let's just say that it's not for
saluting!" Said Jackson playing momentarily
with his trusty lighter!

"What's that over there?" Inari inquired, looking back towards the first entered chamber.

"I'll show you in a minute!" Stated Jackson, for Inari only to now turn her back on the portal walking back. "Inari?!" He stated with concern, calling her back.

"Whoa! Now that's what I call a TV! Remarked Inari. "Can you get pay per view on this!"

"No! Just a view on History!" Said Techy, like a kid who got to play with the best toys in the world everyday!

"Time to check the Looking Gla..." Spoke Jackson taking a pause, placing his hand against the said named Looking Glass!

All silent! Trapped in a frozen moment with the exception of Jackson. both Techy and Inari stood still as if they were statues. As an Earth shattering and super amazing sight was about to be viewed? As with a possessing whisper, breaking itself apart! The gigantic polished like mirror shattered. Throwing itself and it's pieces forward! Only to then instantly reform! As if the whole thing had been filmed in rewinding reverse!

Now swirling inwards on itself with a whirlpool sea of ice like water. The Looking Glass travelled inwards and over itself... Only to then form a crystal clear image of promise Island! As if a live video feed was playing from a spy satellite from a sky high orbit.

"O' Inari, girl! You better check yourself!" She said aloud, beyond amazed. "Now that's what I call astonishing! What place is that?" Asked Inari.

"It's right..." Spoke Techy, only to be interrupted by history itself!

As without warning the Looking Glass now fully activated! Rewinding the time back. Thus displaying present-future day imagery all the way back through a rapid sea of events. That were all showed in glorious eye blinking succession. That were all to quick to be recognized...

STOP THE CLOCK! THROUGH THE LOOKING GLASS...

"Welcome to Media-Net News! And here are this mornings events on the Eve of Christmas... Or Christmas eve as it's more better known!" Stated the newscaster as images of the days tops stories flashed across the screen.

"Terror alert! New York safe and secure! President guarantees commercial flights will not be cancelled for the Christmas Holidays! Europe tightens boarder checks and Channel Tunnel security! Popes Christmas message of peace and goodwill to be read tomorrow! But first..." Voiced the newscaster, as the camera now cut back to him in the studio...

"Was it Anthrax? Was it Ricin? Or a super strain of bird or Swine flu, or something else? That is the question being asked this morning after French anti-terror police... With the aid of Special forces. Sealed off an entire section of a financial district in Paris this morning. With unconfirmed reports of a bio-terror attack by Al-Qaeda, against a French banking Headquarters. That for legal reasons cannot be named." Said the newscaster.

"We now go live to France and our reporter?" He voiced only to now take a collective pause. "My goodness!" He said as if he had just received bad news. "Err? News is just coming from... Austria! That a Château belonging to the C.E.O of Avatar Industries has been completely destroyed by a mysterious explosion! That... That has sadly resulted in the death of said C.E.O and philanthropist, Aryana Avatar. As well as her financial director, Julius Kruger! It is unsure and to early to say if this

incident is terror related! But all signs
do seem to point to Al-Qaeda once more.
With the companies close ties to the US
Military and the Jewish state of Israel.
Err...? We will bring you more on this
story shortly! And now to..."

STOP THE CLOCK... EXIT THE LOOKING GLASS...

Switching itself off with a swirling swoosh
of liquid energy, the Looking Glass now set
itself back to sleep!

"Yesssssss!" Exclaimed Inari like a
football player scoring the winning
touchdown at the Super bowl!
"Motherfucker!!! Burn Nazis burn!" She
cursed with a sexy smile! "O' I don't
believe it! This is to good to be true.
Great, great, guys?" She said turning. As
standing just behind her both Jackson and
Techy looked annoyed at the just said news.

"That's because it is!" Stated Jackson...

"What?" Expressed Inari. Surprised at the
fact that both of them were now not
sporting the total look of victory. But the
look of--"O' Shit! Here we go again!" As
she now walked up to Jackson.

"What's with the sour face, Hero?" She asked, not getting a response at first...

"Stupid!" Said Jackson too himself, shaking his head.

"It's over, isn't it?" Inari questioned only to get an answer she wished she hadn't asked for.

"NO! On the contrary! It's about to get a whole lot worse!" He voiced turning to look at her.

"I don't understand?" Remarked a confused Inari.

"Avatar's not dead... Neither is Dr. Kruger." Said Techy, giving her a few answers.

"Doctor?"

"That's a very, very, very long story!" Stated Techy, giving a know and low-down on Kruger's past.

"We got! I got, played! That scene was just a set-up, the whole thing was one big scam.

One big heist..." Said Jackson with fool me once contempt. "All so she could steal that item, steal it from them!"

"From whom???" Quizzed Inari.

"That's not important, what is... Is that..." Voiced Jackson only then to stop taking a pause. "Techy go back to Temporal Ops and... Go there and run everything we have on Avatar, and Kruger."

"All of it?" He questioned.

"All of it! The stolen items. The fertility clinics scandals in the now. The escape to the past. Possible clues on future town. Everything and anything." Said Jackson with a firm get it done, get it done now, conviction!

"On it!" Said Techy, as Jackson now walked away from them both. "What about Inari, here!?"

Acting as if he was not listening, like a kid who was to cool for school. Jackson now peeled of his white shirt. Throwing it over his left, solid super muscular shoulder.

Walking towards the exit of the chamber,
just before speaking again. "I'll be
inactive for while." He said. "Get Liz to
give her the grand tour of the Island!"

"Okay, J.C!" Voiced Techy obeying orders as
always. As Inari now spoke.

"Island!?" She said, sporting a puzzled
look! "What Island??? Where's he going?
Hey, Hero! Jackson???"

STOP THE CLOCK!

To be Continued...

Jackson Carter will return in...

"The Planetary Patriot and
the Night of the Seven Sisters!"